The Adventures of an Ugly Girl

The Adventures of an Ugly Girl

Elizabeth Burgoyne Corbett

MINT EDITIONS

The Adventures of an Ugly Girl was first published in 1898.

This edition published by Mint Editions 2021.

ISBN 9781513299495 | E-ISBN 9781513223919

Published by Mint Editions®

MINT
EDITIONS
minteditionbooks.com

Publishing Director: Jennifer Newens
Design & Production: Rachel Lopez Metzger
Project Manager: Micaela Clark
Typesetting: Westchester Publishing Services

Contents

I

"As ithers see us."

—Burns

C ome, Dora! I shall never be ready, if you don't make haste. They will be here in ten minutes, and my hair is not half so nice as it ought to be, thanks to your carelessness."

"You are very good to ignore my own claims to attention so utterly. I have been helping you this half-hour and have barely time enough left to change my frock. To make my own hair presentable is impossible now."

"Why, what does it matter how your hair is dressed, or what sort of a gown you put on? You may just as well spare your pains, for unfortunately nothing that you can do seems to mitigate your ugliness. I'm sure I cannot think where you get it. You are—"

But, somehow, I did not feel inclined to wait for the end of Belle's encouraging lecture. Perhaps it was because I was so often treated to my beautiful elder sister's homilies that they had lost the spark of novelty and had acquired a chestnuty flavor. Perhaps I failed to recognize any generosity in her persistent efforts to nip such latent buds of vanity as from time to time tried to thrust their poor little heads above the chill crust of ridicule and contumely. Perhaps I was really as bad-tempered as I was said to be. Anyhow, my behavior could not claim to be either quiet or elegant as I stormily quitted Belle's room, slamming the door behind me with such violence as to elicit from my more well-bred sister a little shriek of affected dismay. So far from feeling sorry that I had given Belle's nerves a shock, I wished viciously that her fingers had been jammed in the doorway, or that something equally disastrous had occurred to take off the edge of her conceit and self-satisfaction. In the corridor I met my brother Jerry, of whom I was devotedly fond. But, although he had evidently some interesting remark to make, I did not stop to speak to him, but hurried noisily to my own room, where I locked myself in, and threw myself on the bed, to give way to a storm of sobs and tears.

"And all for what?" it may be asked. "Surely a spiteful remark from one sister to another is hardly worth all this display of feeling." Ah, well, perhaps *one* such remark now and then might be treated with the cool contempt which spiteful utterances deserve. But does the reader know what it is to be perpetually and persistently snubbed from one year's end to the other? Does he realize how hard it must be for a sensitive and love-craving girl to be reminded that she is ugly and unattractive? Not reminded once in a way either, but pretty nearly everyday of her life. Or does anyone doubt how the heart must needs ache to see all the love and flattery of friends and relations alike showered upon a being whom you know to be empty-headed and frivolous, while everybody seems to regard your plain exterior as sufficient reason why you should be snubbed and neglected?

If the reader has ever had any of these experiences, he will the more readily understand my inability to restrain my tears on the especial occasion just mentioned. For it really was a very especial occasion, and I had been more anxious to look well at this particular moment than I ever remembered to have been in my life. I had hoped that Belle, just for once in a way, would take a little interest in my personal appearance, and that she would help me to create as good an impression as possible upon the newcomer whose advent I had both dreaded and longed for.

But Belle was too self-engrossed, and too firmly convinced of my hopeless unpresentability, to give the slightest thought either to me or to my feelings. Nay, she had even claimed so much of my time in the task of enhancing her own beauty, that, as we have seen, I had only a few minutes left for myself, and even this morsel of time was not utilized by me, as things turned out.

The fact is, I was anxious and overwrought, and Belle's unkind speeches had multiplied all day until they had utterly broken my composure. "Can it really be true," I wondered in abject misery, "that nothing I can either do or wear will help to mitigate the first feeling of repulsion which my new mother must necessarily experience at the sight of my ugliness?"

The question was of very vital import to me, for I longed for the advent of at least one sympathetic woman in the house; and when I heard that my father, now three years a widower, was about to marry again, I hoped, with a fervor that was nearly akin to agony, that his second wife would be the friend I so sorely needed. True, she would be my stepmother, and she would naturally assume the direction of the household affairs, at once placing the daughters of the house in a subordinate position. This being the case, I believe it would have been more orthodox to have railed against the new invasion, and to have followed the prevailing social custom of resolving to make life miserable for the woman who had presumed to step into my mother's place. But I always was terribly unorthodox in many things, and, considerably to my father's surprise, I expressed my enthusiastic delight at the prospect of having a stepmother to reign over me.

He need not have been surprised, if he had ever taken the trouble to understand me. But he was wrapped up in Belle's charms, and never looked at me without regretting either my ugliness or my temper, which all in the house, except dear little Jerry, pronounced unbearable. And yet I can truthfully say, that if I had experienced anything approaching to just treatment, I should have been infinitely sweeter-tempered than my much-bepraised sister, than whom none could have been more unfeeling to the motherless girl whose heart ached for a little love. I generally did Belle's bidding, for she always contrived to make things unpleasant for me if I rebelled against her authority. But to Lady Elizabeth Courtney I felt ready to yield the most devoted service and obedience, if only she would love me just a little in return; and I had anxiously revolved every means of creating a favorable impression upon her. I meant to have taken considerable pains with my toilet, and to have welcomed the home-coming bride with radiant smiles.

And this was how my good resolves had ended. Just when—after working hard all day to see that everything was conducive to a warm and comfortable home-coming—I had begun to hurry through my toilet, I was summoned to Belle's aid, with the result that instead of giving my stepmother a smiling welcome I was up in my own room, with a face red and swollen with weeping, and a heart full of angry feeling, when she arrived. Presently I heard a carriage approaching, and at the same instant Jerry knocked vigorously at my bedroom door.

"Be quick and come down, Dorrie," he cried, in an eager, excited voice. "Papa and Lady Elizabeth are nearly here, and I want you to run down the avenue with me to meet them."

"I'm not coming," I answered, with a sob that was audible to Jerry and provoked him to quick wrath.

"I knew she would!" he exclaimed. "That horrid Belle's been at her tricks again and said something nasty. But don't let her have the best of you like that. Don't you know that you promised to go with me to meet them, and if you don't come they won't believe you are glad about it."

"I can't help it, Jerry," was my mournful reply. "I look so hideous just now that I could not possibly face a stranger. Run off quickly yourself. Say that I have a headache or something of the sort, and that I shall try to sleep it off. Run now, there's a dear boy."

And forthwith Jerry, whose real name, by-the-by, is Gerald Mortimer Courtney, ran along the corridor, down the wide, shallow stairs, across the tiled hall, and into the open air, just as the carriage containing the newly married pair drove into the large graveled space in which the chestnut avenue terminated. In spite of my discomfiture and unpresentable appearance, I possessed my due share of curiosity, and hastily jumped to my feet, crossed the room, and looked through the window at the prancing horses and elegant equipage which bore the newcomers. As soon as the carriage stopped, a liveried footman descended and opened the door with a flourish. By the time he had let the steps down, Belle and Jerry were at the carriage door, and I saw Mr. and Lady Elizabeth Courtney get out and exchange smiles and kisses with my sister and brother, while I, poor pariah, looked on with hungry eyes and an aching heart, and bewailed my luck in seeming ill-natured and inhospitable, after all my efforts to prove the contrary.

Lady Elizabeth, I must explain, had had some love passages with my father a long time ago. But their youthful desires had been taught to bow to the demands of fortune and position. Lady Elizabeth was the daughter of an earl, and could aspire to more material comforts than could have been provided for her by the penniless younger son of a country squire. True, the earl had no money, and what little land was still left him was mortgaged up to the hilt. But he had many friends who possessed sufficient influence to pitchfork his four sons into government sinecures. He had a cousin also, the Duchess of Lyndene, who chaperoned his handsome, clever daughter through two whole seasons, and eventually resigned her charge into the care of Samuel Chisholm, Esquire, once upon a time a shoeblack, now the proud possessor of twenty thousand a year, all made by the judicious advertisement of his prize patent blacking.

Upon the whole, the earl's daughter was supposed to have done tolerably well for herself, and as her husband's fortune steadily increased there was every reason for her to feel satisfied. Even the incumbrance which she had been compelled to take with the fortune was not especially disagreeable to her, for Mr. Chisholm was a very clever man, whose mental and social equipments kept pace with his fortunes, and, in spite of his low origin and antecedents, he was as courtly and well-bred as Lady Elizabeth's nobly-born brothers. The pair therefore lived harmoniously enough together, at least to outward seeming, for many years. Then Mr. Chisholm died somewhat suddenly, and his will was read in due course.

It was during that important ceremony that the unexpectedly bereaved widow first felt real resentment against her late husband. For though he had died a millionaire, he had only willed his wife a life interest of five thousand a year, which was quite a paltry income compared with the princely revenue she had expected to be hers. To her father a like fortune was bequeathed, in addition to a sum of thirty thousand pounds wherewith to redeem his impoverished estate. The widow's brothers each received a gift of five thousand pounds, and to the widow herself was willed all the personal property of the deceased.

All the rest of his vast fortune was divided among a swarm of poor relations, whose existence Lady Elizabeth had never acknowledged, but who no doubt showered blessings on the memory of the dead man who had thus befriended his own flesh and blood. The Earl of Greatlands, too, declared himself delighted with his son-in-law's generosity. But his daughter did not hesitate to say that she had been treated shamefully, and at once proclaimed her intention of resigning the tenancy of the costly London establishment, which it would be a farce to attempt to keep up on five thousand a year. She retired to a pretty place in the country, declining to reside with her father, who, elated by his unwonted prosperity, was actually talking of taking a young wife to comfort his old age.

My father had, meanwhile, married my mother, whose memory I adore, for she loved me passionately, and while she lived I was never humiliated, as was perpetually the case after her death, which occurred some three years before my story opens. I do not remember hearing how my father came across Lady Elizabeth again, but I believe that their early attachment soon reasserted itself, and though he was much the poorer of the two, and encumbered with three children, the match was soon arranged.

Although Lady Elizabeth had been dissatisfied with her widow's portion she was very much richer than we were, and her coming to Courtney Grange was likely to be a very important event to the previous humble inhabitants thereof. In addition to the Grange, which had been my maternal grandfather's property, my father had just six hundred a year, derived partly from what his father had left him, partly from my mother's small fortune. Our establishment consisted of two servants, in addition to the family. Their names were John and Martha Page. They had never seen any other service but that of my father and grandfather, and had lived seventeen years under the same roof before it entered their heads to amalgamate their interests by marrying. They were quite used to the constant scraping and economizing which we were compelled to practice, and did not look upon the arrival of a new mistress as an unmixed blessing, even though she was bringing a good income with her.

As for Belle, she was quite wild with delight at the gorgeous prospect which opened itself before her mental vision. London seasons, presentations at court, halcyon days of brilliant pleasure, and a swarm of dukes and earls sighing for the honor of her hand. These were some of the glowing visions in which she indulged.

"And I mean to get into Lady Elizabeth's good graces, whether I like her or not," she informed me. "She can do so much for me if *she* likes, and I can be amiability itself when *I* like. Besides, my looks will win her over at once. She will soon see what credit I can do to pretty gowns. As for you, you'll be lucky if she tolerates you at all. I'm sure it's a shame that our family's reputation for beauty should suffer as it does through you." And so on, *ad libitum*.

Of course, I was not surprised to see her warm, gushing welcome of my father and his wife, nor to note the glance of surprised admiration which the latter cast upon Belle and Gerald, for they were really both very beautiful, and both tall and well-grown, with lovely golden hair, rich deep blue eyes, and an exquisite complexion, united to perfect features.

Lady Elizabeth, too, I was sorry to see, was a tall, handsome woman, who by no means looked her forty years. When I say that I was sorry to observe this, it must not be imagined that I grudged her her good looks. But I had had a vague notion that if she were comparatively plain she would the more easily sympathize with my troubles, into which no one in the house except Jerry seemed able to enter. Now my hopes in that direction were upset, and I already knew instinctively that my own absence was being commented upon. I saw my father, the very picture of masculine comeliness, glance up at my window with an angry frown, and I knew almost as well as if I had been present what Belle and Jerry were saying about me.

After all, I thought, I had been very foolish to let Belle's ill-nature

ELIZABETH BURGOYNE CORBETT

and my own ill-temper spoil my resolve to make Lady Elizabeth's home-coming as pleasant as possible. Apart from looks, my remaining upstairs would have already made me lose ground with my stepmother. Was it too late, I wondered, to rectify my error, and make my appearance before dinner was served? Answering the question in the negative, I resolved to complete my toilet as quickly as possible, and get over the ordeal of the first meeting without further loss of time.

So I began operations at once, wondering, while I brushed my hair, how it was that I was so different to Jerry and Belle. I pulled faces at my own ugly reflection in the glass, but as that only seemed to make matters worse, I desisted. But I could not banish the discontent which enhanced my ugliness, and made it almost perfect in its own way. Why was I so short and dumpy? I asked myself vainly. And why was my hair so black, and lank, and scanty? And how was it that my complexion was more like Thames mud than anything else? And why was my face covered with freckles? These freckles I always felt to be an especial aggravation of nature; for whoever heard of freckles on a dark, sallow skin? And then, how did it happen that my eyes were of a pale watery-brown hue, while I had hardly got either eyelashes or eyebrows that were visible? And why, oh, why! had my nose got that exasperating habit of looking skyward?

Even as I asked these questions of myself, I felt how hopeless it was to attempt to answer them. So I abandoned them and tried to console myself with the reflection that my mouth was well-shaped and that I had splendid teeth. But then my great red hands obtruded themselves upon my notice, and blotted out all consciousness of my redeeming features. I took considerable pains with my hair, and put on my best dress. Alas! the latter was of a curious brown shade which somehow only seemed to enhance my ugliness. Belle was dressed in a dainty pink cambric; but I was never allowed such a luxury, as it was considered that I was too untidy, and too plain, and altogether too unsuitable to indulge in pretty things. Besides, we had to be economical, and as I could never hope to captivate a lover, no matter how I was dressed, it would have been a shame to waste money upon my futile adornment. So Belle argued, and I had hitherto had no choice but to bow to her arguments.

I was at last ready to go downstairs, when once more Jerry came to look me up.

"Oh, you're donned up, are you?" he remarked. "And, upon my word, you're looking quite spry."

But I was not to be soothed by such negative flattery as this, and sternly asked Jerry what he meant by "looking quite spry."

"Why, spry, you know, spry means—at least, I mean—that you look as if you were going to a prayer meeting; that is, you look so prim, and tidy, and straight. But, Dorrie, dear, I like you far better as you were this morning, and as you generally are. You look real jolly then."

Saying this, Jerry kissed me warmly, and I forthwith resigned myself to the hopelessness of attempting to improve my appearance. This morning I had worn an old lilac print that had originally been made for Belle. It was faded with much washing, and possessed sundry little adornments in the way of frayed edges and sleeves out at elbows. Truly, Belle had been right, after all, and it was sheer folly on my part to rebel against fate, since neither coaxing nor rebelling seemed to propitiate her. Seeing, therefore, how stern and uncompromising she was with me, I resolved to take less notice of her in future, and had no sooner made the resolve than I began to feel peaceful and self-possessed. What if the gift of beauty was denied me, had I not many other blessings to be thankful for? In all my seventeen years of life I had never had anything but the most robust health, and if my school record was anything to go by, I possessed a much more valuable property in the way of brains than Belle did. These should outweigh my physical defects, and prove my passport to the world's good graces.

I dare say Jerry was rather surprised to see me suddenly straighten myself up, and assume a much more cheerful expression.

"What is Lady Elizabeth like?" I asked.

"Looks?"

"No, ways."

"Well, I take her to be rather a brick, do you know. She was as pleasant and as much at home with Belle and me as if she had lived here all her life and had just been off for a holiday. She thinks we are just like pa, and that is high praise, I should fancy."

"Very high praise, Jerry. I wonder what she'll say about me. But it doesn't matter. Is dinner nearly served?"

"Yes; but John was grumbling because you hadn't helped to see that the table was all right, as you had promised to do."

"Oh! Poor John. It was a shame of me to forget all about him. I'll hurry down now and see what I can do. Come on, Jerry."

A minute later we were both skipping nimbly downstairs, and while

Jerry, at my earnest request, ran round to the stable to see how my bull-terrier, Bobby, was progressing, I ran into the kitchen to make my peace with John and Martha. As Martha was somewhat sulky, and protested that they had managed very well without me, I made my way to the dining-room, and began swiftly to re-arrange the flowers which I had culled for the table earlier in the day. John looked rather scandalized, and remarked that he thought he knew how to arrange a table as well as most folks. But I did not heed John's grumbling much, for it was his chronic condition, and I had just completed my little task to my own satisfaction when John rang the second dinner-bell, the first not having been noticed by me.

Just then Jerry came back.

"Bobby will be all right in a day," he said, whereat I expressed my satisfaction, for I had been greatly troubled when poor Bobby had come limping home with every sign of war about him.

"And, oh!" I said, with sudden remembrance, "what has been done with the wonderful carriage and pair, and those gorgeous servants?"

"They went straight home. They belong to the earl. He sent them to meet Lady Elizabeth at the station. Her own carriages are coming after she has seen what arrangements it will be best to make here. I fancy she doesn't like the place very much."

"Not like the Grange?" I exclaimed indignantly. "Why, she must be a veritable heathen—"

"Dora, I regret that you should think fit to behave so badly, but must demand a little of your attention, while I introduce you to the notice of Lady Elizabeth Courtney."

Was ever luck like mine? Here had I quite lost sight of the fact that my father and his wife might enter the room at anytime, and they had actually overheard me speak in tones of contempt of the one woman on earth whom I wished to propitiate! I turned hurriedly round, and saw my father, looking very irate, Lady Elizabeth, looking coldly critical, and Belle, looking ill-naturedly triumphant.

"I beg your pardon, papa. I did not mean it," I stammered.

"No, I do not suppose you did mean us to overhear you," he replied sternly. "But I have no doubt that you had resolved to be intensely disagreeable, and I tell you plainly that I will not have it. You see, my love," he said, turning to his wife, "you will have a little temper and self-will to deal with, but I am sure you will know how to compel it to keep within due bounds."

What could I do or say after that? Nothing, of course, and I sat miserably through the whole meal, while all but Jerry laughed and talked as if quite unconscious of my presence. I would fain have escaped to my own room when the dinner was over. But my father had taken it into his head that I merely wanted to be obstinate and disagreeable, and suggested that I should spend an hour in the drawing-room. I accordingly took refuge at the piano. But my music was so melancholy that I am not surprised that I was asked to desist, for, when you come to think of it, "Killigrew's Lament," and "The Dead March in Saul," haven't a very bridal sound about them.

So far Lady Elizabeth had not spoken directly to me, and whenever my eyes wandered in her direction, I could see that her glance was very critical, but I could not be sure that it was quite so disapproving as I had expected. Yet, although I neither spoke, nor was spoken to, there was no constraint between the others, for my father and Lady Courtney were both good conversationalists, and Belle could chatter by the hour, provided the talk was kept at a suitably frivolous level. Jerry, after being petted and praised a little, had been sent to bed primed with a quartet of kisses, and jubilant in the possession of a bright sovereign which papa had given to him in honor of the advent of a new mistress at Courtney Grange.

"Belle, dear, suppose you play us one of your pretty pieces," said my father. Whereupon I vacated the music-stool, and took refuge near the big oriel window which overlooked the orchard, and which was my especial delight. For it was like a small room in itself, and I did not feel quite so lost among its cozy, faded draperies as I did in any other part of our drawing-room, which always seemed to me to be much too large for the furniture that was in it. Belle, after a great deal of fidgeting and looking round at herself, to make sure that her dress was falling in graceful folds, struck a few chords on what had been a very fine piano in its day, but which even I, who was partial to all that had belonged to my mother, was compelled to admit was getting out of date.

"I really don't like to let you hear me for the first time on an old instrument like this, Lady Elizabeth," said Belle. "If my music strikes you disagreeably, pray make all due allowance for the difficulties under which I labor."

"Pray don't apologize, my dear," answered Lady Elizabeth. "I know how to separate the faults of the instrument from those of the player, and the quality of the piano need not trouble you long, as in all probability a grand of my own will be here in a day or two."

ELIZABETH BURGOYNE CORBETT

"How delightful!" exclaimed Belle, and then she proceeded to give us a specimen of the skill which, times without number, I had been advised to emulate. She played "The Rippling Cascade" in a style that was faultless as regards time and precision, following it up with "The Musical Box." But her playing was utterly devoid of expression. Pathos, tenderness, power, fire, were all unknown musical quantities to her, as they are, alas! to numbers of other conventional players; and whether it was "Home, Sweet Home," or "The Soldier's Chorus," each and everything was played with the same clock-work insensibility to all the laws of expression. I watched Lady Elizabeth narrowly, as she listened to Belle's efforts in the musical line, and (shall I own it?) I was maliciously glad to notice a distinctly bored expression steal across her features. There was one thing in which I could excel my usually all-conquering sister, of which the lady whom we both desired to please was evidently a judge, and I could not help rejoicing in the fact that I was not quite weaponless in the fight for favor, though I had certainly done anything but shine so far.

"What do you think of Belle's performance?" asked my father, either forgetful of my presence, or not caring whether I overheard the conversation or not. Lady Elizabeth's reply, though given in a low tone, and under cover of the music, reached my ears quite distinctly.

"She is just a trifle disappointing there, Gerald. I should imagine your younger daughter, Dora, to be much the better artist of the two. She seems to be a trifle wild and ungovernable, but would, I think, be amenable to reason, with judicious handling."

"My dear Elizabeth, you don't know her yet. Wait until you have seen more of her, and then you will agree with me that she is more than trying. Indeed, she is positively exasperating at times. Belle always has some complaint to make of her, and I am not surprised that this should be so, for it is a matter of impossibility to make her either look or act like a lady. No one would dream that she was a Courtney."

Often and often I had felt my heart ache at the neglect and carelessness with which my father had always treated me, and I had grieved bitterly at the lack of outward comeliness which seemed to be the passport to his affection. But that he was actually so devoid of parental feeling as to show himself positively antipathetic to me had never occurred to me. Now, as I heard him saying things which must make me almost hateful in Lady Elizabeth's eyes, I felt myself harden toward him, and the love which I had hitherto cherished for him fell from me like a worn-out mantle. What! oh, what had I ever done that he should do that which presumably only my bitterest enemy would do to me? Why should he try to prejudice me in the eyes of his wife? Had he no remembrance of the mother who loved me with a love equal to that which she bore for himself and his happier children? Was he quite forgetful of all the little efforts I had always made to increase his comfort? Did he really regard me as quite removed from the sphere of a lady, because I had worked hard, and made my hands red and unsightly, ever since I had realized how difficult it was for Martha and John to manage our big house efficiently without assistance? I, in my blindness, had hoped that he would commend me for my industrious habits, and it was a bitter awakening to discover that he only rated me on a par with, perhaps, a scullery maid.

I could feel my eyes begin to gain the fire they usually lacked, and the hot blood suffused my cheeks as I sat trembling with anger, and fighting madly to prevent myself from uttering the reproaches that forced themselves to my lips. It would be well, I thought, to keep quiet until the end of the play, and hear the verdict which Lady Elizabeth would pronounce upon me. I therefore listened for her answer with tightly clasped hands and motionless form, but with my attention strained to the utmost, Belle having meanwhile reached the most flourishy part of "Household Harmonies."

"Do you think it quite fair to the child," said my stepmother, "to give implicit credence to what one sister says to the detriment of the other, without giving the latter a chance to defend herself? Do not imagine for a moment I have a thought of reproaching you. But I cannot help contrasting the love and admiration you so openly display for Belle with the coldness and actual displeasure with which you look at Dora. May not this have much to do with the girl's presumably bad temper and *gauché* manners? You see, I want to make the best of all belonging to you, Gerald, and I am inclined to think that there is more in your younger daughter than you have given her credit for."

"I should be only too glad to discover a single good quality in Dora," replied my affectionate father. "But I repeat that she is really hopeless, and assure you, for your own future guidance, that her disposition is on a par with her looks, than which nothing could very well be more disappointing, considering the fact that she is the offspring of a house which for generations has been famous for its beauty."

"But a beautiful body does not invariably hold a beautiful mind, and

ELIZABETH BURGOYNE CORBETT

of course the obverse rule holds good. The fact is, I am not sure that I have not taken a fancy to Dora. I have an idea that she is a girl of great possibilities, under judicious management. Certainly, appearances are against her at present, but appearances are but very circumstantial evidence at best."

"And how do you get over her rudeness to you on your arrival?"

"You mean her failure to meet me at the door?"

"Yes."

"Well, I rather fancy that if I had been in her place I should have done the same. It is bad enough to be such a contrast in looks to her handsome sister, without having her plainness accentuated and aggravated by the most unbecoming attire that could possibly have been procured for her. Belle is beautifully dressed, and Dora's frock is simply hideous. Her hair, too, is plastered down in as ugly a fashion as possible. I mean to alter all that, and the result will astonish you, I am sure."

By this time Belle had noticed that she had an unappreciative audience, and was closing the piano, contriving to display, as she did so, a certain amount of well-bred annoyance, as I knew instinctively without looking at her, so well was I used to her little ways. Lady Elizabeth smiled pleasantly and said, "Thank you, my dear." My father, considerably to Belle's own wonderment, appeared quite oblivious of her beautiful presence, a thing she had never had to complain of before. He looked like a man suddenly confronted with a new and mysterious riddle, and as if he were not sure whether he ought not to doubt the sanity of anyone who could deliberately say anything in favor of me. True, old Martha and her husband were sometimes quite ungrudging of their commendation, after I had been specially useful to them. But they were only servants, and it was perhaps natural that they should judge things in a different way to more educated people.

As for me, I sat like one in ecstasy, for I had at last found someone who was not only willing, but actually determined to see that I was treated in a manner equal to the other daughter of the house, and not relegated to the position of a menial. My father had evidently forgotten that I was in the room. Lady Elizabeth thought I had left it, as was evidenced by her parting words to Belle, as the latter was going up to her own bedroom.

"Goodnight, Belle," she said. "Tomorrow we will have a talk about what we will do together in future, eh? And tell your sister that I hope she will be well enough to go on an exploring expedition with me. I'm sure she has a pretty garden and other interesting things of her own to show me. She looks like a real lover of nature."

Had my heart not been so full of conflicting emotion I could have laughed at Belle's stare of surprise. But laughter would have been horrible to me just then, and would have seemed a desecration of the purer sounds that rose to my lips.

Does the reader know how it feels to be in a state of joy so exquisite that it is difficult to restrain the voice from shrieking aloud and the limbs from dancing in wild abandonment? Even so did I feel when I rose from my chair as Belle left the room. But my excitement ran into the channels of gratitude and love, and I soon found myself kneeling at Lady Elizabeth's feet, sobs shaking my frame, tears streaming down my cheeks, and broken words of feeling issuing from my lips.

"Dear, dear lady!" I cried. "Oh, how I bless you for your kind words! You don't know how I have hungered for love! You don't know what a grief it was to me to seem rude to you. You don't know how grateful I can be. I will do anything for you. I will work my fingers to the bone, if you wish it. I will lay my life down for you, if you will only give me just a little corner of your heart, just a little of the sympathy for which my heart has been aching."

"My dear child," said my stepmother, as she clasped me warmly to her breast, while genuine tears of sympathy actually rolled down her cheeks. "My poor Dora! of course I mean to love you. And I want you to remember that I am your mother, to whom you must come in all your troubles."

Then, with an affectionate kiss, she released me, and I fled to my bedroom, sobbing still with excitement, but proud, happy and exultant, as I had never been in my life.

"She is an angel!" I thought, rapturously. "Oh! how happy we shall be now!"

Alas, poor mortal! it is well for thee that the portals of the future are impervious to thy gaze, and that it is forbidden thee to know how small is perhaps thy destined share of happiness, the true elixir of life.

II

*"In the world there is no duty more important
than that of being charming."*

—Victor Hugo

On rising next morning my first thought was that I must dress myself with more care than was usually the case with me before breakfast. Not that I was not always neat and tidy, as far as my personal toilet went. But the old dresses which had hitherto been deemed good enough for me to wear in the mornings would have to be discarded henceforth, and I felt quite proud of the suddenly accentuated importance of my personal appearance, as I rummaged my wardrobe in search of something that would be fit to wear in the presence of Lady Elizabeth Courtney.

But I was not very successful in my search, and was obliged to content myself with a somewhat shabby green striped stuff, that had been bought for Belle, but was made up for me, because she took a dislike to it on seeing it at home. I remembered the remark Lady Elizabeth had made about my hair, and tried, with very indifferent success, to remove the objectionable sleekiness which was its distinguishing feature.

When quite ready to go downstairs I surveyed myself in the glass, but cannot say that I was delighted with the reflection which confronted me for a moment. It was only seven o'clock, and I went to the stable ere going elsewhere, to see after the wants of Bobby and of my dear old Teddy. Teddy was a shaggy pony, whose looks were anything but handsome, but in whose society I had hitherto spent my happiest hours. That I should be the proud possessor of a pony often struck me with surprise; but it was an established fact, nevertheless. My uncle Graham, protesting that no one would buy such an ugly animal, had given him to me, and as Belle would not have been seen on the back of such an inelegant steed, there was no attempt to subvert him to other uses than the donor intended.

Sometimes Jerry and I wandered for miles with him, taking turns at having a ride on his broad back over the wide expanse of moorland in which our county rejoices. Bobby, too, always went with us, and, next to Teddy, perhaps, was the dearest animal alive. I had bought him, for sixpence, from some boys who had been paid a shilling to drown him because he had the mange. He wasn't handsome then, but he improved in looks when he recovered from his illness, and he was so loving, so merry, so clever, and such a jolly companion altogether, that it would have been a terrible grief to me to part with him. Then both Bobby and Teddy were such splendid confidants. To them I poured out all my sorrows, and I always felt better after we had talked things over. They would both look at me so earnestly and lovingly with their beautiful eyes, while I told them whatever I had to tell. And then, to prove that they understood me, Teddy would rub me with his head, and Bobby would first lick my fingers, and then give a short, sharp bark, and look defiantly round him, as if to challenge my enemies.

Both animals were nearly as fond of Jerry as they were of me. But he was only nine years old, and did not understand them quite as well as I did. Whenever we were bent upon a long excursion on the moors we would take a basket of provisions with us. Then, when we got to a suitable spot, we would prepare to enjoy our picnic. Teddy and Bobby would lie down for awhile, or would amuse themselves in their own way, the one by nibbling at such eatables as he might find, and the other by excursionizing in search of rats. But they knew what a certain whistle meant, and returned promptly to our side as soon as they heard it. Then, having unpacked our basket, we would distribute the luncheon. There was always a goodly bone for Bobby, and some apples and a few carrots for Teddy; and though we were no doubt a curious quartet, we were a very happy one, for I had no regrets when in the unrestrained company of my three chums. After lunch, we sometimes had a game at hide and seek among the stones and hillocks, Teddy in particular being very difficult to deceive. It was such fun to see his dear old nose come poking round a corner, and to witness him neigh and prance in his joy at having unearthed us, while Bobby complimented him on his skill by barking his admiration.

It seemed a pity that such beautiful days should have an end, and we were all sorry when it was time to go home again. As for me, I used to feel my spirits leave me as we neared home, for I was always sure to be in some scrape or other on my return. It was very easy for me to get into trouble at anytime, but the head and front of my offending in connection with our picnics was my inability to distinguish between scraps and bones to which Bobby was welcome, since no one else could eat them, and the remains of a joint which Martha had intended to convert into *rissoles*. Teddy's apples, too, had a knack of being of the choicest flavor, whereas the green windstrewn ones were supposed to be good enough for a pony.

As I now went to the stable, I could not help wondering how Lady Elizabeth would regard my pets. But I felt more assured about the matter than I would have done if I had thought about it yesterday. For if my stepmother could actually take a fancy to *me*, she was not likely to take exception to the ugliness of Teddy and Bobby.

"Hallo, Dorrie!" I suddenly heard a voice exclaim, and looking toward the kitchen-garden, whence the sound proceeded, I saw Jerry, hand-in-hand with Lady Elizabeth, to whom he was doing the honors of the place thus early.

"We've been getting some strawberries for breakfast," smilingly said my stepmother, "or, rather, we were going to get some, but either Gerald or I ate all we gathered."

"Well, it wasn't me," said Jerry. "I gathered them, and you ate them. But I can soon pull some more, after you have looked at my white rats and my rabbits."

"And my pony," I put in; adding, with no shade of reserve or shyness about me, "Do you always get up so early, Lady Elizabeth?"

"Not always, especially if I am in town. But I am fond of rising early in the country. Besides, I wanted to explore the Grange thoroughly today. I have been here before, but it is so long since that I have quite forgotten what it is like."

"Do you know," put in Jerry, "that I fancied yesterday you did not like the place?"

"And Dora thought I must be a heathen not to do so."

"Oh, I beg your pardon," I exclaimed hurriedly. "It was very presumptuous of me. But I have lived here all my life, and to me no place can be nicer than Courtney Grange."

"That remains to be proved," said my stepmother, with a smile. "I have an idea that the sanitary arrangements of this place are bad. Should this really prove the case, we shall vacate the Grange in favor of a pretty place of my own."

"Leave the Grange!" I cried aghast. "Why, that would be awful! I should look uglier than ever anywhere else."

"On the contrary, it is just possible, Dora, that this place is to blame for your unsatisfactory complexion. Perhaps your bedroom is a specially unhealthy one. Your father has promised to employ some sanitary engineers at once, to examine the place. Meanwhile I have left my maid at Sunny Knowe, and we are all going next week to pay a visit to that place. Your father is quite willing that you should all three accompany us, and I am sure you will enjoy your visit."

"But I have no pretty clothes to be seen elsewhere in."

"We will soon alter that. I am very glad that Ernestine did not come with me. I can manage very well for a week without her, and it is just as well that neither she nor any other servant of mine should criticise you at present. You will show to much better advantage in new clothes, and may as well create as good an impression as possible, even upon the servants, who can be very neglectful of people who do not strike them as important. I intend you to be considered as important as your sister, who is very lovely, but who must not monopolize all the attention due to you."

"Indeed, I do not want attention or assistance. I am quite used to looking after both myself and others, and cannot expect the same politeness as Belle. See, these are my pets, and I love them dearly, for they both love me."

Bobby always slept with Teddy, and it was no unusual thing to see the two friends come to meet me, as they did on this particular morning, Teddy brushing my arm by way of salute and uttering a delighted neigh, while Bobby barked his "good-morning" quite plainly.

"They have brought you to see some lovely animals," said a voice at this juncture. It was my father, who had joined us, preparatory to going in to breakfast, and who gazed at me with manifest displeasure.

"I'm afraid, my dear," he continued, "that you will be somewhat disgusted at being taken the round of stableyards and back premises. But I should have warned you as to what you might expect from Dora. Her tastes are inveterately low."

"Then I am afraid I am low, too," laughed Lady Elizabeth, "for I have actually been enjoying myself. I was always sorry that I had no children of my own, and a few fresh young spirits about me will complete my happiness in marrying you. Come along, children. We mustn't keep your father waiting for his breakfast."

My father was not severe or ill-natured, except when irritated by the sight of the child who was a veritable eyesore to him, and he would have had to be a churl indeed to resist his wife's sunny ways. He was smiling pleasantly at her, and had turned to walk toward the house, having offered her his arm, when I hastily whispered to her: "Pray excuse Jerry and me for a moment, while we gather those strawberries." And then I ran off, followed by Jerry, and knowing full well that my desire to procure Lady Elizabeth a plentiful supply of the fruit of which she seemed fond would provoke my father's displeasure again, simply because it would strike him as another undesirable exhibition of my notoriously independent manners.

But I no longer felt any particular desire to please him, and only cared to be of service to the dear lady who would permit no prejudices to influence her treatment of me. As far as she was concerned, I meant to follow Victor Hugo's advice, and be as charming and helpful as I could. If I could not make my appearance charming, I would charm her by a solicitous and persistent attention to her pleasures and comforts.

It did not take the two of us long to gather a good supply of "Queens" and "Presidents," and we reached the morning-room before the others had sat down to breakfast. Belle was there, attired in a pretty pale blue print, and was admirably foiled by my altogether unprepossessing appearance. As I saw Lady Elizabeth's glance wander from Belle to myself, I knew that she was wondering what I could possibly wear to make me look pretty; and though I could never really hope to embody such a pleasant adjective as "pretty," I was happy in the knowledge that Belle's unpleasant theories were upset, and that I might possibly show a marked improvement in my appearance ere long.

The rest of the day was chiefly taken up with explorations and consultations, and a good many new arrangements were made. Jerry, I was sorry to hear, was to be sent off to a French boarding school at the beginning of the next term. But when I heard that he was to spend all his holidays at home, just as if he were in an English school, I felt reconciled to the temporary absences of the bright, clever child who liked his ugly sister best. Jerry himself was quite overjoyed at the programme cut out for him, and promised to write us each and all a French letter from the first week of his residence in France.

Belle, who was now twenty, was enraptured by the promise of next season in town, while I was so delighted to hear that I was to have efficient instruction on my favorite instrument, the violin, that I burst into tears, and ran hastily up to my own room, where I might vent my emotion unrestrainedly. You see, my tastes had met with so little sympathy heretofore that I required sometime to get used to unwonted indulgences. I was not sure that my happiness would not yet take unto itself wings and fly away, or that I was not dreaming; for I had never heard of the arrival of a stepmother being so conducive to the welfare of the junior branches of the family as promised to be the case with us.

My father, I noticed during the next few days, was so supremely contented and so happy in the society of his wife, that I contrasted the coldly conventional manner in which he had always comported himself in my poor mother's presence, and was able to see that the feeling he had borne for her was but poor stuff compared to the love he felt for Lady Elizabeth. I remember also having heard that these two were lovers in their youth, and it amazed me to think that they could have deliberately thrown aside the heart's most sacred feelings in order to make a worldly marriage.

I have since then become thoroughly conversant with the fact that Mammon is infinitely the more powerful god of the two, when it comes to a tussle with Cupid, and that even very estimable people lose their judgment when called upon to choose between them. And yet, how can they honestly utter their marriage vows, when the heart is given away from the one they are marrying? Truly, life has many mysteries, which it were unprofitable work to attempt to solve!

In a day or two quite an assortment of new clothes came for me, and it was astonishing to see how different I looked in the reds and yellows which I now wore. I was still the ugly girl of the family, but it was quite possible for strangers to overlook the unpleasant fact for a while, and I even caught myself hoping that I looked rather nice than otherwise, especially when callers began to pay their respects to the newly-married couple.

Both Belle and I were introduced to nearly all our visitors, among the first of them being the Earl of Greatlands. I was rather disposed to like him, until he put his eyeglass up, quizzed me attentively, and remarked: "You are unfortunately very like your mother, Miss Dora, though I believe she had much finer hair and eyes than you have. But everybody improves in the hands of my daughter, and I have no doubt you will be as handsome as your sister by the time you are her age."

"I am only just twenty," said Belle stiffly.

"So I suppose, my dear," rejoined the earl. "But you will find in a year or two that even the slight margin of age there is between the two of you will land you considerably on the weather-side, in other people's opinion."

Belle flashed an angry glance from her beautiful eyes, being careful, however, not to let the earl see it, for did she not desire an invitation to

Greatlands Castle? As for me, I felt nothing less than enraged, although I could not quite decide whether the old gentleman was deliberately rude, or only gifted with an unfortunate knack of making *mal-à-propos* speeches. But he did not notice that he had hurt the feelings of either of us, having turned his attention to Jerry, who, faultlessly dressed in a new black velvet suit, was being introduced to his stepmother's father.

"Ah! a very pretty boy," he said. "But a perfect imp of mischief, I know. Boys who look like him always are. How many times have you gone out ratting?"

"Not so often as I would like, sir. Dorrie can't always get away."

"And does Dorrie go rat-hunting?"

"Of course she does. She has a splendid dog. Teddy is hers, too, and he's just a brick."

"Teddy's a brick? But of what use is a brick on hunting expeditions?"

"Oh, you know what I mean. Teddy is the jolliest little pony in the world."

"You seem fond of Teddy?"

"Rather."

"And of Bobby?"

"I wonder who wouldn't be!"

"And of Dorrie?"

"Why, of course!"

"And of Belle?"

"Belle? Well, yes, I dare say I am, when she doesn't sneak on Dorrie."

"Gerald, I think you are forgetting yourself," interrupted my father angrily. "That girl has made you worse than herself. It is just as well that you are going to be parted. For the present, you have been long enough in the drawing-room."

"Very well, sir," said Jerry, and turned to leave the room at once. Lady Elizabeth, I could see, was more amused than vexed; Belle looked at both Jerry and me with angry disdain, and the earl just laughed as if Jerry had uttered a very good joke.

"Wait a bit, Jerry," he said. "If the others will excuse me for a few minutes, I would like you to show me this wonderful dog and pony. And as they are Dorrie's property she will perhaps be good enough to come with us."

As nobody entered any objection to the earl's proposals, I accompanied him from the room, and five minutes later he and Jerry and I were interviewing Teddy and Bobby, who had been having a gambol at the foot of the orchard. The orchard was not a place they were supposed to frisk about in. But somebody had carelessly left the wicket open, and it was not their fault, poor things, that a choice young "ribstone pippin" had been snapped in two during their frolics.

The earl was certainly a funny man. He was as different from what I had always supposed an earl to be as was possible. In fact, he was more like a jolly old farmer than anything else. But what a gossip he seemed to be! And how inquisitive he was! He laughed immoderately at sight of my pets, but immediately soothed my wounded feelings by stroking and patting them, and I could see that they both took a fancy to him at once. It wasn't everybody that Teddy would sidle up to in the dear, winning way he had, or to whom Bobby would wag his approval. But perhaps they were both in a better humor than usual; for Bobby had uncovered one of the mushroom beds, and had helped himself to a few of the fungi, of which he was inordinately fond, while naughty Teddy, as several broken branches testified, had been feasting on unripe "Dutch mignonnes" and "Duke of Oldenburghs."

"Nice animals," said the earl. "Just the sort I would have expected your property to be, eh, Dorrie?"

"My name is Dora."

"But Jerry calls you Dorrie."

"He is privileged. He likes me."

"And how do you know that I don't like you?"

"You? I don't see how you can. Very few people do."

"Perhaps I am one of the few. At any rate, I mean to call you Dorrie. It sounds nicer between friends than 'Miss Dora,' doesn't it?"

"Now you are making fun of me. And you would make even more fun of me, if I were to believe that the Earl of Greatlands wanted to be friendly with an ugly, uninteresting girl like me."

"Isn't Lady Elizabeth friendly with you?"

"Oh, she is an angel!"

"Well, please to remember that I am that angel's father, and of the same species. Don't you see my wings?"

At this we all three laughed, and we enjoyed each other's society very well for about half an hour, during which time we had shown our visitor all sorts of things that I had never dreamed would interest an earl.

Suddenly he exclaimed: "And now I must go back to the house, or I shall be getting into hot water with the old people, eh? But look here, Jerry, what has Belle got to sneak about?"

"Now, Jerry, don't *you* turn sneak," I warned.

"You don't need to be afraid. But Belle is horrid, after that. She's always saying that Dorrie's ugly. And I'm sure she isn't really ugly, is she?"

The latter question was addressed to the earl. But I did not wait to hear his answer, for I was thoroughly angry with Jerry, for once, and returned to the house unceremoniously, leaving them to go back when they liked. Of course I was not behaving politely. But I am afraid that very polished manners were really a little out of my line at that time, and, after all, it was too bad of Jerry to turn the conversation on to my unfortunate ugliness, just when we were having such a nice time of it. Instead of going back to the drawing-room, I went straight to the kitchen, where I was busily occupied for the next two hours in helping Martha to shell "marrowfats," to prepare salad, to make a pudding and some cheesecakes, and in other ways to do my best toward making dinner a success. Belle never condescended to enter the kitchen at anytime, nor would my father have liked her to risk spoiling the perfect loveliness of her hands. But Martha and John had never suffered from lack of work, and some help was absolutely needed by them. True, a strong girl from the village of Moorbye had been engaged now to do the rougher part of the housework, but even then there was plenty of room for my assistance.

That evening the Earl of Greatlands dined with us, as did also Lord Egreville, his son, who had ridden over to pay his respects to his sister and her husband. He was a widower, and resided with his father at Greatlands Castle, his two sons being at Oxford. I did not like him at all, and he took no pains to conceal the fact that he considered me to be very small fry indeed. But he was quite fascinated by Belle's beauty, and flirted desperately with her. She seemed perfectly willing to receive his attentions, and certain amused glances which I saw exchanged between Lady Elizabeth, the earl, and my father, set my thoughts working in an odd direction.

What a queer thing it would be, I mused, if this Lord Egreville and Belle were to fall in love with each other, and make a match of it! How it would complicate relationships. Why, let me see, Belle would become her father's sister-in-law, and would be a sort of aunt to Jerry and myself, while the old earl could call himself either her father-in-law, or her grand-father-in-law, if he liked. The situation presented so many funny aspects, that I felt it necessary to relinquish my dessert-spoon while I abandoned myself to a fit of laughter that obstinately refused to be repressed.

As there was apparently nothing to laugh at, my manners were again called into question, chiefly by the innocent and unconscious cause of my amusement.

A few days after this, the sanitary engineers were at work on Courtney Grange, and we were all domiciled *pro tem* at Sunny Knowe, a lovely place in its way, but not nearly equal to what Courtney Grange would be when thoroughly restored. Oddly enough, a distant relation, from whom my father had never expected anything, died at this juncture, and bequeathed him several thousand pounds. His income had never been large enough to keep the place up as it ought to have been kept, and the Grange had therefore fallen considerably out of repair. Now that he was married to a lady with an ample income he could spare his newly acquired fortune for repairing purposes, and resolved to spend nearly the whole of it on that object.

Under the circumstances, we were not likely to return to the Grange much before Christmas. But we did not trouble about that, as the Knowe was a very pleasant place to live at. I had, very much to my sorrow, left Teddy under John Page's care, for Lady Elizabeth desired me to ride a more presentable steed while at the Knowe. I was provided with a well-made habit, and had the use of a handsome horse. But the decorous rides I now took, in company with Belle, and with a groom following closely, were not to be compared with the delightful excursions Teddy and I had had together, though Belle enjoyed them, and the altered state of things was evidently regarded by her as a great improvement.

As it had been necessary to leave Teddy behind, I could not be cruel enough to bring Bobby away and leave him without a friend to talk to. John had promised to look well after them both, but I knew that they would miss me sadly, and longed for the time when I could comfort them again with my presence. Lady Elizabeth was very good to me, but at times I was not sure that I did not regret the old spells of unconventional freedom.

So true is it that we are prone to lose sight of the privileges and blessings of the present in the vain longing after a vanished past, in which we could find little to be joyful at, when it was with us. In my case, I was ready to let the memory of our halcyon days on the moors outweigh that of all the days of neglect and misery during which I had craved for the mother's love which had once blessed me.

The Earl of Greatlands and his son spent a good deal of time at the Knowe, and we, in our turn, saw much of the castle, which had been thoroughly rehabilitated since Lady Elizabeth's first husband had been good enough to furnish the money wherewith to do it. It was a fine old place, and it was pleasant to see what pride its owner took in all connected with it. Lord Egreville was very attentive to Belle, but it was difficult to decide how far the element of seriousness entered into the behavior of either of them. There was a prudent reticence on the part of Lord Egreville at times that annoyed Belle very much, because it argued that he was not quite so infatuated with her as she would have liked him to be.

And yet, I do not believe she cared for him one atom, although she gave him more than sufficient encouragement to proceed with his attentions—up to a certain point. Once, when in a very gracious mood, she became quite confidential with me.

"It would be a very good match, even for me, who have always meant to do well for myself," she said. "The estate is quite unencumbered, and in first-class order. Lord Egreville is not very good-looking. But I would tolerate his looks if I cannot do better for myself. Though certainly it would be a great thing to become an English countess."

"But Lord Egreville will not be an earl until his father dies."

"His father, as you seem to forget, is close upon seventy, and cannot live forever."

"How horrid it seems to count upon dead men's shoes like that!"

"Don't excite yourself, my dear. If Lord Egreville were to propose to me tomorrow, I would not give him a decided answer. I must see what my coming season in town brings forth. I might captivate a much richer nobleman, or even a millionaire pill or soap manufacturer. At any rate, I am not going to throw myself away in too great a hurry."

"'A bird in the hand—' You know the rest."

"Yes, I know the rest. But my motto is: 'Look before you leap.'"

"Well, I hope you won't leap into a big bog-hole, that's all."

"Well, no. I will leave that suicidal performance for those who can never hope to leap any higher. How do you like this brooch? Lord Egreville sent it this morning."

"If I were you, I would tell him to keep his dead wife's jewelry a little longer. He might require it for someone else, if you pick up a duke or a millionaire."

Having had my parting shot, I judged it wise to leave Belle to her own devices, and went off to my little room, where I practiced industriously on my fiddle for an hour and a half. There were plenty of servants here, and I had no excuse for offering to help with the cooking, though I would have liked nothing better. Indeed, I had often thought that if I had not belonged to a family in which it was necessary to keep up appearances, I would have become a professional cook. But I had still a little congenial employment to turn to. Jerry was going off to school this week, and I had undertaken to mark all his things myself, besides making him sundry little knick-knacks that would prove useful to him.

I found it very hard to part with Jerry, when the time came for him to go, and was rather hurt to find that he cared less about leaving us behind, than he did about the delights of travel and school-life to which he was looking forward.

"I did think you would be sorry to leave me," I murmured, reproachfully, just as he was being resigned to the charge of the tutor who was going to accompany him to the school, and afterward take part in teaching the boys.

"Well, what's a fellow to do?" Jerry rejoined. "You wouldn't have me to cry and look like a muff, would you? It isn't the same as if I was a girl. It wouldn't matter then if I cried my eyes red."

"No more it would, Jerry. Good-by, dear. And you'll be sure to write often to me?"

"Quite sure. Good-by, Dorrie. Good-by, pa. And, oh! Dorrie, I've forgotten my bag of marbles, and my new top. Will you send them to me?"

There was barely time to answer in the affirmative, and then the child was off. Then my father, having seen me comfortably seated in the waggonette in which we had driven to the station, flicked his whip, and off we started on our return drive, little dreaming of the terrible events which were to come to pass ere the dear boy from whom we had just parted came back to the home he left so blithely.

　　　　　　　ELIZABETH BURGOYNE CORBETT

III

"'Tis the unlikely that always happens."

My life seemed strangely quiet without Jerry for the next few days, and I longed all the more to console myself with Bobby and Teddy. But one gets used to the absence of anybody in time, and Lady Elizabeth's arrangements were so promotive of the comfort and pleasure of all with whom she lived that it would have seemed ungrateful of me to suggest that I should be glad when the time came to go back to the Grange. Still, it was true that, apart from the loss of Jerry's companionship, I had conceived a desire to leave Sunny Knowe. The Earl of Greatlands had become unpleasantly effusive to me. He was constantly paying me compliments, which were all the more galling as they were made with a perfectly grave mien. Had Belle been the recipient, there would have been nothing objectionable about them, as she could have received them in the full conviction that they were honestly meant. But for me, whose ugliness was proverbial, to be addressed as "pretty dear" and "dainty dove," was very bitter indeed; for it was bad enough to be fully conscious of a total absence of all that was dainty and pretty, without being publicly satirized, and held up to the unfeeling laughter of Belle and her admirer, Lord Egreville.

One afternoon my temper, which of late had lain in abeyance, reasserted itself in a startling manner. We were all in the drawing-room, with several of the neighboring gentry, who had come over to confabulate about some *tableaux vivants* that there had been some talk of getting up. Several satisfactory groups had been decided upon; but, apparently by common consent, nobody had suggested that I should take a part in the performances, until the earl remarked: "Look here, there seems to be a strange want of judgment among you. You have left the flower of the flock out of your calculations, and I propose that she and I represent 'Beauty and the Beast.' I can soon dress up as the 'Beast,' and she can fill her part satisfactorily."

"And pray who is the 'flower of the flock'?" said Belle, who was to represent "Guinevere."

"Who else, but winsome Dora?" retorted the earl, whereat there was an undisguised laugh on the part of Belle and a few more of her caliber, while the rest smiled in good-natured toleration of so palpable an absurdity. Just for one instant I turned sick with humiliation. Then I walked up to the earl, and, with my eyes flashing angrily, hissed rather than said: 'You are an old man, my lord. I am but a young girl. You think that you may hold me up to ridicule and laughter with impunity. But I vow you shall do so no longer. Shall I tell you what I will do if you dare to insult me in that manner again?'

"Dora, how dare you!" exclaimed my father angrily. "If you have forgotten how to behave yourself, I must request you to go to your own room at once.—I told you how it would be," he remarked to Lady Elizabeth.

"Tut, tut!" put in the earl. "Let the girl alone, Courtney. This little bit of an outburst is my especial prerogative, and I would like to hear the whole of it. What will you do if I repeat the kind of conversation which seems to rouse your ire? Why shouldn't I call you a beauty?"

"Because I have a right to demand that you should cease to satirize my unfortunate appearance, and because I will no longer submit quietly to listen to compliments which become insults when applied to me."

"But you have not yet told me how you will prevent me from saying just what I please."

"If you are so little of a gentleman as to repeat your conduct, I will—I will slap your face!"

"This is too disgraceful!" interposed my father again. "Once more, Dora—"

"I have to beg you once more to permit me to finish this little affair in my own way," said the earl, who was actually laughing, so utterly insignificant and childish did he deem my anger. "So you would slap my face, eh? Well, there's nothing would please me better. I like a girl with some go in her. And you know you really are the nicest, bonniest—"

Five minutes later I was in my own room, feeling thoroughly ashamed of myself. I had not permitted the Earl of Greatlands to finish his preposterous compliment. But I certainly had disgraced myself in the eyes of my father, of Lady Elizabeth, and of sundry other people who witnessed my exit from the drawing-room and its predisposing cause. For I had really slapped the old earl's face, even as I had threatened to do. He would probably not annoy me in the same way again. Indeed, it was problematical if he would ever speak to me again; for, after all, my conduct must seem inexcusable in the opinion of all but myself. For how could I expect anyone else to understand how bitter it was to me to have my lack of comeliness held up to the laughter and contumely of more favored mortals.

Next morning, when I came down to breakfast, I found my father awaiting my advent in the morning room, and braced myself for the reprimand which I knew to be inevitable. Said reprimand was even more severe than I had anticipated, but my affectionate parent displayed such a total lack of the consideration which I felt was the due of my own wounded feelings, that, somehow, I no longer felt sorry for what I had done, but maliciously resolved to adopt equally drastic measures if ever I should be insulted in like manner again.

"I was never so ashamed in my life," supplemented Belle, who had come in while my father was talking, and had listened with a smile to his lecture.

"I am glad to hear you say so," said the voice of Lady Elizabeth. "It really was a shame to laugh when you saw how Dorrie was being tormented."

"Indeed, it is Dora I was ashamed of, not myself. It is not likely that I shall ever disgrace myself in like manner." So said Belle, and then the very absurdity of the suggestion that she would ever be tormented for the same reason that I had been provoked the girl to irresistible laughter, and served to prove how utterly heartless she could really be where my feelings were concerned.

That afternoon the earl rode over to Sunny Knowe and surprised me by greeting me even more cordially than ever. Evidently he thought me too insignificant and childish to be offended with, while I considered that the best thing I could do would be to make no further allusion to yesterday's *contretemps*. He did not seem inclined to tease me anymore, and the remainder of that day passed pleasantly, as did many more ere we returned to the Grange.

When at last we were installed in our old home again, we were astonished at the wonderful improvements that money and taste had been able to effect in and around it. It was now a grand old place, worthy of the imposing view it commanded and the fine trees by which its grounds were dotted. My father both looked and felt like a rich landed proprietor, as he surveyed the realm which, thanks to Lady Elizabeth's income, he would be able to support in a style becoming the dignity of the Courtneys, who had once owned all the land for miles around. A new wing had been added, for the comfort of Lady Elizabeth, whose rooms were situated here, and who had brought such a quantity of beautiful new furniture with her that the Grange was a veritable palace of delight to Belle and myself, who had never known anything but shabby surroundings. My bedroom was now of my own choosing, and had been furnished exactly like Belle's.

I wrote glowing accounts to Jerry of all that was being done, and was especially careful to give him full details concerning Bobby and Teddy, and the rats and rabbits. Poor Jerry! he was to have come home for the Christmas holidays, and they were close at hand when a serious accident befell him. He had been too venturesome in some of the school sports, with the result that he had a severe fall and fractured his right leg. His father was telegraphed for at once and lost no time in reaching him. Meanwhile, the boy had been treated by a skillful surgeon, and there was every prospect of his progressing satisfactorily toward recovery. But it was deemed inadvisable to move him at present, so poor Jerry had to forego his anticipated holiday at home.

"I felt awfully sorry for Kendall," he wrote in his weekly letter home, "because his father and mother were dead, and he would have to spend his holidays at school. Now I am jolly well glad, for he will be company for me."

It must not be imagined that Jerry was particularly selfish in expressing himself thus. It was only his youthful vagueness that was at fault. The writing, under the circumstances, was hardly legible. But I thought it very brave of the child to write at all.

Meanwhile, Christmas approached and passed with comparative uneventfulness. True, Lord Egreville had proposed to Belle. But she had declined to give him a definite answer, on the plea that she was too young to be engaged just now; the truth being that she was determined not to labor under the disadvantage of being already out of the running when she went to London for the season.

A house in town had been rented for us, and in due course we all migrated thither. I had hardly expected to be introduced to London society yet, and Belle openly grumbled at the idea. But Lady Elizabeth generally got her own way in everything, and when she intimated that there was no reason why I should not enjoy myself like the rest there was no opposition from my father. Arrived in London, however, I found that people were by no means inclined to make a fuss over me, while the "beautiful" Miss Courtney was fêted and courted to her heart's content.

Still, the proposals she had confidently expected were somewhat chary in realizing themselves, and when they did come they were not as superlatively tempting as they might have been. The fact was, it was

　　ELIZABETH BURGOYNE CORBETT

pretty generally known that Belle would have no dowry to speak of, and though plenty of young aristocrats admired her immensely, they deemed it advisable to offer their affections and society at the shrine of Mammon. There were a couple of millionaires in the market. But, incredible as it seemed to Belle, there were other girls in London whose physical charms equaled her own, and to these other girls the millionaires succumbed.

Belle fumed. Belle raged. Belle almost anathematized. Belle hated her victorious rivals. But Belle was wily, and presented an unruffled front in the presence of Lady Elizabeth and her relatives. She made the most of the proposals she did get, but professed her inability to love the proposers. Love, indeed! Could such a beautiful sentiment find an entrance into her cold breast? Impossible! What she coveted was wealth and station, and when, toward the end of the season, Lord Egreville's proved to be the most eligible offer, she accepted him, and had the felicity of seeing her engagement recorded in all the society papers.

I had an idea that the Earl of Greatlands did not care much for Belle, but had never presumed to give utterance to my suspicion. Lady Elizabeth, however, was not quite so reticent.

"I wish you every happiness, dear," she said to Belle, kissing her warmly, "and I think that you and Cyril will prove very congenial companions; but I am not sure that my father will like to see any mistress at the castle, other than his own wife, so long as he lives."

"But your father has not got a wife!" exclaimed Belle, with rising resentment at what she considered Lady Elizabeth's presumption; for, by her engagement to her brother, she was prospectively lifted to the same plane of relationship, and but for the favors which her stepmother could bestow upon her, she would at once have merged the respect due to a mother in the aggressive equality which she deemed a sister-in-law's meed.

Lady Elizabeth's reply startled us all.

"He has no wife at present," she said, "but I have good reason for asserting that he contemplates marriage at an early date, provided the lady of his choice condescends to accept him."

"Condescends to accept him!" I knew very well what was the gist of Belle's thoughts, as she sat with a sullen and dismayed face, without making even a pretense of eating the dainty fare which lay on her breakfast plate.

Who wouldn't condescend to accept him? Wasn't he nearly seventy years old? And wasn't he likely to die ere many years were over, leaving his widow in the untrammeled possession of a title that would give her the *entrée* to any society? He was sure, too, to scrape and save all he could to provide for his widow after his death, and that would mean a considerable curtailment of the allowance which Lord Egreville looked for on his marriage. Besides, if the earl brought a countess to the castle, and Lord Egreville was asked to retire to the dower-house with his bride, her position would be by no means so imposing as she had expected it to be. Residence at the castle, as its nominal mistress, had been one of Lord Egreville's special pleas when urging his suit, and, next to the acquisition of the secondary title, with the prospect of a succession to the primary one, had been one of her chief reasons for considering him much more of an eligible *parti* than her other suitors.

And then, oh, horror! suppose the earl's new wife should be young! Suppose there should actually be a child born! Why Cyril would be still further despoiled to provide for the bringing up of the little brat. True, he could not be robbed of his prospective right to the earldom, as he was the eldest son. But an active fancy could easily picture no end of humiliations for him and his wife, if the foolish old earl were permitted to bring his infatuation for some pretty face into fruition.

That these thoughts flew through Belle's brain in the sequence in which I have recorded them is more than I am able to vouch for. But I knew her temperament and disposition so well that I had no hesitation in guessing the direction of her reflections.

"I believe you are just saying all this to try me," she said at last, looking up at Lady Elizabeth with a face from which she was trying to banish some of the shadows. "Now I come to think of it, he spends the greater part of his time with us, and if he were attracted by anybody in London, he would be more likely to seek her society than ours."

Lady Elizabeth smiled very mysteriously, but did not vouchsafe a more explicit reply.

"Papa," said Belle, impatiently, "suppose you look up from that stupid paper and take a little intelligent interest in what is going on around you. It's perfectly exasperating to see you absorbed in an account of a shooting or fishing expedition, when the future of your eldest daughter is being discussed."

"My eldest daughter, eh? To be sure, I have two daughters, but the future of one of them is considerably in embryo yet, I should imagine. And what do you wish me particularly to say?"

"Have you known anything of the earl's intention to get married?"

ELIZABETH BURGOYNE CORBETT

"Well, really, now you mention it, I did hear sometime ago that he was on the lookout for a suitable spouse, but I fancy the old party hasn't turned up yet."

"Just what I think. Lady Elizabeth has simply been teasing me."

"Why, my dear, do you happen to know anything definite about the matter?"

Appealed to thus directly, Lady Elizabeth replied guardedly, "I have really been given to understand that my father would like to get married. But I am not at liberty to disclose the name of the lady whom he would like to marry."

"At least tell me whether she is old or young," appealed Belle, anxiously.

"Oh, she is several years younger than my father, I believe."

With this answer Belle was forced to be satisfied, and shortly afterward we all left the breakfast-room.

As for me, I had listened to the foregoing conversation with considerable interest, but not with the absorbed attention which might perhaps have been aroused in me, if I had had the least idea that the doings of the Earl of Greatlands could possibly affect myself. After all, I was really sorry for Belle. But perhaps the earl's marriage might not affect her so adversely as she feared.

At eleven o'clock Lord Egreville came to see Belle. I do not know the exact purport of their conversation with each other, but I do know that when Belle's *fiancé* left the drawing-room he looked much less pleasant than when he entered it, and hardly seemed to have time to speak to the earl, who was announced at this juncture. Thinking I would have an hour's uninterrupted practice on my violin, I went up to my own room, but was summoned thence by-and-by.

"Please, Miss Dora," said Lady Elizabeth's maid, "you are wanted in the library."

"*I* am wanted in the library!" I echoed, in surprise. "Why, who can possibly want me?"

"I do not know. It was milady who sent me to ask you to go down to the library."

"Is Lady Elizabeth there?"

"No, she is in her boudoir. Mr. Courtney is with her."

At first it struck me as very singular that there should be a caller who wished to see me alone, and then I reflected that my music-master had perhaps found it inconvenient to give me my music lesson at the usual hour, and had come to ask me to change the time. Full of this thought, I hurried downstairs, but was very much surprised to be confronted, not by Signor Tringini, but by the Earl of Greatlands.

"My dear child, how astonished you look," he said, as, coming forward and taking my hand, he conducted me courteously to a seat.

"Well," I replied, "I cannot conceive what can be your object in desiring an interview with me. But perhaps there has been a mistake, and it is Belle you want."

"Indeed, it is not Belle I want, but your very own self."

"I hope I have not been doing anything to call forth your particular displeasure. I have really tried to be on my best behavior with everybody since I came to London."

"You have not displeased me yet. But you will displease me very much, if you refuse to grant the request I have come to make of you."

"Then I will do the best I can to avert your threatened displeasure by promising to grant your request beforehand."

"Ah, my dear, if I were inclined to take an unfair advantage, I would rejoice exceedingly over that promise. As it is, I am terribly afraid that you may retract it. Do you happen to have heard of my intention to get married, if I can persuade a certain lady to accept me?"

"Yes, Lady Elizabeth spoke of it this morning. But she would not give us any clew to the lady's identity, and I, at least, am very curious about her. I hope she is a nice old lady, and that she will like me. You see, she will be a sort of grandmother-in-law to me—with your permission."

"Grandmother fiddlesticks! She isn't old enough to be anybody's grandmother. Can't you guess who it is?"

"Why, no. How should I? I do not know so very many of your friends, and I really do not know anybody that would seem to be a suitable Countess of Greatlands."

"Well, it seems to me that for all-round obtuseness you beat everything! Do you think it likely that I would seek a private interview with you, in order to tell you of my intention to ask someone else to marry me?"

"Then why have you come to see me?"

"Why? Only to ask you to take pity on a lonely old man, and marry him. Look here, child, don't jump up and look angry, for I really mean it. You are the only woman I would care to marry, and if you refuse to marry me I will have nobody else."

"Good gracious! how can a girl marry her grandfather? Do you forget that you are my stepmother's father?"

"And what of that? We are not really related. Now don't be hasty, my dear. Think of all I can do for you, and of all you can do for me. You shall have anything and everything you want, and be presented at Court. As the Countess of Greatlands you will be courted and sought after. But you can do much more for me than that. You can make the short span of life which yet remains to me perfectly happy. Say yes, my dear, and my love and gratitude will know no bounds."

But I could not say yes for a while. Yet neither could I say no. My astonishment was almost too great for words. Still, I was not displeased at the dazzling prospect held out to me. Reflect, dear reader, before you blame, that I had always been told that I need never hope to win the affection of any man, and that, while those around me basked in the sunshine of family joys, the man did not exist who would care to cast in his lot with mine. True, this man was old, and he was almost decrepit. But he had singled me out from the many others who would gladly have become Countess of Greatlands. In doing so, he had done me an honor of which I was fully sensible, and it was such a joy to me to have become the best beloved of even an old man that my heart prompted me to say "yes," as he desired.

Still, certain scruples would obtrude themselves upon my notice, and counseled a little hesitation.

"Belle?" I faltered at last. "I cannot! It would make such a difference to Belle."

"It will not make the slightest difference to Belle, I assure you, Dorrie. She is too vain and frivolous for me to care about living in the same house with her. Whether I marry or not, Cyril and she will have to content themselves with the dower-house during my lifetime. It is the same with the title. They cannot have it until I am gone, and your present possession of it will not keep them out of it one day after it accrues to them. Come, my dear, end my suspense, and keep the promise you made me a while ago."

"My father? And Lady Elizabeth?"

"Have no solid objections to offer."

Neither had I after that. But, somehow, the enraptured kiss with which my old lover sealed our engagement was not the sort of thing I had pictured in my day-dreams, and I involuntarily shivered under his caresses.

"What is it, my little pet, are you cold?" he asked solicitously.

"Just a little," was my evasive answer. "This room always seems chilly. But that does not matter. Tell me, for it seems so strange, how it is that you actually want to marry *me*, of all people in the world. Look how ugly I am!"

"You are not ugly to me, my dear. Besides, I am past thinking outward appearance the sole recommendation and guarantee of a happy life. I need more than mere outward beauty."

"And you think you have found it?"

"I am sure I have found it! And now, my love, with your permission, I will remain here until your father comes. I shall see you again later in the day."

Having thus virtually received my dismissal, I sped up to my own room, but not before my ardent lover had claimed another kiss as his due.

Did I feel glad?

Or did I feel dismayed?

I was really unable to tell myself which sensation predominated. I met Belle on the landing, and was conscious of a strange feeling of trepidation, which made me slink into my own room like someone guilty of a mean action.

Oh, dear! how could I ever face them all? I thought. How could I ever have the presumption to pose as the superior in rank and family prestige to my beloved stepmother? Why, if I married her father, I should be *her* stepmother. And my sister's mother-in-law! And my father's mother-in-law, too! And—could it be possible?—my own step-grandmother! There were no end of complications involved in the new arrangement; and, as I pondered over them, I became more and more doubtful as to the propriety of accepting the grand future held out to me. And yet, if I could do so without repugnance on my part, and with an honest determination to prove that the earl had acted wisely in selecting me as the wife of his old age, why should I not become a great lady? Why—

But my conjectures were interrupted at this juncture by a very unusual event. Belle had actually come to visit me in my own room! I knew instinctively, however, that her visit boded me no good, and when I looked up into her face, I saw that she was in a demoniacal temper.

"Is it true?" she cried, as she flung herself on a chair just in front of me. "Is it true that you have actually deluded that old imbecile into offering marriage to you? My father has just told me that you are to become the Countess of Greatlands at a very early date. But the news is too monstrous for belief! A hideous little reptile like you to lord it over me! A shrimp of a girl, whose *gaucherie* and ill-manners are proverbial, to dare to assume airs of superiority over me! I tell you it shall not be. I will not have it. Sooner than endure such a humiliation I would—I would—"

"And pray what would you do?" I asked, not with the compunction I had felt a while ago at the idea of relegating my beautiful sister to a secondary position. Nor yet with the anger which had blazed up in me on hearing the commencement of her virago-like harangue. But with the cool contempt of one who feels that her position is impregnable, and that her assailant is beneath consideration. "And how will you prevent an arrangement with which you are not of sufficient importance to be permitted to interfere?"

Perhaps it was astonishment at the unwonted courage with which I met her assault. Perhaps it was a sudden access of prudence. But whatever the cause, the effect was the same. Belle declined to tell me how she would prevent my marriage with the earl. But she continued to revile me for some minutes as treacherous, deceitful and scheming, and wound up by saying that I need not congratulate myself upon my seeming triumph, as Lord Egreville would certainly not permit his father to perpetrate the folly he contemplated, even if he had to swear that he was no longer responsible for his actions.

To all this I steadfastly refused any further reply, and, becoming tired of leveling abuse which seemed to make no impression, Belle left the room as suddenly as she had entered it. Once alone, I found that my own feelings with regard to the coming event had undergone a complete revolution. I no longer entertained the slightest doubt as to the propriety of having consented to accept the earl. On the contrary, I was strongly determined to fulfill my promise, and to remove myself forever from the tyranny of Belle's reproaches and airs of superiority. Very much to my own surprise, too, I felt very indignant at the slights cast upon the earl, and found my heart warm considerably toward him. For, when I came to think of it, he had always treated me kindly, and even when I thought he was deliberately insulting me, he must really have meant what he said. That his taste was peculiar, to say the least, was patent even to myself, but that was all the more reason for gratitude and love on my part.

Gratitude? Yes, that was undoubted. Love? Why not? Surely it is not so very hard for the one to engender the other.

Presently Lady Elizabeth came to my door and asked my permission to enter. This was readily given, though I already felt very much overwrought, and dreaded the coming interview. But I need not have been uneasy about that; for, as usual, my good stepmother had only my welfare at heart.

"I am afraid Belle has been giving you an uncomfortable time of it," she said, drawing a chair toward me and kissing me affectionately. "She is fuming in the drawing-room, and has sent for Cyril to consult with him as to what is best to be done in this remarkable crisis."

"And you?" I asked beseechingly. "Do you think I have been a scheming, wicked girl, and that I have done wrong in accepting the earl?"

"Certainly not, my child. I have known for sometime that my father wished to make you his wife. Indeed, he consulted me as to the wisdom of doing so, and I gave my unqualified approval to his project. Seeing that he had set his heart on having a young wife, I preferred to see you in that capacity rather than anyone else. But I hope that you are fully alive to the duties that will be expected of you."

"Indeed yes," I answered soberly. "I mean to do all in my power to make the earl happy."

"That is right. If you think only of promoting his happiness, your own will come, as a matter of course. But tell me, have you any idea that the ceremony is expected to take place almost immediately?"

"Oh no! how can it? I am too young yet to marry."

"My dear, in a case like this the bride's youth counts for nothing, and the bridegroom's age carries all other considerations before it. Your father also agrees that it is best to make immediate arrangements, and there is really no reason why you should not be married next week."

And somehow it was all decided, almost without referring again to me, that on the following Wednesday I should be transformed into the Countess of Greatlands. I have no doubt that society partially echoed Belle's sneers and voted the earl half crazy. But if it did, its criticisms did not trouble me, and I was supremely happy as I reveled in the lavish preparations that were being made for the great event. Belle's wedding was indefinitely postponed, although it had at first been spoken of as an almost immediate event.

So far as I could judge, Lord Egreville was as bitterly opposed to the earl's wedding as Belle was. He was just distantly civil to me, and I took no trouble to ingratiate myself with him. Sometimes, when the couple sat whispering in a corner, I surprised an occasional glance that was positively malignant in its intensity of hatred. Once or twice I remembered my sister's assertion that she would prevent my marriage, and wondered vaguely if she were really hatching some plot against me. Then a certainty that it was out of her power to harm me consoled me once more, and I pursued the happy tenor of my way, all my time occupied either by the earl's visits or by my initiation into further gayeties of attire.

The wedding itself was to be a very quiet affair, and as soon as it was over my husband was going to take me into Derbyshire for a week. Then we were to go to the castle, which was being rapidly prepared for my reception.

And so the time flew on, until Tuesday came round once more. Tomorrow was to be my wedding day.

Tomorrow! Oh, that dreadful tomorrow! Shall I ever forget it as long as I live?

IV

"There will be no wedding today."

That night I went to bed hoping to the last that Belle would relent and say a kindly word to me. For after all, she was the only sister I had, and I would have been thankful to have been reconciled with her. But she was as implacable as ever, and never uttered one kindly word to me amid all the congratulations of others; although Lady Elizabeth had, I know, remonstrated with her on her unsisterly behavior. My father did not care to interfere in the matter, especially as his sympathies were all in favor of his eldest daughter.

I was up betimes, for we were to be at the church at ten o'clock. I had been sorely exercised about the choice of a wedding dress, as I feared that white would make me look more hideous than usual. But Lady Elizabeth had persuaded me to have a creamy satin, and, somehow, as I surveyed myself in the glass, I was not quite so dissatisfied with the result as I had expected to be. The freckles had found the London atmosphere uncongenial, and had departed, I fervently hoped forever. My complexion too had changed from a muddy hue to a clear dark olive which, though far from being satisfactory, was a considerable improvement on its former condition. My hair, thanks to the skillful treatment of Lady Elizabeth's maid, had grown much thicker, and looked rather nice than otherwise.

But, in spite of these improvements, I was still an ugly, insignificant-looking slip of a girl, and I lost myself in wonderment at the thought of such great good fortune coming to me. There were to be no bridemaids, only a few personal friends having been invited to church, though there was to be a reception at the house afterward. Belle had at first declared her intention of refusing to accompany us to church. But perhaps the thought that she would, by holding herself aloof, betray to the world at large how deeply chagrined she was, induced her to alter her mind.

Still, when I saw her in the hall, just before we started, I could not account for her unusual appearance. She was positively livid, and shook every now and then in the strangest manner. Both my father and Lady Elizabeth conceived the idea that she must be ill, but she assured them that there was nothing the matter with her.

"But of course one feels a little excited at seeing one's sister so

ELIZABETH BURGOYNE CORBETT

suddenly raised to splendor," she said, with a side glance at me which displayed so curious a mixture of fear and hatred that I lost all my good spirits, and was driven to church in an unaccountable state of nervousness and trepidation, which was increased when I saw that the bridegroom and Lord Egreville, who was to officiate as best man, were not here first, according to arrangement.

"I am surprised they are not here yet," whispered Lady Elizabeth. "Never mind, dear, they are sure to come soon."

So I thought, too. But for the life of me I could not hinder the tears which came to ease my head and my heart, both of which were in a state of painful tension. By-and-by, I looked up to see Belle's eyes fixed upon me once more. But what had wrought a change in her again? Her expression was no longer one of fear, but of victory. The hatred was there yet, and that did not surprise me. But how to account for the unmistakable triumph which I had seen manifest itself on her face for a moment?

Like a flash her words recurred to me: "I tell you, it shall not be! I will not have it! Sooner than endure such a humiliation I would—"

Ah! what would she do? What *had* she done? I asked myself anxiously. Something decisive. Something disastrous to me, I knew, or her face would not have worn that momentary impress of a purpose accomplished. Somehow, through all the weary waiting that followed, my powers of observation and deduction seemed strung to their highest pitch. I noticed that as the moments dragged on without bringing the two gentlemen, Lady Elizabeth and my father grew momentarily more anxious. And I also noticed that Belle no longer looked expectantly toward the door, as everyone else kept doing, but that she bore all the appearance of one whose desires were accomplished.

At last, unable to bear the suspense any longer, my father rose from his seat, and, whispering to Lady Elizabeth that he was going to the earl's temporary town residence, to ascertain the cause of the strange delay, he left the church without further preamble, my acutely attuned ears shortly afterward hearing the rattling of his cab-wheels down the street.

Lady Elizabeth, who sat next to me, put a caressing hand upon my own, and whispered: "Do not look so frightened, child. I do not suppose they will be long in coming now."

"They will never come!" was my reply, intended only for my comforter's ears. "They will never come! Something dreadful has happened, and Belle knows it. See how calm and self-satisfied she is now. Remember the state she was in before she came. She vowed that my marriage should not take place. She has made her vow come true!"

Lady Elizabeth cast a startled glance at Belle, but had no time to comment upon my words, for at this moment we heard an excited hubbub near the door, and Marvel, the earl's valet, came down the aisle with a face which advertised bad news.

"Will your ladyship please leave the church as quickly as you can?" he said to my stepmother. "And take the bride with you. *There will be no wedding today.*"

"For God's sake, tell me what is the matter!" she exclaimed. "Something dreadful has happened to my father!"

"An accident has occurred to him," said Marvel, with an attempt to speak as if it were nothing serious. But his voice broke in the endeavor, and he sobbed forth: "Oh, my poor master! it is too dreadful!"

"What is the matter with him?" cried Lady Elizabeth, fairly shaking the man in the intensity of her excitement and dread. "Tell me at once."

When I heard Marvel's reply, I neither shrieked nor fainted. For I had felt sure that he would say what he did.

"He is dead!" he said, and my eyes, flaming and accusing now, at once sought Belle's, flashing my conviction of her guilt in her face. Under that glance she reeled as if from a blow.

I hardly know what else happened that morning. I went home as in a dream, feeling somehow more sorry for Lady Elizabeth than for myself, and wondering if they would hang Belle when it was discovered that she had murdered the earl; for my mind refused to disabuse itself of a conviction of her guilt, although reason pointed to the conclusion that it was impossible for her to have injured the earl, seeing that she had not seen him, or spoken to him, for twenty hours.

The wedding guests returned to their own homes, there to discuss the sensational interruption to what some of them had voted the most sensational wedding of the season. My father reached home soon after we did, and confirmed Marvel's story in every detail. The Earl of Greatlands had been found by Marvel, who had grown alarmed when he did not rise at eight o'clock, lying in ghastly rigidity in the bed which he had sought some hours earlier in apparently unusually buoyant health and spirits. A glance convinced Marvel that life was quite extinct, and a moment later he was rousing the household with shouts and cries. Of course everybody came rushing up to the earl's room. And of course several doctors were summoned at once. But it was

ELIZABETH BURGOYNE CORBETT

only too patent from the very first that there was no hope, and though there was much loud lamentation on the part of the servants, and quite a touching display of sorrow on the part of Lord Egreville, or, rather, the new Earl of Greatlands, it was not of the slightest avail, and the fiat speedily went forth to the world that Lionel, ninth Earl of Greatlands, being in an unusually excited state, owing to his prospective marriage, had succumbed to unsuspected heart disease.

Nearly all the world accepted this explanation of the tragic event which had, at one blow, deprived me of husband, wealth, title, position and influence, and had converted Lord Egreville into the peer he longed to be.

But not for one moment did I believe that the doctors had given anything like a true diagnosis of the cause of the late earl's death. There is a fashion in everything, even in matters of life and death, and nowadays it seems to be an epidemical fashion with medical men to ascribe every sudden death of which they do not understand the cause to unsuspected heart disease. The explanation is plausible, and, in all likelihood, more often than not correct, although there is a strong element of guess-work about it. Post mortem examinations are horrible and unpleasant contingencies to contemplate, and the feelings of relatives and friends are apt to be cruelly wounded by the bare mention of such a *dernier resort*.

Of course it would have been extremely painful for all parties concerned if an inquest over the remains of the Earl of Greatlands had been suggested; but I never doubted for one instant that such a course would have resulted in the discovery of foul play, such as only I—and one other, as subsequent events proved—suspected.

Suspected! do I say? It was no mere suspicion with me. It was a firm and rooted conviction, that nothing but absolute proof to the contrary could ever dispel. And that proof, since no one broached the advisability of an inquest, was not likely to be afforded me. No doubt there was considerable marvel in some people's minds concerning my manner of bearing the sudden reverse of fortune which had befallen me, but their opinion troubled me little, and it was not likely that I would occupy the minds of sensation-mongers long after I had been relegated to my former status of insignificant obscurity. Tears did not often come to relieve the aching weight which oppressed me, as I pondered in what perhaps struck those who were unable to gauge my real feelings as a hard and defiant mood.

How could they tell, however, that the grief I felt for the loss of the man who had loved me outweighed my regret for my lost glories, since I let very few words of sorrow escape me? Indeed, I dared not indulge in comments with anyone, for I feared lest the horror and loathing which I now felt for my sister and her *fiancé* should break the bounds in which I had resolved for the time being to entrammel them, and overflow in a torrent of bitter denunciation and invective. I should imagine that there are few girls of stronger passions for love or for hatred than myself, and I sometimes caught myself wondering how I managed to refrain from publicly denouncing those whom I firmly believed to be the deliberate murderers of my dear old earl; for I hated them with a hatred that was consuming in its wild intensity. Yes, my hatred was of fearful force. But I was swayed by an even stronger passion, which held it at bay.

This was my love for Lady Elizabeth, the first being who, since my mother died, had opened her heart to me, and who was now prostrated by a nervous attack, due to grief at the loss of her father, between whom and herself the strongest sympathy had always existed. She had of late admitted me largely into her confidence, and I had gained so much knowledge of her nature that I knew what a bitter blow such family disgrace would be to her as would overtake us all were my convictions shared by others. For my father's sake I would not have repressed my wild longing for vengeance. For Lady Elizabeth's sake I could have submitted to make an even greater sacrifice.

But even my great love for her could not induce me to hold friendly intercourse with Belle, or to withhold the fierce glances of accusation under which the new Earl of Greatlands writhed in impotent rage. He saw that I suspected evil-doing of some sort on his part, and he resented my glances at first by frowns of defiance. But somehow, when I continued to maintain steadfastly the antagonistic attitude I had assumed, he grew manifestly uneasy, and even went so far as to presume to address words of sympathy to me, which implied that he imagined me to cherish animosity against him merely because he was occupying the place of the man who was to have been my husband, and suggested that he hoped I would no longer hold aloof from him and Belle as if I thought they had done me an injury.

To this misjudged attempt to induce me to bury the hatchet I vouchsafed no response but a cold stare of contempt and a curl of the lip which spoke volumes. Indeed, so potent was this mute answer of mine that the earl almost ceased to visit our house, and my father was informed by Belle that my violence and ill manners had succeeded in depriving her to a great extent of her lover's society.

"Dora," said my affectionate parent to me one morning after breakfast, "I am sorry to observe that you have lapsed into your former ill-conditioned state of selfish ill-breeding. I have made all due allowance for the disappointment you must have felt at being prevented from becoming the great lady you expected to be. But I have noticed with growing displeasure that you are venting your spleen in an unjustifiable manner upon Belle. Certainly, she is going to occupy the position you thought would be yours, but she is doing you no personal injury thereby, for your chances are irrevocably gone, and she was engaged to the present Earl of Greatlands before the marriage between yourself and his father was arranged. It is therefore abominable that you should try to make her life miserable by driving her lover from the house, and doing your best to produce an estrangement between them; and if you continue your present behavior, I shall insist upon your going to live at the Grange until we are ready to leave London."

Lady Elizabeth was too ill to come downstairs, and was, therefore, not present during this harangue. Otherwise it would probably not have been made; for, even in things that wholly and solely concerned me, my father was wont to show that consideration for his wife, who loved me, that he would never have displayed toward me for my own sake, and he treated me with tolerable politeness when in her presence. But when she was not there, he showed the same unbounded partiality for Belle and the same lack of sympathy for me which had always distinguished our intercourse in the past; and it is not surprising that my lately acquired self-reliance prompted me to retort that I was best aware of the motives of my conduct, and that Belle was not likely to lose her lover through me, since their destiny would henceforth be ruled by the promptings of an evil conscience.

"You miserable little wretch!" exclaimed my father. "How dare you speak to me in that tone? And how dare you cast innuendoes against Belle and Cyril which virtually amount to an accusation?"

"An accusation of what, sir?" I asked, with a calm deliberateness which surprised even myself, and caused my father to stagger as if he had received a blow. And, indeed, he had received such a blow as is to be hoped falls to the lot of few fathers. For my looks and manner, more than my words, had struck him with the sudden conviction that his favorite child was suspected of having at least been accessory to a mortal crime. That the suspicion emanated from the brain of another of his children mattered little to him, for he already disliked me too intensely to feel any heart-pangs on my account. It was quite sufficient, however, to cause him to cast aside the last shred of conventionality as regarded his treatment of myself.

What transpired during the next five minutes I prefer not to relate. There are events in the lifetime of most people which possess either too sacred or too painful an interest for discussion with others. The memory of my last interview with my father awakes in me no emotion but that of resentment at the constant injustice with which he had always treated me, and which culminated on this occasion in my expulsion from his house.

Perhaps he thought that I would not take him at his word, and that at the end of the hour which he had named as the limit of time he would allow me in which to pack up my belongings and rid my family of my presence, I would weepingly sue for mercy and promise to be polite and conciliatory to Belle and the Earl of Greatlands. The mere supposition that I, whose passions were of the strongest, could thus do violence to my feelings, and acknowledge the superiority of two people whom I hated and despised with all my heart, for the sake of retaining a home in which I could never hope to be happy again, still serves to excite my indignation and to provoke me to a feeling of resentment which I would fain repudiate in my calmer moments.

For, after all, my father, poor man, was blinded by his partiality for Belle; and although he fully grasped the deadly import of my unspoken suspicions, he never for a moment doubted his beautiful darling's goodness, but accepted my attitude merely as a convincing proof of the monstrosity of nature of one to whom had been denied that outward fairness which in his eyes was equal to the strongest proof of inward purity. Thus I sometimes reason, in attempted palliation of his harshness to me. But, somehow, my reasoning has an awkward knack of doubling upon itself and transforming my would-be kindlier leanings into the old imbittered resentment.

My preparations for departure were soon made, although as yet my brain was in too great a turmoil to permit me to make a definite plan for my future guidance. I must remove myself and my belongings quickly. And I must take my leave of Lady Elizabeth without permitting her to be pained by a knowledge of the permanent nature of the estrangement between myself and my family. The latter was a difficult feat for me to

ELIZABETH BURGOYNE CORBETT

perform. But I succeeded in going through the interview in a manner which it pleased me to recall during my subsequent sufferings; for my dear stepmother was spared the pain which would have been hers, if she had realized the anguish of mind which my love for her caused me to hide.

I found her in her dressing-room, reclining on a couch which was drawn up to the fire, the day being somewhat chilly for the time of year. I noted with a sudden foreboding dread the change which the last few weeks had wrought in Lady Elizabeth's appearance. She was paler, thinner, and altogether much more fragile-looking than when, so short a time ago, she had assisted me to select the trousseau for my own marriage with her father. There was, however, a light in her eyes which had, until lately, been a stranger to them, and which had caused me considerable uneasiness. For it gave me the impression that it had its origin in a feeling deeper even than the grief which an affectionate daughter would naturally feel at the loss of a beloved parent.

Could it be that—oh, no! perish the thought! Why should she be tortured by such suspicions as had fixed their scorpion-fangs in my brain? She could scarcely be so fully convinced of Belle's capacity for evil as I was, since she had never known her until the glamour of her artfulness and beauty was such as to cause nearly everyone who knew her to take a fancy to her. Nor had she such deep reason to distrust one of her own mother's children as was the case with me. Some hidden sorrow was sapping her life's strength. But I fervently and sincerely prayed that it might not be the hideous phantom of suspicion which was bidding fair to wreck my own life.

"I have come to say good-by for a time," I said, speaking with wonderful quietness for one whose brain was in a whirl of stormy emotion. "As you know, things are not as pleasant as they might be between Belle and myself, and father and I have agreed that it will be best for me to return to the Grange for a while. The change will do me good, but I shall be grieved to part from you."

"But, my dear, we are all going to the Grange shortly," said Lady Elizabeth, casting upon me a look of anxious scrutiny. "Come here. Kneel beside me, and tell me all about this sudden arrangement. Have Belle and you been quarreling?"

"Belle and I have not been quarreling," I answered, as I dropped on my knees beside the only woman in the world who loved me, and stroked her white hand between my much less shapely ones. "But you may have noticed that, whether rightly or wrongly, I cannot feel happy in her presence. The earl, your brother, too, seems to be kept away from the house through the antagonism which he and I feel for each other. I feel as if it were wicked to dislike anyone nearly related to you. But, indeed, I cannot help it. So you must forgive me, and let me go from you now with nothing but the kindest and most loving words from you; for, believe me, I am more sorely in need of your sympathy than ever I was, and could not bear to think of an estrangement between you and me."

"Dorrie, I have learned to love you, and I know that you are not likely to form violent antipathies without a cause. I also feel convinced that your treatment of—of—my brother is dictated by the strongest feeling on your part. The nature of that feeling must remain unknown to me, for I dread confirmation of certain thoughts which fill my days and nights with terror. Even should you prove to be actually unjust to my brother, it will make no difference between us. But, if you are really leaving town before the rest of us do, you must promise me one thing."

"I will promise anything to you."

"I know your willingness to serve me, and I think I can gauge your love for me, but I am about to exact a great proof of both. Listen. All my life I have yielded to the dictates of family pride. I have been proud of my ancient lineage and unsullied family escutcheon; so proud, indeed, that I did not hesitate to ally myself with one who had once been one of the humblest sons of the people. I never dreamed of the possibility of my being lowered to his family level by marrying him, but was sure that the prestige of my own connections would over-shadow the possible vulgarity of his antecedents. In marrying a wealthy commoner, of whose personal worthiness I felt thoroughly convinced, I hoped to be able to assist my family to a financial position more commensurate with their social status than the aristocratic impecuniosity which had been our lot for many years, owing to the extravagance of my grandfather, who had mortgaged the greater part of the estate. My expectations were fully justified. My husband was kind and generous, and whatever my original feelings toward him may have been, I can truthfully say that his upright nature won my complete loyalty and respect. I was certainly disappointed to find myself comparatively poor after his death. But I have had time to think the matter over since then, and believe that the people to whom he left the bulk of his money must have needed it more than I did. I see that you wonder why I am

ELIZABETH BURGOYNE CORBETT

telling you all this. I assure you I have a strong enough motive, for I want you to realize that I would sacrifice everything to the honor of my family—love, happiness, even life itself. This being the case, can you picture how terrible it would be to me to see even the shadow of public disgrace fall upon our name? That you have ample provocation for a certain course of conduct which would materially affect the interests of my brother, and of your sister, I know. I also know that you return the love I bear you. Let that love outweigh the resentment you feel at the conduct of others. If you are not inclined to spare *them*, for God's sake spare *me* the anguish which a disclosure of your—of your suspicions would cause me! You are leaving us for a time. I implore you to have mercy upon an ancient name."

By the time Lady Elizabeth had got thus far, she was sobbing in uncontrollable excitement, and clung to me with convulsive apprehension. As for me, I was filled with grief at this disclosure of the suffering which my dear one was undergoing. I could no longer doubt that she shared all my own painful suspicions, and that to her distressed state of mind her recent physical prostration was attributable. And I was stabbed by the remorseful thought that I had been the one to originate the dread suspicions which were doing so much mischief. Was it too late to undo the mischief? Could I hope to remove the terrible burden of dread which oppressed Lady Elizabeth? It was doubtful. But there was too much at stake to warrant hesitation on my part, and my course of conduct was instantaneously mapped out.

"Mother," I said, as quietly as my emotion would permit, "I cannot pretend not to understand the meaning of what you have just said. But, oh! my dear, how could you think I meant all that I implied to you on that terrible morning, when I was beside myself with anxiety and grief? Put away such thoughts from your mind. It is the misfortune, not the fault, of Cyril and Belle, that all the circumstances attending recent events have seemed as if specially guided for their interests. But if even I, who am so great a loser by their advancement, can say that my first suspicions were unjustifiable and wicked, surely you can no longer think them capable of a crime too atrocious for even ready-dyed criminals to think of."

Lady Elizabeth suddenly raised her head and literally gasped with mingled relief and amazement.

"Is it possible," she cried, "that I have been tormenting myself needlessly? That I have foully wronged Cyril and Belle? That I have mistaken your dislike to them for a stronger sentiment—that of a thirst for justifiable revenge for a deadly injury?"

"Quite possible. Think. Our dear old earl could not have been expected to live very much longer. He was happy. So happy, that he was naturally excited. Excitement is not good for weakly old people, and the skillful doctors who were summoned were sure to be able to judge of the real cause of death. You cannot tell how much I regret having given audible expression to a cruel suspicion. But you can do as I have done—and repudiate it."

"Do you repudiate it?"

"Most certainly I do."

"Thank God for that! You have lifted a nightmare from my mind. Do you know that the promise I wished to exact from you was that you would at least spare me the suffering which a denunciation of my brother Cyril would cause me?"

"A denunciation! Ah, well—I don't like him. I never shall like him. But as there is nothing to denounce, I can safely promise you, nay, swear to you, that never, so long as you live, will I, by word or deed, do aught that can injure any member of your family or in anyway jeopardize its good name."

"You swear this?"

"I swear it!"

"You have given me a new lease of life, my darling, and by the time we join you at the Grange you will see me almost as vigorous as ever."

"I hope so. But I must be off now, or I shall not be ready when the cab comes round for me. Good-by."

"Good-by, my dear. I hope the change will do you good. You too have been drooping lately."

"I suppose I have. But country air will work wonders, eh?"

Another minute, and I had hurried out of Lady Elizabeth's room, with breaking heart and whirling brain. Should I ever see her again? To what had I pledged myself? I had, for her sake, forsworn all my dreams of punishing those whom I firmly believed to be the murderers of the Earl of Greatlands. Certainly, I had never intended to invoke the vengeance of the law upon them, for I also had some regard to the maintenance of the esteem in which the two families were held by the world at large. But I had meant to elucidate, by some means, the extent of their culpability, and to show them up to their relatives in all their hideous criminality, leaving them to continue their career stripped of

ELIZABETH BURGOYNE CORBETT

the misplaced love and confidence that had hitherto been so charily bestowed upon me.

Surely this was but a feeble ideal of the punishment due to a great crime which had deprived me of everything that made my life worth living. But I was now bereft of even this small satisfaction, for I had, for the sake of Lady Elizabeth, pledged myself to do nothing that would reflect discredit upon her family. I had even gone so far as to repudiate all my suspicions, and so long as she lived I must do nothing to re-awaken the terrors which had been tormenting her of late.

Does anyone doubt that I found this sacrifice of my personal inclinations very hard to bear? or that it was not a real sacrifice to leave my enemies to gloat unrestrainedly at the success of their evil plotting? Or do they imagine that the feelings I harbored were unjustifiable? If so, let them imagine themselves in my position. Let them picture all that I had lost and suffered, and contrast my lot with what would have been my condition had the earl's life not terminated when it did. True, I had as yet not the slightest practical evidence to support my opinion of the culpability of the new earl and his *fiancée*; but as my personal conviction never admitted the slightest doubt on that score, I found its virtual abandonment all the harder to bear, though nothing would now make me disregard Lady Elizabeth's wishes. And this I mention, not for the sake of demonstrating my powers of self-sacrifice, but to show how gratefully I reciprocated the kindness of my stepmother, and to show how my heart hungered for love, since the lavishment of a little of it upon me had power to arouse in me a feeling so passionate as to be almost akin to worship.

And now I was about to leave, probably forever, the one being who cared for me. Small wonder that the hard feelings which had hitherto enabled me to keep my composure should break down, and that the quick tears of utter lonesomeness should chase each other down my pale cheeks as I hurriedly gathered my belongings together, and began to pack them in the substantial trunks which had been provided by Lady Elizabeth to hold the trousseau with which her loving liberality had provided me.

"Excuse me, Miss Dora, but my lady has sent me to see if I can be of any use to you. You are packing everything up? Then pray let me do it for you."

I looked up through my tears, and saw Agnes, my stepmother's maid, standing ready to relieve me of my task. She was in such evident sympathy with me that at sight of her kindly face my last shred of composure left me, and I wept in such an abandonment of grief as only a feeling of utter desolation can produce. Agnes was frightened at the violence of my emotion and did her best to console me. But I presently became calmer, and thanking her for the trouble she was taking, gladly availed myself of her help in packing my boxes. I felt no hesitation in taking everything that belonged to me, for all I had worth having was due to the generosity of Lady Elizabeth or of her father. To my own father I owed nothing of which I was now possessed, the last item of the unbecoming garments which he had so grudgingly bestowed upon me having disappeared long ago.

In another half an hour I was ready to go, and a few moments later the cab for which I had sent was at the door. As I stepped into it I glanced at the upper windows of the house which was no longer a home for me. I saw Lady Elizabeth, who had come to her window to wave me a smiling good-by. Evidently no one had yet told her that I was permanently banished from my father's house. I smiled and kissed my hand to her, resolved that her last glimpse of me should be as pleasant as possible. Then my eyes sought the level of the drawing-room windows, to see—what? My sister standing there by the side of the Earl of Greatlands, both of them displaying the greatest delight at my departure, and both of them casting contemptuous glances of triumph on a poor, homeless girl whose presence near them was a continual reproach.

But their malevolence did not get all the satisfaction it sought, for my glance wandered swiftly upward again, and rested on my stepmother's smiling face, until I was driven out of sight altogether, with such apparent unconsciousness of their presence that they could not know I had seen them. And thus I entered upon the battle of life on my own account.

ELIZABETH BURGOYNE CORBETT

V

"A maiden's fancies."

In spite of the turmoil of mind under which I had labored since my interview with my father, I had already formed somewhat definite plans for my future.

I had made all my arrangements as if I were really going to the Grange, and had had my boxes labeled accordingly. Thus Lady Elizabeth had not alarmed herself about me, knowing that my comfort would be looked after at the Grange. My father, if he had taken the trouble to make any inquiries about me, would also think he knew whither I was bound; and, even if visited by a faint feeling of compunction on my behalf, would consider that I was as well off in one place as in another.

But since he had ordered me from his house, I meant to take him literally at his word, and had resolved never to cast my shadow within any threshold of his again. I was but ill equipped for earning my livelihood, but I had a certain determination of purpose at whose bidding I was prepared to cast aside all false pride, such as might possibly throw obstacles in the way of my progress. Thus I realized that it might become necessary for me to adopt a means of living perfectly honest and honorable in itself, but which had hitherto never entered into the calculations of a Courtney.

Circumstances had precluded my having many friends to whom I could turn in my present need. But I felt that I could rely upon the vicar of Moorbye and his kindly wife. Both the Rev. Horace Garth and Mrs. Garth had always shown some interest in me and in my doings, and they were among the few people who seemed to be uninfluenced by the physical disadvantages which were such a sore source of trouble to me. It was to the Moorbye vicarage, therefore, that I resorted for aid and counsel in this my great extremity. I felt some trepidation as I was swiftly whirled along in the second-class compartment, for which a sense of the necessity of economizing the money I had at my disposal had induced me to take a ticket. As to what kind of traveling companions I had, it is impossible for me to say, for I was too much engrossed with my troubles to take notice of my surroundings.

"Will the Garths welcome me, and do their best for me; or will, they consider me to blame, and wash their hands of me?"

This was the question that was uppermost in my mind, and I could scarcely refrain from putting it into so many words, when, on alighting at Moorbye Station, whom should I see but the vicar himself welcoming two ladies who had evidently traveled from town by the same train which had conveyed myself.

Leaving the porter, who gave me a respectful recognition, to see after my luggage for the present, I hurried up to the vicar and accosted him.

"Mr. Garth, can you give me a moment's private conversation? If these ladies will kindly excuse you, I will not keep you long."

"Why, Dorrie! What brings you here just now?" Mr. Garth exclaimed, as he, fortified by the permission of his friends, walked along the platform with me. "And how do you happen to be traveling alone?"

"My father has turned me out of his house. Until I can find some means of earning my living, I have no one to whom I can go for counsel but yourself. I hoped to have been able to stay with you tonight, but I see you already have visitors."

"Tut, tut, child! As if that mattered. You would always be welcome. Now, not a word of all this until we can talk the matter over later on. Meanwhile, come and be introduced to my friends.—Oh, I say, Thompson, see that Miss Courtney's luggage is sent up to the vicarage with the rest.—Ah, here we are! Mrs. Marshall, I am glad to introduce to your notice Miss Dora Courtney, who has kindly come to cheer her old friends up a bit. Miss May, you will be pleased to have a clever companion of your own age while you are down here. Dorrie, these are old friends and near relatives of ours, Mrs. Frank Marshall and Miss May Morris."

What wonderful power there is in generous good nature combined with tact! Five minutes before I reached Moorbye Station I was among the most miserable upon earth, wondering whether even a civil welcome awaited me. Five minutes after my arrival I was being bowled toward the vicarage in Mrs. Garth's funny little governess car, and was laughing merrily with the others at the small space at our individual disposal.

"My dear, I have an unexpected pleasure in store for you. Here are our cousins, and here is Dora Courtney, also come to favor us with a visit."

Thus said the vicar, on our arrival at his home. There was a warm welcome from Mrs. Garth, supplemented by a somewhat boisterous one from Master Vincent Garth, who betrayed great curiosity concerning my outward appearance.

ELIZABETH BURGOYNE CORBETT

"Do come right into the middle of the hall, just for one minute," he demanded, "while we have a real good look at you."

Quite unconscious of the purport of his impetuosity, I laughingly obeyed him, the rest meanwhile standing by in indulgent amusement. For some seconds the child looked at me gravely. Then his face became quickly clouded with disappointment, and, considerably to the surprise of us all, he burst into loud lamentations, of which it was sometime before we could gather the meaning.

"We don't like her any better," he sobbed. "Susie said Miss Dora was to be a grand countess, and we've looked at her, and she isn't turned grand. She's just ugly."

I believe Mrs. Garth hoped and fancied that I had not been able to understand Vinnie's comments. But I had not found it very difficult to do so, and felt quite as much hurt as if this little stab to my vanity had proceeded from a responsible individual, instead of from an impulsive child, though I strove to hide my humiliated feelings as much as possible.

"What a horrid child," whispered Miss Morris, as we passed up the fine old staircase, in the wake of our hostess, on the way to the rooms allotted to us. "He ought to be whipped for insulting anyone like that."

For a moment I was tempted to second her remark. Then my better nature prevailed, as I remembered how frank and generous Vinnie really was.

"I do not blame him," I answered, somewhat soberly, it must be confessed. "Vinnie was only giving way to a natural disappointment, and did not dream of hurting my feelings, I am sure."

"Now look at the accommodation I have for you, and tell me if you think it will do," called out Mrs. Garth's rich voice from a room which she and Mrs. Marshall had just entered. "I have only two spare bedrooms, which open out of this dressing-room," she continued. "I had intended the large room for Madge, and the small one for May, but I am afraid I must ask two of you to use one bedroom jointly."

"Oh, how delightful!" exclaimed May, who was evidently a very impulsive young lady. "Madge can have the small room, and Dora and I will sleep in the other. I may call you Dora, mayn't I? I hate ceremony, and, do you know, I have taken quite a fancy to you."

Of course all Miss May's propositions were cheerfully acquiesced in, and we were all three soon occupied in unpacking our dinner-gowns. In the dressing-room a cozy little fire shed its comforting rays upon the pretty furniture and draperies, and gave an aspect of cheerfulness to the place which was by no means reflected in my own heart, though I strove to banish all outward semblance of dejection.

"Fancy a fire in June!" laughed May, as she insisted I should at once call her. "It strikes a Londoner as rather odd; but, do you know, I'm not at all sure that it isn't quite cool down here. I gather that you are a native of these parts, Dora. Is it a usual thing to need fires in summer?"

"At the Grange," I replied, as I fastened the dinner-dress which I would rather have been excused from wearing this evening, as I was both tired and overwrought, and would gladly have gone to bed, "at the Grange we seem to need fires all the year round in some of the rooms. Some parts of the neighborhood are inclined to be rather marshy and damp, and as coals are cheap about here, nearly everybody keeps the chills off in the only possible way."

"Good gracious! I hope it isn't a fever-and-ague sort of a neighborhood! What shall we do if it is? We are invited down here for a month, but if there is any danger in that direction, I shall betake myself off again. Fancy jerking your limbs first in one direction and then in another, and pulling grimaces at people just at the very moment when you want to be most polite! It's too awful to think about, and I dare not risk it."

"Why, you goose," exclaimed Mrs. Marshall, "you are mixing up fever-and-ague with an entirely different complaint, called St. Vitus's Dance. It is a nervous affection, not likely to be brought on by a chill."

"And," I added, "I don't think you need alarm yourself about fever-and-ague, either. None of the Garth household have ever been troubled with it, and we have always enjoyed the same immunity at the Grange."

"The Grange. That's where you live, isn't it?" inquired May. "It sounds quite old-worldish and jolly. I can fancy all sorts of spirits and hobgoblins disporting in its interminable corridors and secret chambers. What is the ghost like? Is it a woman dressed in gray silk, and with a heartbroken look on a beautiful face? And does she wring her hands, and cry, 'Woe is me!' Or is it a man, looking fierce and vengeful, and dragging clanking chains after him? They are mostly either one or the other, and oh! I forgot, the woman turns into a cat sometimes, and stands mewing over a place where there is a buried treasure. Isn't it delightful to think of? Dora, you must take me to the Grange, and let me sleep with you one night. Then we'll watch for the ghost, and perhaps we may solve the mystery of the treasure and become rich beyond the wildest dreams of avarice. And then I'll write the ghost's history. Mr. Stoach is great on ghosts lately, but our ghost tale will be much better and much

ELIZABETH BURGOYNE CORBETT

more thrilling than any he has got hold of. I wonder if there are heaps of rubies and pearls and diamonds and sapphires among the treasure. It always is the case. Oh, won't they be gorgeous! Dora, we must go not later than tomorrow night! I really cannot bear the suspense any longer. What do you say?"

But for a little while I was beyond saying anything, for everytime I tried to speak a fit of laughter prevented the utterance of a single intelligible word. Mrs. Marshall, too, though she laughed like one who was more familiar with Miss May's flights of fancy and vagaries than I was, enjoyed the situation thoroughly.

"That's the way with May," she smiled. "You will get used to her by-and-by, no doubt. She pictures the wildest things, and accepts the freaks of her own imagination as gospel truth."

"But," interrupted May, whose face looked comically anxious. "There is a ghost, isn't there? And there is a treasure, isn't there?"

"I'm afraid that the Grange possesses neither of those hall-marks of antiquity," I responded, as gravely as I could. "At least, I have never heard of them."

"That's just it!" cried May, renewed hope sparkling in her eyes. "Perhaps you are rather nervous, and they didn't like to tell you about the ghost. But it's there, all the same. Have you never heard it pattering along the deserted corridors, or tapping gently against the window panes, to attract your attention, or sighing mournfully through the keyhole, or—"

"May, do be less absurd," pleaded Mrs. Marshall. "You will not be ready to go down with us to dinner if you do not hurry up, instead of standing chattering about rubbish."

"Rubbish, indeed! Ghosts are not rubbish. Treasure is not rubbish. I wish I had some of the latter now, so that I could have a maid to dress me. Dora, you must, you really must, let us make a start at solving the mystery tomorrow."

"But there is no mystery."

"That remains to be seen. At any rate, you will take me to the Grange tomorrow, will you not?"

I was glad that just at this moment we were summoned to dinner, as May's persistence about visiting the Grange worried me a little, and I did not want to commit myself in anyway until I had had the private talk with Mr. Garth that had been agreed upon. So "We will see about it" was all the reply on the subject which May received just then. But it satisfied her for the time being, for she immediately went off into ecstasies of thanks and speculation, which bubbled over even after we had sat down to dinner.

"What do you think?" she exclaimed to Mr. and Mrs. Garth. "I'm in for no end of adventure. Dora has promised to take me to the Grange, to exorcise the ghost and recover the buried treasure. And we're going to spend our wealth abroad. We shall wear our diamonds at the foreign courts, and I intend to marry nothing under a duke. And my children will be princes, and perhaps—Good gracious! who's the next heir to the throne of Germany?"

By this time the whole company was convulsed with laughter, which Miss May did not seem to appreciate; for she froze up immediately, cast a withering look of scorn at the callously inappreciative company, and spoke not another word for at least two minutes, at the end of which time her tongue was languishing for exercise.

"And how did you leave Lady Elizabeth?" inquired Mrs. Garth, during this momentary break in the conversation.

"I do not like her present condition at all," was my reply. "She has fretted a good deal ever—ever since the earl died."

It cost me much to utter these words quietly, for the mere thought of my poor old lover's mysterious death always moved me to sudden anger.

"But surely she is not fretting herself ill?" said Mr. Garth, in some surprise. "We know that she was much attached to her father; but, after all, he was really old, and she has many compensating blessings, if I am not mistaken."

"You are not mistaken," was my answer. "But Lady Elizabeth's grief is not selfish or unreasonable, though it may be incomprehensible to all but herself and me."

"Then you think you understand fully why she is allowing it to prey on her health?"

"God help me, yes!" I cried passionately. "Why do you torture me like this? Cannot you understand that the whole subject is too bitter for me to talk of more than can be helped?"

"Poor child!" exclaimed Mrs. Garth penitently. "Of course it is. I ought to have known."

"No, no, I am the one to blame. How can you possibly know all that occupies my mind? Forgive my hasty words, they were foolish and unwarrantable."

Mrs. Garth protested against this last assertion of mine, but I need hardly remark that our party was not quite so cheerful as it had been, and that we were all somewhat relieved when it was time to adjourn to the drawing-room.

"Dorrie," said Mr. Garth, "can you spare me a few moments before we join the others?"

"Certainly."

"Then we will have a chat in my study."

And to Mr. Garth's study we went. Here, so far as it was advisable for me to do, I confided the details of my history and perplexities to my host, who listened with the greatest attention to all I had to tell him.

"Do you think I am much to blame?" I asked at last.

"I cannot think that you have much to reproach yourself with, as, though somewhat impulsive at times, I believe you to be very fair and just. But, to be candid, I do not quite realize the necessity for all this extreme feeling. That, I suppose, is because I do not know all the workings of the case. Is that so?"

"You are quite right. But I cannot be more explicit than I have been. I have no right to press the subject further on anyone's notice. But I can assure you honestly that I have done nothing of which I need be ashamed, and that it would be utterly impossible for me to live in the same house with my sister again. Not that she need be blamed much, either. But we seem to be naturally antagonistic to each other and are best apart."

"But what will you do with yourself, child? That you should earn your own living has never been contemplated for you, and you are consequently handicapped at every point."

"I am not afraid of work. Teaching is not much in my line. I believe I can play the fiddle sufficiently well to perform at an occasional concert, but that would not do much toward keeping me."

"You might teach the violin—"

"Oh, dear no. I am afraid I should find myself rapping the knuckles of my pupils if they should turn out extra stupid. That wouldn't do at all. I could go out as amanuensis, or companion, or something of that sort; for I write a neat hand, have more than a smattering of French and German, and am A1 at making Everton taffy and pickled cabbage."

"Two very indispensable acquisitions for an amanuensis! Still, your other qualifications might fetch somebody. What do you say if we advertise? Would you mind going abroad?"

"Just what I would be best pleased to do at present."

"Now about Mrs. Marshall and Miss Morris. It will be necessary to tell them something—"

"We will just tell them that I have had a deal of trouble, that I wish to turn my back on the scenes of my trouble for a time, and that while away from home I have a fancy for earning my own living. Such part of my troubles as are already public property you may of course confide to them."

"Then things are settled so far. I will see about the advertisement being sent off for you, and you must understand that we are by no means in a hurry to get rid of you. You will be more than welcome to stay here until you find something to your liking to do."

Somehow all this kindness robbed me of the composure which a strict business-like attitude on Mr. Garth's part might have helped me to preserve. I could only thank him brokenly, and beg him to excuse my appearance in the drawing-room, as I felt fit for nothing but solitude and bed. He readily promised to do what I wished, and at length I felt at liberty to retire for the night. But by this time I had a distracting headache, and though I bathed my forehead with eau-de-cologne, and tried various other infallible specifics, I found it impossible to go to sleep, or even to subdue the pain which tormented me. From below I could occasionally hear the sound of singing, though I was unable to judge whether the vocalist was the elder or the younger of the two visitors.

About twelve o'clock, as judged from the periodical chiming of the little clock in the dressing-room, it became evident that the other visitors were coming up to bed, and I forthwith feigned the sleep which refused to come at my bidding, lest voluble Miss May might expect me to talk with her. The two ladies made as little noise as possible in the dressing-room for a while, and I was just thinking that my bedfellow would soon join me, when I heard the most blood-curdling shriek imaginable, and a white figure fairly flew into the bedroom, jumped into the bed, drew the clothes frantically over her head and ears, and moaned in a state of shuddering terror. My own natural alarm was speedily quenched by the appearance of Mrs. Marshall, bearing every evidence of extreme anger.

"I do believe you are losing your senses altogether!" she exclaimed, giving her sister's shoulder a vigorous shake, which, so far from pacifying the young lady, only sent her into a fresh paroxysm of terror, and caused her to give a louder shriek than the first. By this time Mrs. Garth had run into the room, to see what was the matter, while at the door could

ELIZABETH BURGOYNE CORBETT

be heard the voices of a startled group of people, composed of the vicar, the cook and the housemaid, all of them wondering what on earth the commotion was about. Inside the bedroom, the tableau was not without interest. Mrs. Garth stood with a lighted candle raised above her head, looking almost as frightened as May seemed to be. Mrs. Marshall was trying to convince her sister that there was nothing to be afraid of. May was steadily trying to bury herself under the bedclothes, and I was sitting up in bed, vainly struggling to wrest my legitimate share of sheets and blankets from the frantic clasp of their unceremonious appropriator.

After a while May grew calmer and popped her head from under the clothes with a sudden jerk, which caused it to come into contact with the chin of her sister, who was bending over her, in an attempt to pacify her. The result was somewhat painful for Mrs. Marshall, and caused May to scream out again in terror.

"Keep it off! Keep it off!" she cried wildly.

"Keep what off? What on earth do you mean?" I shouted, feeling utterly unnerved and vexed at the same time.

"Oh, the ghost! the ghost! Keep it off!" was the shuddering response.

"How can you be so silly," I said, out of all patience. "What do you mean by a ghost?"

By this time, May began to seem more rational, and cautiously sat up, surveying the room with a scared look. "I heard it," she said, solemnly. "And I felt it touch my shoulders."

"It was no ghost other than myself who touched your shoulders," spoke up Mrs. Marshall, still hugging her jaw in an attitude of pain. "I wish I could shake some sense into you."

"Oh! it was you, was it?" quoth May. "But it wasn't you who gave three unearthly taps at the window. I heard them quite distinctly, and I'm sure it was all done by a ghost."

"It was done by the Virginia Creeper which climbs all over this side of the house," said Mrs. Garth. "You will very likely hear it again, but may go to sleep comfortably."

"And let other people go to sleep," added Mrs. Marshall, as she went back to her own room.

Mrs. Garth, after bidding us both goodnight, also retired, and May subsided angrily into a recumbent position. "Just like Madge, to try and make me look ridiculous," she grumbled. "All the same, it was a ghost, and I won't stay here after tomorrow."

And this was the girl who, only a few hours before, had talked of laying a ghost and unearthing the ghostly buried treasure with which her prolific imagination haunted the home of my childhood!

Certainly her escapade had had one good effect. It had banished my headache, and I did not suffer anymore from insomnia that night.

When I awoke the next morning, May Morris was looking at me with a comical expression of disgust on her pretty face.

"Do you know," she said solemnly, "I believe I made a perfect idiot of myself last night. I can't think what it was that so unnerved me. The fact is, it was the unexpectedness of the whole thing. Now, if I had known beforehand that the house was haunted, I shouldn't have been frightened a bit. You wait and see what a bold front I shall put on when we see the Grange ghost."

"My dear," I said, with a smile born of a conscious superiority in matters nervous, "there are two reasons why I cannot show the Grange ghost."

"And what are they?"

"I am not likely to visit the interior of the Grange, and, if I did visit it, I could not show anyone its ghost, because it hasn't got one."

"Hasn't it, really?"

"No—really."

"What a pity! And just when I thought I was going to have a share of the treasure! Never mind, I shall find another some day. Oh, by-the-by, Mr. Garth told me a funny thing last night. He said that you, a rich young lady, belonging to a county family, and, as one might almost say, the widow of an earl, wanted to take a situation and earn your own living!"

"He is quite right in what he has stated."

"Then I believe I know just the sort of thing that would suit you, that is, if you would care to go to Russia."

"Why not?"

"Well, you see, it is such a queer place. It swarms all over with nihilists, and anarchists, and spies, and caviare, and bomb-shells, and there are prisons at every street corner, into which they clap you without so much as a minute's notice, if you don't happen to salaam humbly everytime a government official goes by in his amber gown and scarlet turban. In fact, it's just a horrid place, where they can't speak English, and where they murder everybody who can't pronounce the word 'Peccavi.'"

"Upon my word, May, you'll be the death of me yet! You seem to

ELIZABETH BURGOYNE CORBETT

get awfully mixed up in your information. Somebody must have been slandering Russia to you a little. Of course, it could never be half so nice as England at its best; but even the Evil One, you know, isn't half so black as he's painted, and we'll give Russia the benefit of doubt. Anyhow, your description hasn't frightened me, and, if you don't mind, you shall give me the particulars of the situation you were speaking of, while I complete my toilet."

"All right, I'll tell you about it. But if you are put in prison and tickled to death, don't say I didn't warn you. I dare say you have heard that when Madge and I are at home we live at South Kensington. Now next door to us there lives a Russian lady with her little daughter and a whole swarm of servants. We met Madame Kominski at Lady Tranmere's At Home last week, and heard that she was looking out for a useful companion to take back to Russia with her. She wanted somebody who was a real lady, who could be treated on a family footing, and who could speak French or German. She had had several applicants for the post, but none of them suited."

"I wonder why?"

"Well, between you and me and the post, I think I know. They were all too good-looking. Madame is both young and beautiful, and does not want a companion who will eclipse her."

"Then I suppose I shall stand a chance of securing the coveted post, since I am almost ugly enough to serve as a foil even to a plain woman."

"Now that is nasty of you, for I don't call you a bit ugly. Only just unbeautiful enough to prevent madame from being jealous."

"Very well. I will go back to London tomorrow and interview Madame Kominski, if you will furnish me with her address."

"But why not write?"

"A letter would not describe my appearance accurately enough. If madam desires someone who is unbeautiful, as you put it, a sight of me will go far to convince her that she has found the treasure she is in search of."

"I don't quite understand you, but of course I will write the address down for you, and if you really get the appointment, you must write me regular accounts of your adventures. Then I'll have them printed in a book, and if I can't find a buried treasure, I shall perhaps be famous as an authoress."

"A valuable wrinkle, my dear. I must be careful not to write anything that isn't intended to become public property."

"Oh, but you are sure to be in such a perpetual state of excitement that you will not be able to weigh all your words when you are writing. There is one difficulty. Suppose they put you in prison, how will you manage to send your letters off?"

"You must trust me for that. I am sure to find some way of dispatching all the letters I am likely to write to you while in prison. On your side, you must never mention anything about Russia or the Russians in any letter you may dispatch to the czar's country. Then we shall be all right."

"Very well, then that is all arranged. But before you go downstairs I am going to show you the loveliest, most ravishing, most delightful thing you ever saw in your life. Look here!"

As May spoke, she jumped up and dived into one of her boxes, whence she fished out a whole handful of photographs. I naturally expected to behold the presentment of a superlatively beautiful member of my own sex, and was not a little astounded to see a dozen portraits of a popular but by no means wonderfully handsome actor.

"Isn't he bewitching?" May rhapsodized. "Did you ever see anyone in your life half so handsome? Oh, he's simply adorable!"

"And did he give you all those photographs?"

"Oh, dear no! I bought them all with my own pocket-money. I love him so dearly that I dream of him almost night and day, and I buy a copy of every fresh portrait of him that is issued. Oh, if you could only imagine how I love him!"

"And does he return your love?"

"Unfortunately for me, he does not know me. He has never even seen me."

"Then I suppose you fell in love with him on the stage."

"No, he is nearly always on tour, and I have never seen him act. Indeed, I have never seen him at all. I just saw a photograph of him in a shop-window, and straightway fell in love with it. You may think it only a passing fancy. But I feel that if I could only look upon his face, my greatest dreams of earthly bliss would be realized, and I would be content to die."

"Mere romance, my dear girl. You will come across someone in the flesh who will prove much more charming than the counterfeit presentments of your adorable actor, who, by-the-by, becomes engaged to a fresh young lady about every six months."

"I can't help it. He is just all in all to me, and I shall never marry so long as he remains single. If, after all my devotion, my hero marries another woman, then I may think of accepting a gentleman who proposes to me every three months. Meanwhile, I have a little consolation. I often take a look at his house at Kensington, in the hope of catching a glimpse of him through one of the windows."

And in this style May meandered on, the while I wondered whether she were really sane or not. She was evidently badly smitten, and by mere portraits, which must have revealed to her many beauties of expression which were hidden to me, for I could only look upon them as the faithful presentments of a man whom I had heard spoken of as selfish, conceited and unscrupulous in his dealings with women.

"I suppose you are quite disburdened of all the particulars of your wonderful romance by this time," was Mrs. Marshall's cheery greeting. "I knew it was no use interrupting you before you had confided the whole story to Miss Courtney. And what do you think of it, Miss Dora, now that you have heard it?"

This last question was addressed to me with such a humorous twinkle in Mrs. Marshall's merry dark eyes, that, for the life of me, I could not help responding to it, and my comments were expressed in a burst of hearty laughter, which not all my latent worries could rob of its spontaneity. I was not sure that May might not resent our irreverence, but she took it very good-humoredly, and five minutes later we were all greeting our host and hostess at the breakfast-table.

As both the sisters were in quite a merry mood, they cheered the rest of us up wonderfully, and no one, to look at us, would imagine that we had ever become acquainted with care.

VI

"When venom'd gossip shows her poison-fangs,
the watchword is, 'Beware!'"

B ut as soon as breakfast was over, I had a private confabulation with Mr. Garth, in which he fully approved of my intention of going to see Madame Kominski at once.

"Let me see," he said by-and-by. "There is a train from Moorbye at 12:52. This would enable you to reach Kensington by 4:30, a good time, I should imagine, for catching the lady at home. If you fail to see her this evening, you can either return here, or put up at a hotel which I can recommend for the night. If you do not come to an arrangement, you will return and stay here, of course, until something else turns up. Should you, on the other hand, find the appointment one that you can accept, your future proceedings will be arranged between Madame Kominski and yourself."

"The 12:50 train will suit me admirably," I said. "I shall have time to pay a visit to Bobby and Teddy. They, at least, will remember me with affection."

"Then suppose you get ready at once, Dorrie. I will go with you, as I want to see John Page. He has had frequent touches of rheumatism lately, and I promised to take him some liniment. I can talk to him while you interview your pets."

"Miss Morris is anxious to go to the Grange. But I would much rather go without her this morning."

"My wife will amuse her. I can take her, together with her sister, to have a look at Courtney Grange tomorrow."

Half an hour later the vicar and I were walking briskly toward my old home, and I was feeling happy at the mere sight of the waving corn-fields and smiling hedge-rows which stretched on our right hand, in vivid contrast to the semi-barrenness and sober but quaint coloring of the moorland on our left. I found it impossible to pass all the floral treasures which greeted me by the way, and my heart presently grew heavy at the thought that it might possibly be years before I was able to gather another bunch of wild flowers on my native heath. When the chimneys of the Grange came in sight, I had a fierce battle to fight with my avowed determination not to enter its doors again, and I found that sentiment was, after all, a much stronger passion in me than wounded pride.

"Oh, I must run in and see Martha," I exclaimed, when at last we emerged from the long avenue. "Do wait a minute here, while I run round to the back and give her a surprise."

Suiting the action to the word, I left the good-natured vicar to his own devices, while I hurried round to the kitchen entrance, anxious to see Martha at her usual avocations, in order that I might fancy this hurried visit to my home more homelike. Somewhat to my disappointment, Martha was not half so surprised as I had fancied she would be.

"Eh! is that you, Miss Dora?" she exclaimed, dropping the potato she was peeling, as I impetuously sprang into the kitchen and gave her a warm greeting. "I thought maybe you would come today; and you'll find your room quite ready for you."

"But how could you know I was coming?" I inquired blankly. "I never sent you word that you might expect me."

"No, but Mr. Courtney did. We got a letter from him this morning. Here it is."

I took the letter, which she pulled out of her pocket for me, and read it, feeling as if all the romance were knocked out of me again.

"Prepare Miss Dora's room. If she is not already at the Grange, you may expect her soon."

That was all, and I could not help a slight feeling of vexation at its tenor. True, it implied that my father had not really intended to banish me altogether. But it also evinced such a determination to ignore any mental distress in which I might be submerged that it convinced me more than ever of the hopelessness of ever expecting my father to show the least spark of true affection for me.

"And how is John?" I asked soberly.

"John! Why, John's pretty much as usual, I think," said Martha, with a sharp touch of asperity in her voice. "But somehow he seems to be everlastingly complaining of late, and it's 'Oh, my leg! Oh, my back!' nearly all day long."

"Then he must be really ill."

"Not he. He's just taken a lazy fit, and wants pampering, that's all."

"Which he isn't likely to get from the wife o' his buzzim," broke in John's voice at this juncture.

"Oh, John, I quite forgot!" I exclaimed penitently. "The vicar is waiting for you on the steps. He has got some liniment for you."

John hobbled off at once, calling out, as he did so: "There's a letter waiting for you upstairs, Miss Dora."

Aroused to sudden curiosity, I at once ran up to my old room, and almost cried with joy to see Lady Elizabeth's beloved handwriting. If my father's missive lacked sympathy, his wife's made ample amends for it, for it breathed of nothing but love and anxious care for my well-being. It had been taken for granted by my stepmother that I would come straight to the Grange and wait quietly there for the return of the rest of the family. I resolved to perpetuate her comforting delusion as long as I could, and forthwith wrote her a letter, in which I thanked her warmly for all the nice messages she sent me, and assured her that she need have no uneasiness about me, as I should make myself quite comfortable while at Moorbye.

Then I sallied out to the stables, having wondered already how it was that I had seen nothing either of Bobby or of Teddy. Even as I got quite up to the stable door they were both still invisible, and a vague feeling of impending calamity seized me, as the old familiar whistle, to which my erstwhile playmates had been wont to respond so joyously, failed to evoke the usual boisterous signs of recognition from either of them. I certainly did hear a feeble whine, but could hardly credit it to be Bobby's usually clamorous voice.

"Oh, my God!" I thought dumbly, "is a new trouble about to befall me?"

Then I walked slowly forward, feeling a leaden weight on limbs and brain alike. With quaking heart and anxious eyes I peered in the direction of Teddy's old stall, and when I failed to see the dear little ugly companion of my happiest frolics, I only felt the mist which covered my eyes to be the outcome of a dreary conviction which had been stealing over me ever since I emerged from the house. For a moment a deadly faintness almost overpowered me, so that I had to seize the nearest available support, in order to prevent myself from falling. While I still stood, feeling half dazed with a newly added sense of misery, I once more heard the feeble imitation of a whine which had already attracted my attention. Then, looking down, I saw, painfully rolling toward me, a little round body that must be, could be, nothing but my darling Bobby. Hastily stepping forward, I stooped and lifted the object, and oh! how can I ever describe what I felt when, taking it to the light, I discovered it to be none other than my beloved pet! Poor fellow! he had recognized me, and, though almost at death's door, had made a desperate effort to meet me once more.

ELIZABETH BURGOYNE CORBETT

I sat down with him on my lap and bent over him in an agony of grief. He, in his turn, fondly licked my fingers and looked at me with a piteous, all-adoring love shining out of the beautiful eyes which were already fast glazing over with the last dread film.

"Oh, my darling!" I moaned, as I kissed his dear little head over and over again. "What have I done that I should lose everything I love? I would give ten years of my life to see you frisk about me in the old happy way. Can't you really get better, now that I have come?"

Did the poor thing understand me, or was he only making a supreme effort to make me comprehend how glad he was to see me? Perhaps it was both, for he always was more intelligent than some human beings I have encountered. Be this as it may, he suddenly rose to his feet, and stood looking in my face for a moment almost the picture of his old excitable self, with sparkling eyes and quivering body. Then he gave a sharp, glad bark, and dropped, lifeless, on the lap of one of the most desolate human beings on earth.

How long I sat there in my misery I do not know, but was at last interrupted by the voice of the vicar, who, perceiving what had happened, asked me no questions, but, gently lifting poor Bobby's body into a basket which stood close by, suggested that we should bury him ourselves before we returned to the vicarage. As one in a dream, I let him lead me whither he would, and together we went down to the old orchard, where, presently, my kindly friend took upon himself the office of grave-digger. Concerning Teddy, I asked no more questions just now, for I no longer believed him to be alive.

When I had marked Bobby's resting-place, I turned to John Page, whom, for the first time, I noticed to be standing near me. "And now," I said, my voice still shaken with sobs, "tell me how it is that you never sent us word that my pets were ill."

"Indeed, miss, I did," answered John, with a sympathetic look at my grief-stricken face. "I sent the master word about everything. You had only been gone a day or two when Teddy began to fret and go off his feed. He would seek you in the yard, and in the orchard, and in all sorts of likely and unlikely places, and when he couldn't see anything of you, he would whinny that pitifully that neither Martha nor me liked to hear him. We used to try to pet him up a bit. But it was no go, and we could see that if he went on fretting like that things would soon go wrong with him. Bobby, too, hung his head, and walked about looking the picture of misery. When you were away at my lady's place, before, they both took on considerable. But you were not quite so long away, and it hadn't such an effect on them as it's had this time. It was only last week that Teddy died, and Bobby has never been out of the stable since. I have done what I could for him, but anybody could see that he wouldn't be here long. The master knew Teddy was dead, and I'm sure I thought you knew all about it. I buried him just at the foot of the paddock, feeling that that was where you would have liked to put him, if you had been at home."

I couldn't speak. But I gave John a look which would show him that I exonerated him from blame and that I was grateful to him for what he had tried to do for me. Then I walked down to the paddock, to take one last look at poor old Teddy's resting-place. And here a fresh idea seized me. My two pets had been such inseparable friends during life that I felt it cruel to part them in death, and returned to John, to ask him to bring Bobby's body to be finally interred beside that of his friend and companion. My wish was soon accomplished, and then, without looking back at the old home even once more, I walked away toward the vicarage, followed by the vicar, and hardly knowing whether grief at my loss, or resentment at the callousness which had prevented my father from telling me the true state of the case, was predominant.

I had not walked far before I was overtaken by Mr. Garth, but there was very little said between us until we were nearly at the vicarage.

"Did you know that my pony was dead?" I asked him.

"Certainly not," he replied. "I saw John last week, and he never mentioned either of your pets, though I do not doubt that he has taken good care of them. Very likely your father did not wish you to be told much about them, lest the news should unsettle you."

"Yes, of course. That is the true explanation of the case. My father was actuated by tender regard for my feelings, and I ought to feel proportionately grateful. But, somehow, I don't feel particularly moved in the direction of gratitude, and the sooner I am away from the neighborhood of Courtney Grange the better. I shall not regret my absence from it now, since my presence near it could only foster painful memories. The past is dead, and I must let my dead past bury its dead."

"You have youth and energy on your side, my dear. I predict that in six months you will yearn for your old home again and be as happy as ever here."

"Never! You do not know me, Mr. Garth. My experiences since I went to London have been such as to develop and increase the latent passions of my childhood, besides endowing me with others toward which I never suspected myself to have a leaning. Among the latter are self-reliance, independence, and firmness of purpose. They alone will forbid my early return to the Grange."

"Well, I will not argue the point with you, child, as of course you know more about the matter than I do. But has it struck you that while we have been lingering at the Grange, time has been flying, and that you have missed the 12:50 train for London? You will have to put off your journey until morning, as the next train from here arrives in London too late to enable you to call at Madame Kominski's house this evening."

"Then what shall I do? How soon can I get there in the morning?"

"If you do not mind rising early, you can leave by the 6:30 A.M. train. That will land you in Kensington in good time."

"If you and Mrs. Garth—"

"Pray don't mention it, child. We are only too happy to do what we can for you. Oh, there they all are!"

"They" of whom he spoke were Mrs. Garth, Mrs. Marshall and Miss Morris, who were walking leisurely toward us, their hands full of wild roses and honeysuckle, which they had been pulling in the hedgerows. Master Vinnie was skipping alone in front, and having an occasional race with Leo, a splendid St. Bernard, who looked as wise as any of us.

The whole party looked so handsome, so happy, and so thoroughly satisfied with their lot in life, that my own isolation and loneliness struck me more forcibly than ever. I am not sure that I was not going to give way to another outburst of grief, when I chanced to look up into Mr. Garth's face, and saw that the erstwhile sad and sympathetic expression of his countenance had vanished as magically as do morning mists before the power of the rising sun. He was smiling at the pleasant sight which greeted his gaze, and in an instant I was confounded by a sense of the selfishness of my own conduct. What right had I to obtrude my private griefs upon my friends? True, they were kind and sympathizing, but that did not deprive them of their due claim to consideration, and life does not hold so much happiness for any that one can afford to exchange the flowers of joy for the withered leaves of sorrow, even though the sorrow may more closely appertain to another.

I believe that great changes of character may be brought about in susceptible and highly-strung natures by trifling incidents, and a suddenly conceived resolve of my own was no particularly noticeable departure from a somewhat general rule. "If I cannot be happy myself,"

I reflected, "I can at least conduce to the happiness of others by presenting a bright and cheerful front to the world. And this I will try to do in future, God helping me."

It was in conformity with this resolution that I walked smilingly up to Mrs. Garth and her guests, and apologized for having kept the vicar so long away from them. Then I challenged Vinnie and Leo to a race, and, before Mr. Garth had time to conjecture the cause of the abrupt change in my demeanor, I was scampering down the lane with the delighted boy, and the no less delighted dog, who instantly entered into the spirit of the diversion suggested, as did also May Morris, who laughingly exclaimed that she saw no reason why she should not join in the fun, and promptly followed in our wake. We had half an hour of scampering and laughter, and returned to the vicarage breathless, rosy, and hungry. Perhaps Leo could hardly be accused of being either breathless or rosy, but he was certainly as ready for his midday meal as any of us. As for myself, I noted with surprise that my effort to appear cheerful and happy had recoiled upon myself, and that I no longer felt so miserable as I had done earlier in the day.

"You're just a dear, jolly girl," said May to me, as we were rehabilitating our toilet, previous to going down to lunch. "I'm awfully sorry you are going away so soon, and I'm awfully afraid lest those horrid Russians should lock you up in one of their dungeons. Just fancy how awfully horrid it would be if they were to hang you up by the thumbs, and flog you with a bundle of knouts!"

"My dear girl," I said, unable to refrain from laughter at May's limited and slangy vocabulary, as well as at her hazy and mixed-up notions of things Russian. "It is not by any means sure that I am going to Russia, and even if I do go, it is of no use anticipating unlikely contingencies."

"Perhaps not," retorted May sapiently. "But one may as well be prepared for possibilities, and then they don't overtake one as a surprise. And, after all, there are perhaps worse things than the knout."

"Hardly," I rejoined. "The knout so generally proves an instrument of death that it must be regarded as the extreme punishment."

"But suppose they banish you to Siberia?"

"I don't see any probability of such a disaster, as, if I am lucky enough to secure the appointment I am seeking, I shall be very careful about what I say and do. And now—suppose we go downstairs?"

After luncheon the vicar announced his intention of paying some visits which he owed to a few of the poorer of his parishioners. "I do not

ELIZABETH BURGOYNE CORBETT

care to inflict myself upon them in the forenoon," he added. "They are generally busy, either cleaning or cooking, and do not care to be bothered by callers before they have had time to don themselves up a little."

"But why should you trouble yourself to visit them at all, when you have a curate who could look after your poorer parishioners?" asked Mrs. Marshall. "The vicar of St. Dungaree's Church only associates with, or speaks personally to, the well-to-do people of his parish. He never goes to any house of which the rent is less than seventy pounds per annum."

"Then I suppose he does not think people with small incomes possess souls?" I exclaimed.

"Oh, dear, yes! of course they have souls. But you can't attach as much importance to their conversion as if they were in a position to be of service to the church, as rich people can be, and a curate's attentions are as much as they can expect."

"Then we may conclude that the objects of a curate and of a vicar are entirely dissimilar. The curate wishes to save souls. The vicar is anxious to wheedle money out of his parishioners. Fie, Mrs. Marshall, how can you so depreciate Mr. Garth's calling?"

"Good gracious! Miss Courtney. It's you who are doing it, not me. I never thought of the matter in the light you are throwing upon it. And I am sure Mr. Garth understands my meaning very well."

"To be sure I do," responded the vicar, good-humoredly. "No doubt the vicar of St. Dungaree's is swayed by motives which outsiders do not understand. For my own part, I am quite convinced of my own unfitness for a city living, as I have what some would consider inveterately democratic notions. For instance, I am far happier when chatting with old Mrs. Murfree, who has been bedridden for six years, and who nevertheless earns a precarious livelihood by knitting and coarse needlework, than when conversing with Lady Smythe, who imagines herself to be the greatest lady in the county. And I would much rather have a talk and a smoke with old Grey, our cobbler-poet, than be invited out to dine with the lord of the manor."

"And that reminds me," put in Mrs. Garth, "that Lady Smythe and her daughters are coming this afternoon for a game of tennis. The Worthingtons will probably be here, too, so I hope you will try to get back before they leave."

The vicar, having promised to use his best endeavors in that direction, now hurried off. I would rather have been excused from meeting the coming guests, if I had consulted only my own inclination; and it required a little mental struggle on my part to induce me to persevere just then in my lately-formed resolve to be as cheerful as possible at all times. May Morris, superficial and shallow as she seemed, was a bright, merry girl, who did nothing to foster either lugubriousness or reserve, and with whom it would have been difficult for me to maintain a silent mood for any length of time. Vinnie, too, seemed to have taken immensely to me since the morning and eagerly importuned us for another romp. Thus it happened that when the Smythe family drove up to the door they were rather scandalized by seeing two young women, who were evidently utterly regardless of appearances, scampering along a sidewalk, laughing and panting, followed by a fleet-footed child, who was pelting them with daisies which had a few hours before bespangled the tennis lawn, and by an excited St. Bernard, whose occasional tugs had utterly ruined the fresh appearance of their gowns.

"There now," I said at last. "I really must sit down a bit. Vinnie, hadn't you better run in and ask nurse to sponge your hands and face, before any visitors see you? I think I must go in also and straighten my hair."

"That's just how I feel," said May, so we all adjourned, in order to present a better appearance by-and-by.

An hour later both courts on the vicarage tennis lawn were occupied with players, most of whom wielded their racquets in such a way as to indicate considerable practice in the health-giving pastime upon which they were now engaged. The two brothers Worthington, sons of a local landed proprietor, were worthy partners of the Misses Smythe, and Mr. Graham, the doctor's assistant—whose aider and abettor in all social functions at which they could both be present was Mr. Wix, our curate—was so evidently smitten by May's charms that I caught myself wondering whether he would be able to supplant the fascinating actor. Mrs. Marshall had offered to let me play in her stead, but a reaction from my previous excitement had set in, and I craved quiet and repose. Leaving her, therefore, to a game which I knew she would enjoy, I strolled further away from the house, and presently sat down on the forked arm of an apple-tree which grew just behind the hut that had been erected for the accommodation of those who preferred to watch the game rather than take an active part in it. The branch of the tree hung so low that I had no difficulty in fixing myself comfortably upon it, and I soon found the repose of my situation so conducive to drowsiness that I think I must have gone to sleep for a little while.

ELIZABETH BURGOYNE CORBETT

At any rate I was roused by the sound of voices which I could not localize for a few moments, as I had not noticed the approach of the speakers, who were evidently now sitting in the hut close to me. My own name fell on my ears with somewhat startling distinctness.

"Miss Dora Courtney," said a voice which I recognized as that of Lady Smythe, the wife of an ex-wine merchant who had chanced to be the mayor of a neighboring town on the occasion of the Queen's Jubilee, and had consequently dropped into a knighthood. "Miss Dora Courtney surprises me by her behavior."

"In what way, Lady Smythe? And who is the young lady, that she should evoke interest in *you*?" asked another voice, which was strange to me, but which had such a liberal allowance of flattering unction in it, and which laid such emphasis on the second person singular that I set its owner down for a toady of the first water at once.

"My dear Miss Grindle," was the reply, "I am certainly exclusive. But I am able to take interest in many people whose position in society scarcely warrants notice from me. Otherwise you would hardly find me mixing indiscriminately with people at parties like this. It pleases commoners to be noticed by persons of title, and I pride myself upon being looked upon as more condescending than the rest of the nobility hereabouts."

"Oh, you're just an angel! If only the Mountmerlyns were like you."

"Ah, yes! poor things! I feel sorry for them. What's the use of their asthmatic old earldom, without money to keep it up? Such a struggle as they must have! And, between you and me, they're dying to know Sir Robert and myself, but are overawed by a sense of the great difference in our position."

"You mean—Lady Smythe?"

"We are so rich, and they are so poor. No wonder they are afraid of intruding upon us."

"And this Miss Courtney?—"

"To be sure, we were talking of Miss Courtney. Well, she was brought up at Courtney Grange, and has a sister and brother who are perfectly lovely, strange as it may seem when you look at her plain face. I believe they pride themselves upon being a county family, but they were a very poverty-stricken lot until the father secured for his second wife a rich widow, the daughter of the Earl of Greatlands. Then one startling announcement followed another. Lady Elizabeth's brother, the heir to the earldom, became engaged to the beautiful Miss Courtney. Then the wedding was put off because the old earl was to be married to the ugly Miss Courtney, the one who is here now. While all society was opening its eyes in amazement at this freak of the old earl, it was startled by the news of his death on his wedding-morning."

"How shocking! And had the marriage taken place?"

"How could it? This girl would then have been the Countess of Greatlands."

"Poor thing! What a dreadful disappointment for her."

"Yes, you may well say so. And that is what surprises me so about her. She seems to be quite happy and merry. Look how she was running about the garden when we came—a perfect tomboy."

"So she was. It's really very indecent of her, when one comes to think of it. She ought to keep herself as quiet as if she were really a widow."

"H'm! widows! I don't think much of them. They are a flighty lot. But what do you think people are saying about the 'Greatlands Romance,' as it is called?"

"I'm sure I don't know. You see, I have been abroad, and—"

"And you can't afford to buy the newspapers. Yes, I know all about that. Well, they say that the earl's son—that is, the present earl, and his intended bride, Miss Belle Courtney, were furious when they heard of the old gentleman's infatuation, and that they swore the marriage should never take place. One of the servants overheard a desperate quarrel between the two sisters, in which the elder vowed all sorts of horrible things. After that it was queer, to say the least, that the poor old man, who had gone to bed the night before quite healthy and happy, should be found to be dead when his valet went to rouse him on his marriage morning."

"Good heavens! why, they must have murdered him!"

"Well, it certainly looks like it. They vowed he shouldn't get married, and he didn't live to get married. Of course, the other couple, now that all obstacles have been swept out of their path, will get married soon and share the wealth and title. But I wouldn't like to stand in their shoes.—Oh, here is Mrs. Garth! Mrs. Garth, we have just been saying what a good thing it is for poor Miss Dora Courtney that she can be so cheerful after all her troubles."

"Yes, she bears up wonderfully, poor child. But I have not seen her for sometime. I thought she was perhaps in here with you. Where will you have your tea? Here, or in the drawing-room?"

ELIZABETH BURGOYNE CORBETT

"I think I would rather go indoors for a while. I want to look at some new prints Mr. Garth was telling me about."

A few minutes later the hut had changed occupants, and May Morris, hot and excited after a victorious game, was pouring tea for the tennis players out of an urn which a servant had placed on the table, while the young men were handing the bread and butter plates round, amid a chorus of laughter and merry rapartee. I alone sat unobserved, lonely, and now once more thoroughly miserable, heedless of aught else save my own bitter reflections, and feeling as incapable of moving as I had done during the conversation between Lady Smythe and Miss Grindle.

That the tragedy of my life should be talked about did not surprise me. But that my own dreadful suspicions should have found an echo in the breasts of others was to me a most horrible revelation, which created in me so great a revulsion of feeling as to paralyze my energies *pro tem*. I could do nothing for a while but sit and wonder vaguely what would be the end of it all. Would the conviction of my sister's guilt spread from one to another until the authorities felt bound to interfere, with the object of arriving at a complete solution of the mystery? Should I have to give evidence? And would Lady Elizabeth be called upon to witness against her brother and her stepdaughter? Would the name of both families be dragged through the mire of the criminal courts, and be gloated over by pothouse politicians in polemical discussions *in re* the immorality of the aristocracy? And, horror of horrors! suppose things were to come to the worst, was it possible that my beautiful sister, the pride of her father's heart, and one of my darling mother's children, could be sentenced to a shameful death! A murderer's death is not more shameful than his crime, we know; but, alas! how many hearts bear witness to the agony inflicted on friends and relatives by the mandates of justice. It would kill Lady Elizabeth if the case were brought to trial, and this reflection was itself enough to strengthen my determination to avoid publicity henceforth. My very presence, it seemed, was sufficient to set the tongues of conjecture and suspicion wagging. My temporary absence might perhaps help people to forget the existence of myself and my history.

For the future, if I would avoid a crisis, I had better be seen and heard as little as possible; and this reflection made me so feverishly anxious to quit the country that I sprang from my seat in excitement and hurried toward the house as if thereby I could hasten the interview between Madame Kominski and myself. As I might have expected, I was intercepted on my way and besieged by inquiries as to where I had been hiding myself. My pale face and heavy eyes indorsed my plea of the desire of seclusion on the score of a violent headache, and I was allowed to go to my room, where Mrs. Garth soon followed me with a cup of tea and words of sympathy. Left alone once more, I meditated earnestly as to my future proceedings, finally coming to the conclusion that for the sake of Jerry and Lady Elizabeth, if not for the sake of my father and Belle, I must never divulge aught that could harm Belle, but must do all in my power to prevent the suspicions of others from being fostered.

In spite of my desire to appear as cheerful as possible, I felt myself unequal to the task of going downstairs again that afternoon. Evening found me able to appear more sociable, and the next morning saw me, primed with good wishes and affectionate "good-bys" from my dear good friends, Mr. and Mrs. Garth, both of whom had got up to escort me to the station, en route for Kensington, where I arrived in due course.

VII

"From prying eyes and fingers defend us, good Lord!"

Is Madame Kominski visible?" I inquired of the smart servant-maid who answered my ring at the bell of the house to which I had been directed to go.

"Is it an appointment, madam?"

"No, but I have reason to think that Madame Kominski will see me."

"If you will step inside, I will ask her. What name shall I give?"

"Miss Dora Saxon."

This change of name was the result of my deliberations while on my way here. It struck me as desirable, in Belle's interests. In Belle's! How strange it seemed that I should have to resort to trickery and subterfuge for the sake of one who, though so nearly related to me, was yet my mortal enemy! Yet so it was, for was not the happiness of those whom I loved best on earth involved in her immunity from punishment, if she were guilty; and in her protection from false accusation, if she were innocent? Ah! would to God I could have thought the latter! My course of conduct would then have been much easier for me.

"You wish to see me?" was the question addressed to me after a while, in such a musical voice that I glanced at the owner of it in pleased surprise, as I answered somewhat eagerly: "Yes, Madame Kominski. I have been told that you are seeking a companion, and would like to secure the post. I can give you good credentials."

"And references to former employers?"

"I have never lived away from home before."

"And why, may I ask, do you wish to come to me now?"

"My home associations have become painful. I was to have been married a month ago, but—"

"The old story. Your lover forsook you?"

"No, my lover died."

There was a quick glance of sympathy, and a few moments' pause. Then Madame Kominski resumed: "Your story is very sad. But I am afraid that for that very reason I cannot entertain the idea of making you my companion. I want someone who will be cheerful and bright, not a woman whose bearing will wear the impress of a tragic past. Pray do not think me unfeeling, but I often have to leave my little daughter for days together, and would not like her to be made melancholy."

"You would find me as cheerful as you could desire. I intend to cast my past from my mind as much as possible."

"If I could think that—"

But there is no need to give the whole conversation in detail. Suffice it to say that I prevailed upon Madame Kominski to write to Mr. Garth for further particulars of me, and that I obtained her promise to engage me, should his reply prove satisfactory. Feeling quite sure that this would be the case, and that Madame Kominski was a woman who could be trusted, I told her that my real name was Courtney, but that I preferred to be called Miss Saxon for the future, as I did not wish it to be known that I had left home to go to service. As it happened, it was well that I took my prospective employer into my confidence. She had heard something about my history from the newspapers, and my candor seemed to win both her sympathy and her good-will.

She insisted upon my having lunch with her, and introduced me to her daughter Feodorowna, a girl of ten, who could not boast of a much more attractive appearance than myself. But by-and-by, as she grew to womanhood, her looks might improve, and she might possibly become more like her mother, who certainly was a very beautiful woman, being tall, stately, and inclined to embonpoint, though as yet being only sufficiently stout to make her voluptuously perfect. Her fine dark eyes, Grecian features, clear skin and purple-black hair, which waved and curled about her brows in charming disorder, would seem to disclaim a Mongolian origin altogether, and were all in harmony with her musical voice and graceful gait.

Two days later, a very satisfactory reply to madame's letter having come from Mr. Garth, all arrangements were completed. My luggage had been sent for, and I was formally installed as companion-governess in the household of Madame Kominski, who readily agreed to my wish that my true appellative should be discarded for the present, and that I should be introduced and known to others only as Miss Saxon. I had not forgotten May Morris's idea that absence of good looks was the best recommendation to madame's favor. But I did not let the notion worry me. I was by this time convinced that nature, when denying me beauty, had given me some compensating qualifications, and Madame Kominski was so kind and friendly with me that I found no difficulty in being comparatively happy and wholly cheerful.

ELIZABETH BURGOYNE CORBETT

Feodorowna, or Feo, as she was called by her mother, seemed to have taken quite a fancy to me, and I won her heart altogether when I proposed teaching her to play the violin. I found her to be an apt and docile pupil, but as masters came to the house to teach her many of the branches of her education, such portion of it as fell on my shoulders did not prove onerous.

"We start for St. Petersburg on Monday," said Madame Kominski, the Friday after I had become a member of her household, looking up from a letter which she was reading. "I suppose you have no objection to go there, Miss Saxon?"

"None whatever, madame. I shall like it very much, I am sure."

"I have no doubt you will, for you will have every possible comfort and will mingle in the best society St. Petersburg affords. And you, Feo, now that you are going to see your cousins again, must not neglect your English. I shall depend upon Miss Saxon to insist upon constant practice in that and in French."

"You may depend upon me, and upon Feo, too. We have already made a compact to speak nothing but English together one week, and nothing but French the next."

"And, mother, what is the use of saying Miss Saxon everytime? Why don't you call her Dora, like I do? She will really seem like one of the family then."

"Well, Dora be it, with all my heart, child. Ah! what's this? Dora, I find that I have to go out of town today. I may be back tomorrow, but cannot be sure. You will see that the servants push on with the packing."

"Certainly. I will do my best to make up for your absence."

Madame Kominski had evidently read something in the last letter she had opened which had caused her to form the sudden resolution of leaving home that day. She hastily gathered the papers which had come by that morning's post together, and was leaving the breakfast room with them, when Feo exclaimed: "Oh, mother, it is too bad! You promised to take us to the theater this evening."

"My dear child, I cannot help that. This journey cannot be postponed. You shall go to the Grand Theater soon after we arrive in St. Petersburg. You know that I never willingly disappoint you or break a promise to you."

"Forgive me, dear mother. I won't complain again."

From this it may be gathered that Feo was a docile, affectionate child, and such I always found her. I could not help hazarding a faint conjecture as to the nature of the business which took madame from home at a time when one would suppose her presence to be more than usually necessary in it. But it was no business of mine, and I found sufficient to do to occupy all my thoughts and time for the next few days. It was Monday at noon before the mistress of the household returned to it. She seemed tired and somewhat dispirited, but insisted upon starting for St. Petersburg that night, as had already been arranged.

A week later we were all comfortably installed in a splendid house, on the Nevski Prospekt, and my eyes were fairly dazzled by the magnificence of some of the houses to which I was introduced. I was very glad that my wardrobe was so liberally furnished, and that I was at least possessed of the means of mitigating my plainness as far as was possible. I was also spared some of the humiliation which had been so often meted out to me in England. Whether it was that I was surrounded by more people, whose chief characteristic was lack of physical beauty, or whether it was that less importance was attached to the possession of mere outward charms, I cannot say. But it is certain that my personal deficiencies were less often brought home to me here, and, greatly to my surprise, I seemed to promptly win the favor of several cultured aristocrats, who apparently never dreamed of discounting my few mental attractions because I was only a hired companion.

Many of them spoke English, and showed great interest in our social laws and customs, so different to those prevailing among themselves. To the best of my ability, I answered all the questions put to me, sometimes; I fear, forgetting that to extol English institutions was to decry the systems of the land in which I had temporarily found a home. One evening madame, always good to me, had taken me with her to the house of a certain Prince and Princess Michaelow, both of whom welcomed her with great warmth and affection. The princess, who proved to be English, and only a few years older than myself, was a girl of strikingly imposing figure and lovely appearance. Her rich, glittering auburn hair framed a face of the purest oval. Her arch, piquant features were set off by a complexion of exquisite fairness and purity, the cheeks reminding me of nothing so much as of the dainty pink dog-roses I had so often delighted to gather at home. Her teeth were white and even, and were given plenty of opportunity for display by their smiling owner. But her eyes struck me as her chief charm. They were large and limpid, fringed by dark lashes, and were of the deepest azure, with a bright-rayed amber iris that gave them an almost uncanny beauty. She was dressed in a gown of soft pale blue surah, and her only jewels were pearls. But such pearls! And such a mass of them, in ropes, strings, sprays and festoons, which helped to put the finishing touch to as fair a vision of human beauty as I had ever beheld.

I was half inclined to stand in awe of her at first, and to shrink into a pained comparison of her appearance and mine. But her frank, cheery smile and demonstrative welcome at once put that nonsense out of my head, and I was henceforth content to worship her as the embodiment of all that was good and beautiful. My admiration must have shone in my eyes, for the prince bent down to me, and said smilingly, in rather broken English: "I perceive that Miss Saxon's tastes are similar to my own. I hope she will often favor us with a visit. My wife has been looking forward to meeting Madame Kominski's new friend."

New friend! Was that Prince Michaelow's delicate way of putting the case, or did he really not know that I was madame's paid companion? I caught myself revolving this conjecture even while conversing brightly and with outward ease. But it was not destined to trouble me long. Later on in the evening, Madame Kominski, who was a brilliant conversationalist, and an evident favorite wherever she went, being surrounded by a group of admiring friends, I found myself somewhat isolated and thrown upon my own resources. Yet I was by no means tired or dull, for I watched the ever-varying panorama in the brilliant salon in which I found myself with considerable interest.

One man in particular attracted my notice by his somewhat sinister aspect and gloomy bearing. He stood, half concealed by the draperies of a large portière, with erect figure and folded arms, looking at Madame Kominski with an expression in his eyes which I found it difficult to fathom, but which gave me an uneasy conviction that it boded her no good. He was tall, of fine build and bearing, and would, I think, by most people be considered handsome. But there was a depression of the eyes and upper part of the nose which I did not like, and which seemed to me to argue the possession of a cunning and perhaps malignant nature.

My inability to fathom the meaning of his frequent glances in Madame Kominski's direction began to irritate me. Was it love that he felt for her? Or was it hate? If the latter, why did such a look of desire shine from his eyes when they rested on her sparkling beauty? If the former, why did he frown and clinch his hands at the sound of her merry laugh?

"You seem engrossed in contemplation of Count Karenieff," said a voice at my elbow. "Does his appearance charm you so much?"

"By no means," I replied quickly, turning to the Princess Michaeloff, who seated herself by my side. "On the contrary, he strikes me as rather repellant than otherwise. I have been wondering if he hates Madame Kominski."

"Certainly not. He is madly in love with her. Unfortunately for him, our friend's tastes lean in another direction and she has been compelled to reject his suit."

"Then he does hate her, and his glances mean revenge."

"I hope not. He is a dangerous enemy. There are several people now doing penance in the fortress of St. Peter and Paul who have been doomed to their awful fate through his denunciations. Only last week the son of one of these, a mere child of fifteen, was banished to Siberia, and there is little doubt that Count Karenieff has a hand in this business also."

"But what could he, a boy of fifteen, have done to deserve so horrible a fate?"

"He has done nothing to deserve it. No one pretends to say that he has. But he is a bright and intelligent lad, who might some day be seized by a desire to avenge the wrongs of his parents, and he is the heir to a vast property which is now confiscated by the State. Of course the man who has given the State an excuse for increasing its revenue has also come in for a share of the spoil."

"What a monstrous system! What a monstrous—"

"For God's sake, be quiet! If you are overheard talking like that, we are lost! How could I have been indiscreet enough to dwell on tabooed subjects like that? I think it must be through meeting with someone who is as unsophisticated as I was myself when I first came here, only twelve months ago."

"So short a time as that?"

"Yes, so short a time as that. I came out here as Madame Kominski's companion. Thanks to her goodness, I had as many social advantages given me as if I had been a sprig of nobility, instead of being merely the daughter of a poor country curate, who had found it necessary to leave home to earn a livelihood. How kind fate has been to me! I was scarcely here before I won the love of the man who is now my husband. I have surely all that woman can desire. I love and am beloved, and I revel in unlimited wealth and comfort. Better still, I am able to free my parents from the harassing anxieties against which they have hitherto had to contend. Still—"

"You must be perfectly happy."

"I have only one wish ungratified. I would dearly like to live in England, and to escape the constant espionage to which we are all subject. But this cannot be, so I spend as much time in the company of English people as I can. Do you know, Madame Kominski brought an English companion out here three years ago. She was very fond of her, and was somewhat cut up when Miss Vernon, a very handsome woman, by-the-by, left her to get married. When I left her, she said that she would have no more companions, as she grew fond of them only to lose them. I am very glad that she has altered her mind."

So then, madame had been actuated by no petty feeling of jealousy when she declined to engage a pretty girl as her companion. She had few relatives, felt somewhat lonely in the house, and desired to secure a companion who would be likely to remain a member of her household for sometime. Struck with this conviction, I felt more assured than ever of the real kindness of madame's nature, and actually felt glad for the moment that there was no likelihood of her being disappointed in me as she had been disappointed in her other companions. Little did I dream how soon she would stand in dire need of loving friendship, she, to whom the world seemed to wear so smiling and benignant a front!

While we had been talking, there had been a slight movement of dispersal, and some of the guests now claimed the attention of the princess, who had certainly given me a disproportionate share of her attention. Soon afterward, we also took our leave, and both madame and myself seemed to have plenty of food for pleasant thought during the short drive home.

The next morning it was found a difficult matter to rouse Feo at the usual time, and her maid expressed the opinion that the child must be ill. I went to see her, and found her pale, sick and languid, possessed of a violent headache and consuming thirst. Somewhat alarmed, I announced my intention of summoning a doctor at once. But to this plan Feo entered very strenuous objections.

"Indeed, Miss Dora, I am not really ill," she protested. "I shall soon be all right again, and I'll never, never do it again as long as I live."

"Do what, child?"

"Oh, that would be telling, and I promised Olaf that I wouldn't tell."

"That mischievous little cousin of yours! You have been up to some naughtiness together. Tell me, have you been out and caught a fever, or something of that sort?"

"Oh, dear no, Dora. At least, we caught something, but it isn't a fever, and we didn't have to go out for it. Oh, dear, my head!"

"Well, I must just go and see if madame knows what will cure you."

"Oh, Dora, dear! pray don't! She would be so vexed. Look here. I'll tell you all about it, if you'll promise not to let mother know what is the matter with me."

"But suppose you should get worse. Madame would blame me then, and serious mischief might result from delay. I really think we must call a doctor in."

"Oh, Dora, you are so silly! Why can't you understand? I see I shall have to tell everything. But do give me a drink of lemonade first. I shan't get worse, that is certain. They never do; Olaf says so."

"Let Trischl fetch you a cup of coffee."

"Bah! Do you want to make me sick? I want lemonade, and you might—yes, I wish you would get me some vodki to put in it."

"Vodki! Is the child crazy?"

"No, I'm not crazy. But I think you must be, or else you would understand that it's just the Katzenjammer that's the matter with me."

"Katzenjammer! What a queer complaint. I hope it isn't catching."

But at this point Feo suddenly became convulsed with laughter, provoked thereto, I think, by the comical aspect of Trischl, who had all this time remained in the room, and who had thrown her hands up in horror at the name of the mysterious disease. The sight of Feo's mirth began to make me feel angry, for it struck me that she had been hoaxing me a little. But all at once the laughter ceased, and was replaced by sobs, amid which I heard an occasional protest to the effect that she would "never do it again—no, never!"

I now deemed it wisest to keep silent for a while, and presently Feo raised a repentant and shamefaced countenance to mine.

"I'll tell you all about it," she said. "But you must promise not to tell mother."

"If it is nothing very bad."

"Of course it isn't."

"Very well, then, I promise."

"I knew you wouldn't be nasty with me. And now I'll explain what the Katzenjammer is. You get it after you have been tipsy."

"Feo!"

"It's quite true. You see, last night, after mother and you had gone out, Uncle Feodor and Aunt Anna called with Olaf to take me to the theater, as they had promised to do. But Olaf didn't want to go to the theater, and asked me to stay at home and play with him. He knew of such a splendid new game, he said. So we got permission to stay here, for I thought Olaf's new game was something wonderful, he made such a fuss about it when he ran to my room to persuade me to agree to his plan. Then, when we were alone, he said: 'I have a short story to tell you first. Our old isvostchik, who has been with us so many years, has got dismissed today for getting drunk. He has often been drunk, and he was told that if he did it once more he would lose his place. Old Hans, who is a German, knew the penalty of offending again, and he was always troubled with what he called the Katzenjammer after he had been tipsy. But this seemed to make no difference. He got tipsy yesterday, and couldn't drive the carriage when mother wanted to go out in the afternoon. So he was packed off about his business, in disgrace. Now don't you think, Feo, that it must be delightful to get drunk? If it were not, do you think a poor man would risk so much for the sake of drinking vodki? I'm sure he wouldn't, so I'm determined to try what it feels like to be tipsy, and I want you to share the fun. We'll pretend to be two friends, who haven't seen each other for a long time, and we'll keep inviting each other to have a drink with us.'

"'But suppose it makes us have the Katzenjammer after it?'

"'Oh, then we have only to take a little drop more vodki, and then we shall be better again.'

"So at last I agreed and Olaf reached a decanter and some glasses out of a sideboard, and we made ourselves tipsy. It was great fun, too, for we grew quite jolly, and we danced, and we sang forever so long. Then Olaf fell asleep on the floor, and I came to bed. I don't know whether Olaf wakened up or not when they came to fetch him. And it isn't half so jolly as I thought it would be. My head aches awfully, and I'm never going to get drunk again."

Now was it very wrong of me to be so stricken with laughter that I found it necessary to turn away to hide my emotion? I'm afraid a strict moralist would hardly approve of my behavior, and I must have felt some twinges of conscience, or I would not have tried so hard to recover a stern demeanor. Finally, I succeeded, and drew such a picture of future horrors, that would certainly be the consequence of indulgence in a taste for strong drink, that Feo was almost frightened out of her wits and was not likely to transgress again in a hurry. Of course I tabooed the idea of giving her anymore of the pernicious stuff which had made her ill. As Trischl appeared to know all about the matter, I purchased her silence by the gift of a silver rouble, which she received with many manifestations of satisfaction. Then I ordered some hot extract of beef to be brought for Feo, advised her to lie still for an hour or two, and went to the morning-room in search of madame.

I found her looking somewhat disturbed. She always had a surprising amount of letters, seeing that she was a private individual. I had once or twice offered to take some of the fatigue of correspondence off her hands. But to this she would never consent. Indeed, I never even saw the addresses of the letters she sent away, as might have been the case had she cared to trust me with the duty of writing them down to her dictation. There was much that was mysterious in her way of receiving and dispatching her postal communications, and she was so good-natured with me on every other point that I knew she must have a good and sufficient reason for keeping me aloof in this respect. On this particular morning one of her letters had brought her tidings which necessitated a sudden change of plans on her part. As had been the case when in London, she left home for a few days, scarcely allowing herself time to have a small portmanteau packed, and giving us not the slightest idea of where she was going or how long she would be away. I was told that she depended upon me to take her place in the household as far as possible, but specific directions she had not time to give me.

That afternoon, I was writing a letter to Mrs. Garth, when Feo came into my room.

"I wish you would take me for a drive, Dora," she said. "My headache has nearly gone, and I believe fresh air would cure it altogether."

So I put my half-finished letter on one side, ordered the carriage, and prepared myself to go out with Feo. We both enjoyed the drive, and as I was still fresh to many of the sights of St. Petersburg, there was plenty of subject matter for conversation.

On arriving home again, I repaired at once to my own room, as I was anxious to finish the letter which I had begun to write to Mrs. Garth. I took the key of my room door out of my pocket. As I did not want the prying eyes of any of the servants to glance over my correspondence, I had taken the precaution of locking my door instead of putting my papers into my desk again.

I was somewhat surprised to find that the door was not locked, after all, and thought for a moment that I might have been mistaken as to having turned the key. But no. Reflection convinced me that there had been no mistake. I distinctly remembered that, after taking the key out of the lock, I had tried the door-handle. It would not yield to my touch. Therefore, the door had been locked. It was not locked when I returned. It was evident, then, that it had been tampered with during my absence. But who could have taken such an unwarrantable liberty? The question puzzled me, until I recalled to mind a figure I had seen on the stairs as I came up. It was the figure of a man whom I had not seen before, but who was walking leisurely downstairs, as if he felt assured of a safe and familiar footing in the house.

Who, or what could he be?

A servant in the house?

I thought not.

What then, a spy?

At the mere thought of being subject to the government espionage of which I had heard so much my limbs trembled under me and I fairly gasped for breath. I thought of May Morris and her gruesome predictions, and the wildest consternation seized me as I wondered if I had written anything that could compromise me. Had my letter to Mrs. Garth been overhauled? I must ascertain, if possible. I examined my blotting case and papers. They did not look as if they had been disturbed. I was putting them down again, half-reassured, when I perceived the faint impress of what must have been a dirty thumb on the edge of the sheet of note-paper on which I had been writing. I disclaimed the idea of having soiled the paper myself; but resolved to apply a test, in order to be quite sure.

Taking another sheet of paper, and wetting my right thumb with ink, I lightly grasped the paper between my thumb and forefinger, leaving upon it a slight mark. Then, taking a magnifying-glass from the table, I observed the two marks with its aid. The veinings on them were totally different. I had not soiled the half-written letter. A spy had been in my room. Could it be that trouble was in store for me, and that I had already fallen under the ban of suspicion?

Madame was away a week. When she returned, I was struck by the anxious expression of her face and still more by the evident effort with which she strove to be her old bright self.

"Are you not well?" I asked her, feeling considerable solicitude on her behalf.

"Quite well, Dora. Only a little tired after traveling. Tell me, has anything notable occurred during my absence?"

"There have been several callers."

"Were the Prince and Princess Michaelow here?"

"Yes. They came on Thursday, and took Feo and myself for a drive. We spent a very pleasant afternoon. Feo is spending the day with them again."

"And Count Karenieff. Has he been here?"

"No."

"Ah! I thought so! I must be on my guard against him. Is that all you have to tell me?"

"There is something else. But I am not sure that it is worth mentioning, or that the circumstances warrant the uneasiness they have caused me."

"For Heaven's sake! tell me all there is to tell. You little dream all there may be at stake."

"I am convinced that there is a spy in the house. Hush—what was that?"

As I uttered the last words, I sprang to my feet, and ran toward a large portière, which seemed to me to have moved while I was speaking. The door behind the portière was open, and I was just in time to see the figure of a man disappear round an angle of the great corridor into which all the rooms on this floor opened. When I turned and faced madame again, after carefully shutting the door, I saw that she was deadly pale, and that she was literally shaking with nervous apprehension. I hastily gave her a glass of wine, which she just as hastily drank, and then sat looking at me with a mute question in her startled eyes.

"A man has just run away from this door. He has been listening," I whispered, feeling as if the raising of my voice might bring ruin on the unnerved woman of whom I had already grown fond. Then I rapidly related how I had been driven to the conclusion that the house was under espionage.

"Was there anything in the letter that could be construed as matter of a mischievous tendency?" madame asked anxiously.

"Nothing whatever," was my confident reply. "I had merely said that my life in St. Petersburg was being made very pleasant, and that I had met a great number of very nice people. After I discovered that my correspondence had been overlooked, I destroyed the letter and resolved not to dispatch another in its place until I had consulted you. On Thursday I wrote out a page from Milton's 'Paradise Lost,' and left it, together with my blotting-book and writing materials, on the escritoire in this room. When I examined the things on my return, I found that the page of poetry and the top layer of blotting-paper out of my blotter had disappeared. Ah—that door is opening!"

The door, which slid on noiseless hinges, was quite concealed by the portière, but a very slight motion imparted to the latter by the incoming draught had not escaped my watchful attention, and the spy, whoever he was, was baffled again for a time, for madame sprang up, and drew the large curtains to one side, so that it was impossible for the door to be moved again without our being aware of it. To make assurance doubly sure, we slid the bolts that were on the inside. Then we explored the room which opened out of the large morning-room in which we had been sitting. We soon satisfied ourselves that nobody was there, and then, after locking the doors of that room also, to prevent unwarranted intrusion, we sat down to discuss the matter more fully.

"Dora," said madame, "just reach me my desk, will you?"

Willingly I obeyed, and then the desk was carefully overhauled by its owner, who became still more agitated when she failed to discover certain papers of which she was in search.

"I am lost!" she said despairingly. "I have been mad to keep those letters. And yet, how could I destroy them, when they were as life itself to me! My God! have I been too late, after all? Is he already in the hands of those cursed, bloodthirsty devils? Holy Mother of God! save me from going mad!"

My own bewilderment and alarm were momentarily increasing, but I used my best endeavors to soothe the distracted woman at my side.

"For pity's sake!" I implored, "be calm. To lose your self-control may help to bring about the very disaster you fear. And think of Feo. She will still claim your attention, whatever may be the demands upon your fortitude."

"My darling Feo! God help her, if anything befalls me, for those ravening wolves, my enemies, will have scant mercy upon the child of a suspect. Dora, can I trust you? Dare I put my secrets in your keeping?"

"God helping me, I will do all I can for you."

"I believe you. Now listen."

Madame Kominski spoke in a low voice, but with a painful concentration of purpose and a nervous clasping and unclasping of her hands which could only be the result of extreme agitation and dread.

"Listen," she said once more. "I belong to a family which has given many martyrs to the cause of freedom, and from my earliest youth I was taught to hate that merciless Juggernaut, the Russian autocracy, with all its vile ramifications of pillage and murder. Pah! Curse it! What does government do for us? It revels in luxury and splendors drained from the life-blood of millions of groaning victims. It grinds the people into nothingness as remorselessly as the millstones crush the wheat with which they are fed. But the day will come when even that mighty thing of evil will be numbered among the curses of the past, and when wealth and happiness are no longer all absorbed by the thin crust of society, while all beneath it is one mass of rotten, seething corruption and misery. They talk of hell! What hell could display sufferings equal to those which have been endured by my people? What hell could be big enough to hold all the accursed wretches who have for ages helped to trample out the lives and souls of a vast nation?"

"Madame! madame!" I whispered, in renewed alarm. "Think how dreadful it will be if you are overheard!"

"Why, yes," she said, sinking her voice again. "I believe I must be mad! And is it not enough to drive one mad, to see the downfall of all one's hopes; the failure of all one's plans; the utter hopelessness of trying to rescue even one unit among all these millions from the remorseless fate which an iron autocracy metes out for it? Where are now all my struggles? Lost! Wasted! Gone! Crashed by the foul harpies who bloat themselves on the miseries of others!

"But I forget that you do not yet know my history. Listen. I will tell it to you."

VIII

"Brave hearts and willing hands may foil even Satan himself."

I had," continued madame, "father, mother, sister, and two brothers, all of whom were sacrificed to the Moloch of oppression: My father's estates were confiscated, and his castle was handed into the possession of his betrayer, to whom was also given a title, and who was henceforth known as Count Karenieff. I, a babe in arms, was surely spared in fiendish irony of purpose, and was consigned to the care of a childless couple in St. Petersburg, who had strict injunctions to bring me up as their own offspring, and who, in consideration of the small income they received with me, kept the secret of my birth until I was nineteen. Then Paul Galtioff died, and his wife Marie, having confidence in my discretion, and a premonition that her own end was not far off, showed me my true vocation. She told me of all that my relatives had suffered, and how my mother had been subjected to imprisonment, torture, the lash and personal degradation because she would say nothing that would incriminate my father. I have often since heard of the horrors of St. Peter and Paul. In your country they speak with bated breath of banishment to Siberia as the extreme compass of human suffering. *We* know that it is the one ray of hope which gleams before the eyes of those who are denounced. Complete freedom will never be theirs again, but there are gradations in even the lowest ruts of misery, and I would pray for the devil himself to be saved from the anguish endured by those condemned to the fortress.

"What wonder that, thinking of all these things, I should pant for vengeance, and that I should devote all my future energies to foiling some of the plots against my compatriots! But Marie Galtioff infused in me some of her own caution and cunning. Both she and her husband had belonged to revolutionary societies for years without once exciting suspicion of their loyalty. Henceforth I derived my chief satisfaction in hoodwinking our oppressors. I habitually met kindred spirits, among them being Feodor Kominski, who afterward became my husband. Perhaps it was well for him that death claimed him soon after Feo was born. His spirit was too ardent to have worked in the dark much longer.

"For some years after I became a widow I supported myself in various ways. Then my opportunity came from a quarter least expected. A member of our society, who possessed great influence at court, where he was supposed to be one of the most loyal supporters of the throne, was asked to recommend some lady who would make an efficient government spy. He nominated me for the office. The pay was on a princely scale. The social advantages attending the post were great. There was no circle deemed too high for my entry into it on apparent terms of equality with the most exclusive. My credentials were indisputable, and my own conversational ability did the rest. I became a general favorite in society, and might have been happy, could I but have faithfully performed the day's duty for which I was paid. My employers gave me every opportunity of spying and denouncing suspected persons. I denounced a good many when I saw that their discovery by others was inevitable. But I always contrived to let them have sufficient warning to escape before the bolt fell. I was doing good work for my people, under the mask of an alien to patriotism. Above all, I was occupying a place which will soon, I fear, be occupied by a substitute whose aims and aspirations will not be as mine have been.

"When I was in St. Petersburg in the early spring, Count Karenieff, the son of my father's old enemy, was introduced to me, and I found it a terribly difficult matter to be civil to him. It was, however, necessary that I should curb the anger which his very name aroused in me. But when the caitiff's whelp actually dared to propose marriage to me, my scorn and hatred over-stepped the bounds of prudence, and my rejection was so fierce as to astonish him.

"'I see, madame,' he said, his face glittering with the evil with which his heart is full to bursting. 'I understand you better than you understand yourself. You see in me a man of strong feeling, and you think it necessary to use strong words with me, in order to drive me from my purpose. But I tell you that your beauty has aroused my passions, and I will gratify them even though you raised ten thousand objections. You are so unnecessarily vehement that I conclude you have a more favored lover. One, moreover, who resembles me not at all. And you think to marry him? I swear you shall marry none but me! Nay, if you do not beware, I will bring that about which shall make you turn to me for help, which shall make you only too happy to throw yourself into my arms and yield yourself to my embraces. As for your lover, I shall find him, and I shall silence him, never fear. His golden hair shall turn gray with horror, and his blue eyes shall become dim with anguish.'

"'He has neither golden hair nor blue eyes,' I cried, trembling with the awe the man's fierce words evoked.

"'Thank you,' was his reply. 'I thought that, as you seemed so disgusted with my proposal, your inamorato must be my antithesis. Now I am sure of it. If it had not been so, you would have been glad to permit me to retain an erroneous opinion. Good-day, madame. Perhaps, when next we meet, you will have become wiser.'

"With this the viper left me, and I sat bereft of all my usual fortitude. For I knew him to be capable of as much villainy as his father before him, and I had practically betrayed Victor Karniak to him; for his instinct had led him to form a correct idea of the appearance of my intended husband. That he would hound him down, I had no doubt. But I was not so paralyzed by Karenieff's threats as to hesitate long about what I must do.

"That night I attended a meeting which was held by Nihilists not far from here. I had difficulty in reaching the place unobserved, and, carefully disguised, I saw Karenieff and two of his myrmidons watching my house. I explained the impossibility of my further attendance at the meetings for sometime, as my presence might lead to the discovery and betrayal of my associates. There were those among them who swore that, if there must be a victim, it should be Karenieff himself. I would have rejoiced anytime since then to have heard of the removal of the pestiferous carrion; but he bears a charmed life, or, rather, he is too well aware of his danger to go anywhere unguarded, for he has denounced too many people not to fear vengeance from some quarter.

"Victor Karniak was persuaded to leave St. Petersburg for a time, and it was considered wisest for us not to meet again until we could do so with more safety.

"I was sent to England, on what was deemed important business, soon after this, and hoped that Karenieff's mischievous intentions were rendered impossible of achievement. Meanwhile Victor, having been imprudently active in Odessa, narrowly escaped capture by shipping as a common seaman on board a steamer, in place of a drunken sailor who had fallen overboard. In due time he reached London. We found means of meeting, and have been married in an English registry office.

"But we dared not return together, and I dared not delay my own return, as I had much information to give concerning many Russians who have escaped to England, some of them with Victor's help and mine. They are safe where they are, and will assuredly never return to Russia, having been warned of what they might expect; so I feel no twinges of conscience because I have convinced the government beyond doubt that they are out of Russian territory and beyond Russian jurisdiction.

"My husband, anxious to be near me sometimes, and having considerable property which he wishes to realize, if possible, followed me here. He was at the Princess Michaelow's reception, and though we were studiedly cool to each other, I once saw Karenieff looking at us with such an appearance of malicious conviction on his face that I felt sure he suspected our secret. Victor, who had been called by an alias in Odessa, believed himself to be recognized, and would have tried to leave the country again, but was taken ill and has been unable to quit his bed for more than a week. I have been with him the greater part of the time, and he is only since yesterday strong enough to rise and dress himself. This morning I saw him, disguised as an old peddler, and armed with a license and pass which a friend had procured for him, start on a journey, every inch of which is fraught with danger of detection and death. God grant that, shaken as he is with his recent illness, he may find himself once more in your land of freedom ere long.

"But I fear, I fear! For my enemy has been active. He has been missing from his usual haunts, and has been trying to discover my husband's whereabouts. This I have been told by the people who, on my behalf, have been watching Karenieff. He did not come here to seek me, because he knew I was not here. That he has not known exactly where I was, I can but hope, for the sake of Victor and the friends who have helped us. But that he has already denounced me as a traitor and Nihilist I was told today on my way here. I would not have entered the house again, but would have tried to escape, had I had means of travel with me. Besides, I could not, in any case, have left Feo. Had I done so, my child would surely have fallen under the vengeance of those who have gloatingly crushed out the lives of other innocent children.

"I had hoped to get away under cover of night, but alas! what you have told me since I came home has served to convince me that I am already too closely watched to be permitted to escape. Dora, my friend, help me, for the love of God! for I already feel, in anticipation, all the horrors of the fortress, and I can no longer plan clearly."

All this had been spoken in a voice too low to penetrate as far as the door, but clear enough for me, whose head was bent close to madame's, to distinguish every word of it. For a few moments I could only continue to gaze at my friend in blank dismay. Then, as certain possibilities presented themselves before my mental vision, I clasped my hands angrily, and exclaimed: "Great Heaven! why am I not tall and beautiful, when so much size and beauty is wasted on people who do not know how to use it?"

Recalling that time, I am not surprised at the change my apparently irrelevant lament wrought in Madame Kominski's demeanor. She sprang to her feet, and fairly hissed at me in her wrath: "Fool! fool that I have been, to imagine my troubles could really interest a comparative stranger! I betray all my secrets to you, and implore your aid, and only succeed in evoking from you a lamentation concerning your own lack of beauty. God! what small minds there are in this world!"

"Madame," I cried, springing to my feet in my turn, "you mistake me. I am devoted to you, and will do anything to help you. I expressed myself clumsily, but I meant to say that if I were more like you I would change places with you. As it is, the plan is hopeless. But we will think of something else. God is not always on the side of the mighty."

As I spoke, I put my arms round madame and kissed her affectionately. The revulsion of feeling produced in her mind by my words and actions broke the intense strain under which she had labored, and she embraced me convulsively, a perfect storm of sobs shaking her frame. I strove as best I could with my own emotion and let madame cry on. I knew it would do her good. Presently she grew calmer, and after a while her sobs ceased altogether.

"I am better now," she said. "I feel as if a great cloud were rolled from my brain. I can think and plan once more. My mother, they say, had the courage of a martyr. If I fall, my enemies shall not gloat over my cowardice. Suppose we open the doors again. It is not wise to show a spy that we fear him."

I had just opened the door, and put the portière into its usual position, when Trischl, the German nurse, came to see her mistress. She walked into the room without invitation, but preserved nevertheless her usual respectful demeanor. "I believe madame needs friends," she said in a low, cautious voice. "I have seen that which makes me think so. Madame has been good to me. If she will not be angry at my presumption, I will be her faithful helper."

As Trischl ceased speaking, she looked at her mistress anxiously, as if half afraid of reproof. But of that she met none, and the friendly clasp of the hand with which madame tried to show her appreciation of the risk the faithful creature was running in offering to help a suspect was to her a seal of allegiance. For a little while we deliberated together, forming and rejecting one plan after another. Presently an unusually vigorous peal at the visitor's bell made itself heard even here, where the sonorous reverberations seldom penetrated. We all turned pale and the same unspoken question was in all our eyes: "Is the enemy already upon us? Is it too late to escape?" Even evils are welcomed at times, when they come in the place of a still more dreaded one, and we were all positively relieved when a footman presently came to ask madame if she would see Count Karenieff in the salon.

"Tell him I will see him immediately," said madame. Instinctively both Trischl and I knew what should be done, and we hastened to bathe madame's face with eau-de-cologne, to brush her hair, to alter her toilet a little, and to give to her face the appearance of quiet composure by means of a little powder and rouge. The results were arrived at quickly. The effect was good, and madame's bearing and appearance, as she went down to interview her mortal enemy, were the reverse of those of a betrayed and despairing woman, who anticipated a horrible fate in the near future.

"Temporize with him," I had counseled while hurriedly assisting with her toilet. "Feign ignorance of his cruel intentions. If he asks you again to marry him, do not insult him, but seem as if you had altered your opinion of him. Ask him to give you a day to deliberate. It would be so much time gained for us."

The nod of comprehension with which she left us showed that she considered my advice to be good, and I felt more hopeful of the result of the interview between the courageous woman and the dastardly man than I could have believed possible half an hour before.

"And now," said Trischl, "there is no time to be lost. There are spies in the house. But we can be as clever as spies, if we like, and we must prepare things for madame's departure as soon as possible. All her jewelry must be hidden somehow, so that she can easily carry it away."

I felt that Trischl was right, and that a desperate emergency like this was not the time to stand on ceremony. Fifteen minutes later a strange face peeped in at the open door for a moment. We were both diligently employed. To all appearances we were both innocently employed. Trischl was quilting some silk, of which she purposed making a kind of cuff, to be tied above the elbows. I was indulging in the prosaic occupation of mending a pair of corsets. Could the fellow who had glanced at us have

ELIZABETH BURGOYNE CORBETT

seen that a pile of jewelry lay underneath the aprons Trischl and I had donned, he would perhaps have been slightly surprised. Had he had a suspicion that I had just stitched a parure of diamonds into the corset, and that Trischl was quilting the silk over a beautiful pearl necklace, he might perhaps have thought it advisable to report the occurrence to his superiors. As it was, he passed on, in blissful ignorance of our real occupation, and it was certainly not our business to enlighten him.

"Here is madame," said Trischl presently; and I looked anxiously at Madame Kominski, to see if I could tell the result of the interview from her bearing. Trischl rose hastily to her feet, seemingly overwhelmed with confusion at having been caught occupying her mistress's seat. She had forgotten that her quilting task was not finished, and some valuable rings rolled across the floor, the incident evoking a little surprise in the mind of their owner. But while Trischl hurriedly tried to recover the runaways, I explained what we had been doing.

"What a clever idea!" said madame. "I should never have thought of such capital hiding-places myself. If I manage to quit Russia, I shall probably be in great need of money, and will be glad to realize the value of the jewelry."

"I hope things are not so desperate as we have feared," I hazarded.

"You shall judge," was the reply. "Karenieff was evidently prepared to find me more antagonistic to him than I showed myself, and I think my bearing convinced him that my suspicions concerning him were not aroused.

"'I am sorry to have kept you waiting,' I said, 'but the truth is, I was busy with my toilet and could not come before.'

"He cast upon me a swift look of surprise, and then, apparently much gratified by the civility of my reception of him, dosed me with a few compliments, adding that he hoped I had forgotten the wild, foolish words he had uttered to me months ago. I actually found it possible to laugh, as I remarked in my turn: 'Ah, yes! We all alter our opinions of things as time goes on. I have learned to esteem where I once despised; and you—you, no doubt, take things more coolly than you did.'

"'My love for you has not grown cooler,' he exclaimed. 'Consent to marry me, and I will secure you immunity from trouble in the future.'

"'Marry you! Is it possible you still wish me to become your wife?'

"'It is not merely my wish. It is the one passion of my life! Say you will be mine, and remove my suspense.'

"'I do not know,' I said, pretending to hesitate. 'You see, I hardly thought you would favor me again with a proposal, after my former rudeness to you.'

"'The woman who hesitates is lost! Have I really supplanted my fair-haired rival?'

"'Bah! Fair men are so insipid.'

"So they are. But you will not find me insipid, my beauty. I hate, or I love, to madness, and either passion finds in me an ardent votary. It is well you have chosen me for your lover rather than for your enemy, since I have more power than you dream of.'

"'Indeed! I did not know that you had any special vocation. You said just now that marriage with you would bring me immunity from trouble. I do not see how that can be, since we all have our troubles; but I wish it were true.'

"'It shall be true. Listen. You are in the pay of the government. The private fortune you are supposed to have is non-existent. I know exactly what is paid you, since my position in the secret service is so high as to be one upon which devolves the regulation of these little things. With one stroke of my pen I can make or mar many a life that fancies itself secure at this moment. Now, information has been brought to me that you, so far from being a faithful servant of the Crown, are in league with those vagabond Nihilists. As my wife, you shall be proved innocent. As my enemy, you would be crushed. Which is it to be?'

"I believe I acted my part very well. I was overcome by sudden terror. I clung to the man. I wept and implored him to save me. I promised to marry him as soon as he liked. I suffered him to embrace me. His kisses, hot, passionate and scathing, have been showered on my face and lips. I have listened to burning words which have made me ashamed of my womanhood. Had I alone been concerned, I would have died rather than have undergone the humiliation of the last half hour. But there is Feo and Victor. For their sakes I must escape from this accursed country."

"And you shall escape," said Trischl, with decision. "I think I know how it can be managed." In another moment she had left us, hurrying away as if struck by a fresh idea, while madame and I eyed each other anxiously.

"Has he gone?" I asked.

"For a time. I believe he has gone to stop extreme proceedings against me. But the relief will be only momentary. I should go mad if I had to endure his caresses often, and he may at any moment discover that I am already married. His vengeance would then be more terrible than ever."

"It is not to be thought of. We must act at once."

"Here is Ivan Dromireff, madame," said Trischl's voice. "I met him on the staircase."

Both madame and I looked at the new arrival with surprise. He turned out to be none other than her coachman, and he stood bowing awkwardly, the while holding out a note between fingers that were much less clumsy than his vocation would have led one to imagine them to be.

"A letter from Prince Michaelow," he said quietly.

"How is it that it has not been sent up in the usual way?" inquired madame sharply, receiving for answer a word of which I could not catch the meaning, but which wrought a great change in madame's behavior.

"Sit down," she said eagerly, "while I read the note. And you, Trischl, secure the door against intruders, and wait here until we decide what is best to be done."

Trischl, having obeyed her mistress's order, came and stood beside Ivan. It struck me that the footing upon which they stood was a very familiar one, for they smiled at each other in quite an affectionate manner. Meanwhile, madame's proceedings were somewhat curious. She opened the note, upon which were merely written a few lines to the effect that Feo was enjoying herself and would remain for the night where she was. Then she took from her pocket a bunch of keys and unlocked a small medicine chest. From this she took two phials, each containing a colorless fluid. Her next proceeding was to fetch a small china tray from a side-table. Into this she emptied the two phials. When the liquids were thoroughly mixed, she immersed the note in them and let it remain a few seconds. When she lifted it out of the tray again, it was seen to be closely covered with writing, some kind of sympathetic ink having been used which had required acids to develop it. This is what was written on the note:

My Friend

Our cause is lost. We are betrayed. Nothing but prompt flight can save us. Count Karenieff has much in his power. If you can dupe him for a while it will be well. Victor will elude his enemies, I think. I have long feared this day, and have been prepared for it. Ivan will give you a pass that will be of good service to you. But it must be used tonight. Tomorrow every departure from the city will be closely watched. By the time you get this we shall be well on our way. Feo will go with us, and I trust we shall all arrive in England safely. You know the rendezvous. It will be better for you to be unencumbered by the child. I would advise your companion to get away, too, if she has helped you in anyway. Ivan has already made his preparations.

M.

After passing the note on to me to read it, madame asked Ivan if he were aware of its contents.

"I know how we are all circumstanced," he said promptly, "and what the prince told me will be something similar to what he has written."

In a low, rapid voice madame read the letter over for the benefit of Trischl and Ivan, who were now too much implicated to be excluded from confidence. Then she struck a match and burned the note and its envelope until they were entirely consumed. Meanwhile, I returned the acids to their receptacles, wiped the tray, and removed every trace of the chemical operation, giving madame the key of the medicine chest when I had done.

"And now," said Ivan, "for action." A minute later he had divested himself of his overcoat, and had made himself much less stout by the removal of some clothes which he had had packed round his body. Then he coolly took off his big, bushy beard and mustache, and his tously black wig. Such a transformation as all this wrought in him! He had seemed a rough specimen of humanity, not far removed from serfdom. He stood before us slim, erect, fair and smooth-faced, but bearing the witnesses of an indomitable spirit in his determined mouth, no longer hidden by the disfiguring hair, in his fearless glance, and in his square jaw.

"Now you know me; but no names, please," he said warningly, as madame seemed about to exclaim aloud at sight of him. "The prince, having induced you to accept a certain position, has always been convinced of its danger, and has always been prepared with plans to rescue you. For this purpose, he recommended me to your notice as coachman, in order that no symptoms of menace might escape your friends. I have seen that you have no more time to lose. Here is our passport. It is made out for August Krämer, a German mercantile agent; Anna Krämer, his wife; Wilhelm Schwartz, commission agent, and Karl Schwartz, son of the latter."

"But that will not do for us. We are three women, not three men," said madame.

"If circumstances do not fit us, we must fit ourselves to circumstances, and I think we can manage it," said Ivan. "Trischl is my foster-sister, and will go with us, I know. She is big enough and strong enough to personate Schwartz, senior. You, madame, will have to figure as Herr August Krämer, while I will do my best to make you a suitable spouse. The young English lady will make a very nice boy. Here are some of the things you will require. Put on as many as will be hidden by outer clothing. Take the rest with you. In fifteen minutes follow me. I will have the carriage waiting at the door. It shall contain a few necessary articles which will have to be put on in the carriage. You must give me your order to drive to one of the theaters. But be very careful. Someone is sure to be on the watch. We will drive away openly. As soon as we have driven off, draw the curtains and complete your disguise the best way you can. After a while I will stop the carriage. You must then get out, leaving nothing in the vehicle, and keeping your mantles well wrapped round you. Walk on a few yards until I join you. The horses will stand for sometime, and I have a man ready to take them to a place agreed upon. It will not do for them to return home too soon, and it is just possible that we may need them. Now I must be off."

Another minute, and he had replaced his beard and top-coat. Still a minute more, and we three women were trying to induct ourselves into garments such as we had never been used to. In ten minutes we had stuffed our pockets full of wigs, beards, jewelry, papers, money and other etceteras. I had had time to run to my room and secure my own money and jewelry, as well as a large cloak and a hat. Everything else I must perforce leave behind. Trischl fetched her big cloak and bonnet, and went down to the carriage a yard or two in front of us. Punctual to time, we stepped inside. Madame told Ivan to drive to the Alexander Theater. Ivan touched his hat obsequiously, mounted his box, cracked his whip, and we were started on our perilous journey.

There was no loss of time among us, after we drove off, for we knew that promptitude on our part was a matter of life and death. It was a somewhat cramped place in which to transform our appearance, but we had to make the best of the situation. With hurrying, trembling fingers we wrought at our disguise. Madame donned a tow-colored curly wig, beard, mustache and eyebrows, and exchanged her mantle and bonnet for a top-coat and slouch hat. Trischl adorned herself with a black beard something like Ivan wore, and likewise donned a rough overcoat, which she surmounted by a felt hat. I was not proud of my hair, anyway, so, seeing what trouble the others had in disposing of theirs under their wigs, I ruthlessly cut mine off with a pair of scissors I had brought with me for emergencies. It was surprising how small and slight a boy I seemed. It would be easy to pass me off as a fifteen-year-older.

When we had done our best to transform ourselves into as presentable representatives of Messrs Krämer and Schwartz as was possible with our resources, we commenced strapping up the cloaks and hats, the latter being mercilessly crushed during the operation. We had barely completed our preparations when the carriage stopped and Ivan opened the door. "Now is our time," he said hurriedly. "We shall barely catch the Cronstadt boat. Go toward the boat-landing. I will follow you in a minute."

Without another word we obeyed Ivan's directions. We had almost reached the landing, when a fair-faced, rather good-looking woman grasped madame somewhat unceremoniously by the arm, and addressed her in the whining, ill-used tone which is the special prerogative of certain carping, dissatisfied wives.

"I'm sure, August," she said. "It's easy to be seen that we've been married this six years and more. I have seen the time when you wouldn't stalk on half a mile in front, leaving me to follow as best I could. But times are different now, and a man isn't above making his wife carry his top-coat in these days. But I won't stand it any longer. You may carry it yourself."

So great was the transformation that for an instant we did not see that it was Ivan who was personating the ill-used wife. As soon as she did become fully alive to this fact, madame took the top-coat on her arm, instinctively apologizing for her apparent rudeness.

"No, no, that will never do," muttered Ivan. "You are far too polite. Keep up your rôle of a careless husband and growl harder at me than I growl at you—if you can. There must be no appearance of haste or anxiety to escape notice. Boldness is our best weapon.—Herr Schwartz, that son of yours looks too much like a girl—too quiet and shy.—Here, Karl, my boy, have a cigarette, and walk with a little more swagger—as if the place belonged to you. Take a peep at the pretty girls you pass, and be politely courteous, if any old ladies seem to need your services.— Herr Krämer, you are as fidgety about that hair of yours as if you were a woman. It is dangerous to appear too solicitous about your personal

ELIZABETH BURGOYNE CORBETT

appearance. Now, all three, please. Follow whatever cue I may think it desirable to give you."

Thus grumbling, admonishing and advising, the pseudo Madame Krämer talked until we were close to the ticket-office, near which a goodly number of people were waiting to pay their fares, have their passports viséd, and receive their tickets to go on board the river steamer which lay waiting for its living cargo.

I am afraid that I must confess myself not nearly so brave as I had imagined I was, for, now that the crucial moment had come, I trembled in every limb; whereas the others, either more habituated to the exercise of courage, or more alive to the irretrievably fatal consequences of a false move on their part, walked up to the barrier as nonchalantly as if traveling by this route were a matter of daily occurrence with them. Fortunately for us, there was an unusually large number of passengers, many of them being of the Jewish persuasion. Upon these the rancor of the officials seemed to concentrate itself, and while apparently well-to-do people were merely treated unceremoniously, the followers of Israel were harassed and insulted beyond patient endurance. Many of them had been prosperous, but had been hounded from their homes and driven to beggary by a cruel and rapacious tyranny that found ready helpers in its horde of greedy, money-grabbing, red-taped myrmidons.

My heart ached for the sorrows of one miserable couple, who were accompanied by six children, and who seemed to be bewildered by the insults which arrogance in office heaped upon them. But I also felt especially grateful to them. For the officials had no time to spare to examine our passports with anything like care when there were so many downtrodden Jews upon whom to exercise their spleen. Thus it happened that without much fuss or questioning we soon found ourselves seated in the deck saloon, en route for Cronstadt, the second-class passengers being huddled forward, where they were not likely to be spoiled by the luxury of too much comfort or accommodation.

I saw madame scan the other occupants of the saloon very searchingly. Perhaps she thought that her daughter was among them, and it was difficult to augur well or ill from the fact that she was not there. I wonder if ever anyone watched the endless twistings and turnings of the Neva with more impatience than we did, or if anyone ever longed more devotedly to get beyond the oft-recurring view of St. Isaac's golden dome. But even as times of joy have their ending, even so is the period of suspense and danger never interminable, and we at last found ourselves close to Cronstadt.

We had not considered it safe to talk about our position while sitting in the saloon or pacing the deck, lest we should be overheard and betrayed. But we all felt breathless anxiety as we filed off the boat on to the landing-stage, holding our tickets in readiness for the collector.

Suppose we had been missed at St. Petersburg! Suppose Karenieff, baffled and enraged, were already on our track! Suppose a wire had been sent here, conveying orders to detain and arrest us!

Anticipation presented numberless possibilities, all of which, as we walked ashore without hindrance, seemed as if they were to be happily negatived by the reality.

ELIZABETH BURGOYNE CORBETT

IX

"How fain are we to turn our backs on that which likes us not."

It struck me at the time as a remarkable coincidence that after walking about fifty yards we should come across a droschki, into which we all stepped, being driven away without a word of explanation to the driver, unless a peculiar, thrice-repeated nod by Ivan be considered sufficient explanation.

It would be useless to pretend that our drive was in every respect a comfortable one. The droschki was, in the first place, so small that we had to sit on each other's knees. And it was so shaky that we had to hold on to each other to avoid turning a somersault on to the roadway. But that was not the fault of the droschki. The ill-used vehicle was compelled to do duty as a sledge in winter. In summer the runners were unshiped and laid to rest for a few months, while the clumsy wheels were hauled out of their hiding-place and tied to the body of the droschki with ropes. When you take a carriage of this description, and drive it helter-skelter through streets paved with rough round cobble-stones, the result cannot be expected to be conducive to comfort.

In my case, the miseries of that drive were intensified, as I was already feeling very sick, in consequence of having been rash enough to cap my first cigarette with a second one. But it was all in the interests of patriotism and freedom, and the memory of the sufferings of that day and night has been wiped out by the recollection of their satisfactory ending.

We had been driving, as nearly as I can remember, about half an hour, having branched off from the streets into the public park known as Peter the Great's Gardens, when our driver drew his horse up close to the edge of some dark, stagnant water. We were beside the new Mole. The last remnant of daylight was now gone, so far as it does go altogether in these latitudes in summer. But we were quite able to see that in the huge basin before us lay hundreds of steamers of various nationalities, in one of which at least we hoped to find a haven of refuge.

Seeing us get out of the droschki, several uncouth-looking boatmen, dressed in bright-colored print shirts, immediately importuned us to employ them. After a little preliminary bargaining between them and the droschki-driver, the two least villainous-looking boatmen were employed to row our party to an English steamer named the *Beacon*.

A liberal *douceur* was given to the driver by Ivan. We stepped into the gaudily-painted boat, carrying our scanty store of luggage with us; the men bent to their oars, and we were soon skimming the surface of the Mole, while the sounds of the droschki's wheels died away in the distance.

"Keep a sharp lookout," muttered Ivan in English. "These fiendish boatmen would brain us all, and pitch us into the water, if they thought that, by catching us unawares, they could land a few roubles and a watch or two. That sort of thing often happens, but none of the villains are ever brought to book. They bolt off to their winter quarters as soon as they have done a stroke of that sort of business, and when they come back in the next boating season the whole affair has been forgotten by the officials."

After this, I sat with my eyes glued on the boatmen, anxiously noting what a number of ships we had to pass before we reached the one we wanted, and wildly longing for the time when I could bid an eternal farewell to misery-haunted Russia. I supposed, the *Beacon* being in the inner Mole, the men would be rowing half an hour before they reached it. To me the time seemed an age ere we pulled up beside a black-looking steamer, and one of the men shouted "Ahoy!" to the watchman on deck. There was a speedy reply to the summons, three or four dark heads popping themselves over the side to have a look at us. There were no questions asked, and it almost seemed to me as if we had been expected, though one could not complain of the preparations for our reception being too elaborate. A rope-ladder hung from the ship's side, and for a moment my heart sank within me, when I was told that this was the only means of boarding our ark of safety.

Trischl confessed to me afterward that she almost fainted at what seemed to her to be courting certain death. But we were both possessed by an even greater dread than that of falling back into the water, and nerved ourselves to appear as "manly" and unconcerned as possible, lest our terror should betray how totally unused to our present surroundings we were. As for madame, she seemed to be endowed with super-human courage and calmness.

In due course this fresh ordeal was over. The boatmen grasped the end of the ladder, which had wooden rungs, in order to steady it, and one by one we sampled its precarious footing, swaying from side to side with the motion of the boat, and sometimes being turned almost with our backs to the steamer before we reached the rail at the top.

ELIZABETH BURGOYNE CORBETT

Here many hands were ready to seize ours, and to help us to descend the short ladder which led from the rail to the deck. It is contrary to all custom for a woman to be left to the last to come on board in this fashion, and Ivan, in spite of his assumed transposition into a member of the weaker sex, would fain have seen the supposed German merchant board the ship before him. This, however, would of a certainty have roused the suspicions of the boatmen.

So madame was left to give the boatmen their stipulated pay and to come on board unaided. The boatmen, knowing with what facility seafarers usually mount these hanging ladders, pushed their boat off without further delay, and paid no more attention to the individual whom they left dangling in mid-air. Being thus unceremoniously thrown upon her own resources, madame exerted herself to secure a more stable footing, and when at last she stood upon the deck, shaking with sudden nervousness, I firmly believed that nothing short of a miracle had saved her from falling into the water.

"Pray come down below at once," said the voice of a man who had taken an active part in our reception, and who proved to be the captain. "I began to be afraid that you would not save the tide. It will be high water in an hour, and there is nothing to hinder us from weighing and starting at once. We must pass out when the gates open. You will have to excuse the quarters to which I am compelled to consign you until we are out of Russian jurisdiction. We may possibly be boarded again by government officials before we are clear of the docks, and you must all be alike invisible and inaudible. So be perfectly still until I come down to you again. You will find someother refugees in the ship. They will help to make you comfortable. Take care!"

While the captain was talking, he had been leading us through the ship's saloon; thence through the steward's pantry to what he called the lazarette, whence we emerged, through a cunningly concealed sliding door, into an apartment that was so narrow that two stout people could barely have passed each other in it, and so dark that the reader may reasonably excuse the momentary panic which overcame me, when, before we had quite comprehended that we were at last at the end of our journey, we were pushed further into the passage-like space. Then the captain hurriedly left us to our own devices, and the door closed with a peculiar click which advertised some patent spring action.

We were doubtful what step to take next, and were so imbued with a sense of the deadly danger that would attend any noise on our part, that for a few moments we dared neither move nor speak. It was a great relief when, in a few minutes, the captain returned with a scrap of candle—warranted to go out in five minutes.

"Daren't allow more. Might be seen," he whispered, and then clicked the door after him.

We eagerly availed ourselves of the dim light which had been put into Trischl's hand to glance around our temporary prison, which eventually proved to have been contrived by means of double bulkheads, which traversed the ship from side to side, but were only two feet apart from each other. The reason for this economy of space will be obvious when it is remembered that the object of the shipbuilders had been the provision of a secret chamber of which the existence was not to be even suspected by those not in the secret.

The long, narrow passage thus obtained was furnished with rugs and cushions, and such other means of comfort as the exigencies of space and practicability allowed.

But we did not dwell long upon the view of our place of refuge, for we speedily caught sight of that which filled us with the liveliest joy.

We had been enjoined to keep silent. Surely it would have been a superhuman task to refrain from a few exclamations of thankfulness at the surprise in store for us. For here were the Prince and Princess Michaelow, madame's daughter Feo, and a fourth person whom we soon knew to be none other than Victor Karniak, my mistress's newly-wedded husband.

Surely tears, and sobs, and smiles, and exclamations of gratitude were never more rapturously blended than in the small, stuffy hole in which we were all reunited! But prudence soon reasserted itself, and ten minutes later a Russian spy might have listened at the door without hearing a sound from within. Yet a little while longer and we could hear the vibration of the screw. We had entered upon another phase of our adventurous journey.

Excitement and danger are prone to make one forget or ignore bodily claims which weigh very seriously with us at other times. But when these unwonted stimulants are withdrawn, nature is apt to take a little revenge for the temporary slight put upon her. Thus it is not surprising that, the happy reunion of friends and relatives being accomplished, the quartet of newest arrivals should become conscious of extreme fatigue and of the need of some kind of refreshment.

The latter was soon forthcoming. A larder at one end of the room

ELIZABETH BURGOYNE CORBETT

we were in was stocked with a liberal supply of eatables and drinkables, and there were plenty of willing hands to serve us with a meal to which some at least of us did full justice.

"And now, Miss Dora," said Trischl, "the best thing we can do is to lie down and sleep for a while. Everybody else has much to talk over with friends, and we shall not be missed."

It was quite true. We could, for a time, at least, be easily, perhaps gladly, spared. While traveling, and sharing mutual dangers, we had all seemed tolerably equal in our claims upon each other. The situation was altered now. Trischl was kindly and warmly welcomed. But her welcome was the one which generous employers would naturally extend to a faithful servant. I was treated in every respect as an equal, but was still conscious of the fact that I was not actually one of the family, as seemed to be the case with Ivan. That madame should appear all in all to her husband and child was natural. But that Ivan, whom I had admired while I thought him madame's very humble assistant, should turn out to be none other than Count Sergius Volkhoffsky, the cousin and bosom friend of Prince Michaelow, was a great surprise to me. They all had much to talk about, or rather, to whisper about, for great caution was necessary, and I felt no compunction in following Trischl's advice.

But it was long before I could sleep; for the motion of the vessel, combined with the unpleasant vibration of the screw, which seemed to be almost under me, soon made me feel sick again, and I underwent a period of intense but silent misery, too ill to lift my head, but not too ill to feel a fresh accession of terror everytime the motion of the ship ceased.

I did not know then that the coming out of dock of a merchant steamer is a tedious business which involves many fresh starts and stoppages, if collisions with quay walls or ships are to be avoided. Had I been aware of this fact, I should not have kept fancying that the *Beacon* had been detained by Russian government officials, and that pursuers were about to discover our hiding-place.

When at last sleep did visit me, it performed its work so effectually that on awaking I had no trace of fatigue or illness left. My cushions were at one end of our curious room, which was no wider than an ordinary bunk, and would hardly have permitted anyone to pass me without disturbing me. As it was, I had slept uninterruptedly for hours, and was quite refreshed when I opened my eyes and saw that a lamp was casting its brightening rays around me. Trischl stood by my bedside, if such I can call it, smiling with joy, and holding in her hand a cup of fragrant coffee.

"I have brought you some coffee and a ham sandwich," she said. "You may get up as soon as you like now, and come on deck when you have had some breakfast. We have left Russia behind us and have got rid of the Russian pilot. The captain says there is no more fear of pursuit."

This was joyful news indeed, and I lost no time in preparing myself to go on deck.

"If you will follow me, miss," said Trischl, "I will show you the berth that is to be yours till the end of the voyage. You will be able to wash and dress comfortably in it."

Even the little den to which I promptly betook myself was of somewhat circumscribed area, but it was as a very paradise to me, by reason of the delightful feeling of security which I felt as soon as I stepped into it. I soon discarded the raiment which had served me so well, and at once lost myself in the delight of making myself more suitably presentable. Every necessity seemed to have been foreseen and provided against, and I found an ample stock of clothing placed at my disposal.

I was very glad that I no longer needed to masquerade in boy's attire, and took especial delight in robing myself in a pretty pink morning gown Trischl brought in for me. My hair afforded me some trouble, though. If I had been an ugly girl before, what must I be now? I thought. My little berth was lighted by a swing lamp, fixed to a bracket in the bulkhead. There was also a mirror hanging near the bunk. But I could not judge very well of my appearance, and it was with a sense of regret at the thought that my cropped hair negatived the advantages of my pretty dress that I eventually followed Trischl into more airy and lightsome regions.

I found the ship's cabin well occupied. Madame and her husband, together with the Prince and Princess Michaelow, being deep in consultation concerning future arrangements. So I did not encroach long upon their time, but, after exchanging pleasant greetings with them all, went on deck. Here Feo was having a merry time with Count Sergius Volkhoffsky. I am not sure that I wasn't sorry to find that the latter was a grand sort of an individual, after all. I would much rather have been able to call him Ivan, especially as he looked so very handsome, now that he was dressed in a manner befitting his station, while I felt painfully conscious that I must be looking a bigger fright than ever.

ELIZABETH BURGOYNE CORBETT

"Oh, Dora, I am glad you have come up at last," exclaimed Feo, bounding affectionately toward me. "They would not let me wake you when the captain first came to tell us that it was safe enough for us now. Isn't the sea pretty? And isn't this a jolly ship? And isn't everybody in it jolly? And, ho; isn't Sergius jollier than anything?"

I have been told since that if my lips did not indorse the latter sentiment, my eyes did. But I must warn the reader that the individual who made the statement is not to be trusted with regard to anything he may say about me. For he is unduly prejudiced in my favor. The latter fact, when it was first brought home to me, came upon me as a huge surprise. I still feel surprise, when I think of it, but am better accustomed to it by this time.

There was much to explain and to talk over concerning our recent flight, and, while Feo rambled hither and thither, in thorough enjoyment of the situation, I listened to the explanation of much that had seemed inexplicable to me. The whole party with which I had become so closely associated was of Nihilistic proclivities, and had been spending much energy and a great deal of money in facilitating the escape from Russia of such members of their fraternity as from time to time fell under the ban of suspicion. It had, however, of late, struck them that the limit of their own safety had been spanned, and their flight had not been nearly so hasty and unpremeditated as it had seemed to me, though Mme. Karniak, as I must now call my employer, had been reluctant to recognize her own extreme peril. There was some special mission to perform, for which a considerable sum of money was still needed. Madame could only contribute her quota after handing in her report and receiving the check with which government rewarded her imaginary services once a month. She resolved that once more, and only once more, she would run the risk of a return to St. Petersburg.

She achieved her purpose, but narrowly escaped falling a victim to her patriotic zeal. Prince Michaelow, less sanguine than she, had foreseen her danger, and provided for her escape, his cousin having considered it by no means derogatory to his dignity to assume the rôle of a coachman for the nonce. The Princess Michaelow, or Nina, as she has since asked me to call her, had taken no active part in Nihilistic plans and consultations, and had been as genuinely surprised at the sudden necessity for the flight to England as I had been, but was by no means downhearted at the prospect of having to spend the rest of her life in her own country. As for Mr. Victor Karniak, he had deemed it wisest to avoid the river steamer, and had not reached the *Beacon* much sooner than we had done ourselves.

Needless to say, the visit of the *Beacon* to Cronstadt was not the result of merely mercantile speculation, but of a thoroughly systematized plan of campaign, by which refugees in the secret had their escape from Russia facilitated. The vessel usually made four trips between England and Cronstadt in the season, taking coals out from the Tyne, and returning with a mixed cargo of wheat, timber, and refugees, London being the discharging port. The after hold was docked of two feet of its legitimate length, this space being utilized for the hiding-place in which we had spent our first night on board.

I used to imagine myself an ardent lover of nature. During this voyage I sometimes wondered if I had turned Goth or Vandal. For I no longer took the all-absorbing delight in my surroundings that had hitherto accompanied me when among fresh and unconventional scenery. The ever-changing panorama of views of first one country and then another, alternated by the numerous islands which are dotted about the Baltic, would have aroused my enthusiasm at any other time. That they did not do so on this occasion must be laid to Count Sergius Volkhoffsky's charge. He was so clever and so brilliant that when talking to him I naturally overlooked the unobtrusive claims of scenery. I might possibly see a great deal more of the world in time to come, I thought, but I should never have such a wonderful traveling companion again. Therefore it would have been foolish to refuse the opportunities which were mine of enjoying his society. Certainly these opportunities seemed to last almost all day, for, strangely enough, Count Volkhoffsky never seemed to tire of my company. I knew that things would be very different, when we reached London, and he was introduced to cleverer and better-looking girls. Meanwhile, I felt happy in the present, and tried to banish the oft-recurring vision of my own probable future of lonely lovelessness.

Alas! the time sped all too quickly for me, though by everyone else on board our arrival in London was hailed with unmixed relief. The Prince and Princess Michaelow went to the Hôtel Metropole until they could complete their arrangements for residing in a home of their own furnishing. Their cousin, Sergius, went with them for a time.

Mr. and Mrs. Karniak, Feo, myself and Trischl were soon located in Kensington again, being fortunate in securing a very nicely furnished house pro tem. I was not sure that madame's financial position was such

ELIZABETH BURGOYNE CORBETT

now as warranted my remaining with her, but I hardly knew how to introduce the question of my departure. It relieved my embarrassment considerably when madame, having probably partially gauged my feelings, spoke to me one morning about Feo's future.

"I find," she said, "that Feo shows considerable facility for learning languages. She is so young yet that she may safely postpone a good many of the ordinary branches of her education, and she is getting on so well with her French and German that I hope you will not leave us for sometime. To lose you would be a serious break in my child's education, and I hope you know how anxious I am to retain your companionship, especially as Victor has much traveling to do before his financial affairs are all satisfactorily arranged."

"Surely he is not going to Russia again?" I exclaimed.

"No, not to Russia, but to South America. He has money invested in shares there, and is also concerned in some California speculations. For sometime he has foreseen that it would be as well to invest his capital out of Russia. But his agents have been rather lax, and he is going to inspect both nitrate beds and gold mines, in order that he may realize his legitimate profit on them. This will take him many months, and we want you to promise that you will stay with me at least until he comes back. Both Feo and I need you."

Stay with them! As if it were a favor on my part, too! Put in that way, the request certainly surprised me.

"Stay with you!" I said gratefully. "I shall only be too happy to do so. Where else have I to go to, since my own father declines to welcome me?"

Madame had a knack of being tantalizingly mysterious at times, and I puzzled my head for sometime to unravel the meaning of the curious smile with which she greeted my last question. But my immediate future was now arranged for, at all events, and the least I could do in return for madame's kindness was to set about my duties, light as they were, with all my heart and all my soul.

Meanwhile, I felt anxious to learn how things fared with Lady Elizabeth. At times, when I remembered the mysterious nature of the illness from which she was suffering when I last saw her, I almost feared the worst. Then my naturally hopeful temper reasserted itself, and I reflected that she would now in all probability be quickly recovering her normal strength in the bracing air of Moorbye, whither my family would be sure to have returned ere this.

And Jerry! Dear little Jerry! How ardently I longed to see him. He would be spending his holidays at home now, and I wondered if he had made such progress with his French as he seemed to anticipate before he left us. What a long time it seemed since father and I, both with such light hearts, had seen him leave our little station in the care of the tutor. And what a round of events had taken place since then. I had suffered much, and felt years older, although the last few weeks seemed to have softened my regrets for the past in a wonderful degree.

Belle, too. Somehow, I was now able to think of her without feeling such anger as had formerly haunted me, though I can never pretend to a return of loving, sisterly interest in her. That was dead forever, but so also was my former determination to make her suffer as keenly as I had been made to suffer. Such a determination I looked upon now as unchristian and unnatural, since the object of my vengeance was my own mother's daughter.

Better let sleeping dogs lie, I thought, since any revelations concerning the death of the late Earl of Greatlands, if they tended to substantiate my idea of willful culpability on the part of Belle and her fiancé, would be productive of great grief to many others.

Feeling anxious and unsettled, and being doubtful of the wisdom of writing home to ask for news of my people, lest my father should compel me to give up my present life of honorable independence and freedom from petty insults, I took advantage of a spare hour or two shortly after my return to London, and went to the house my father had rented in town. It was tenantless. I had not intended really going in, but I believe I should not have been able to resist trying to see Lady Elizabeth, if she had still been living here, and I felt more disappointed than I could have believed possible, since I had not really expected to see her. To go to Moorbye was out of the question just now, I thought, as I did not wish to trespass upon madame's good nature yet awhile to the extent of neglecting my duties for a couple of days.

I was walking through the park, on my way home again, revolving the propriety of writing to ask Mrs. Garth to let me have all the news about my people, when I accidentally jostled against someone else who was evidently as preoccupied as I was. Hastily looking up, with an exclamation of apology, I saw, looking at me with a face upon which was pictured the greatest surprise, an elderly man, in whom I recognized none other than Dennis Marvel, the former valet of my dear old earl.

"Oh, miss!" he said eagerly. "I am glad to see you. For I have that on my mind which will drive me mad, if I keep it to myself, but which I dare tell to nobody but you. I am fairly pulled to pieces with the misery of the thing. One minute something in me says, 'Tell all you know, and let justice be done. Let not the guilty flourish while the innocent are cast aside.' The next minute it seems as if the wickedest thing I could do was to make more trouble for them that has had enough already. Oh! miss, you will be able to help me to decide what should be done. Though you had such bitter enemies, you won't let hatred of them lead you to be cruel to their belongings, and oh! how it will ease my mind to tell you everything. I have been to the house to inquire for you, but the servants could not tell me anything about you, except that they thought there had been a quarrel, and that Mr. Courtney had turned you out—you, who had been robbed of wealth and title! It made my blood boil to hear it; but of course I could not say what I thought, and I never hoped to come across your ladyship that was to have been like this—so lucky, after all."

I had let the old man talk on so long without interruption, for my inward dismay had literally bereft me of the power of speech for a time. I did not even try to pretend to myself that I misunderstood Marvel's meaning, or that I did not know exactly to what event he was alluding. At last the mystery of the earl's death was going to be cleared up for me. My suspicions were to become proved facts, and upon my shoulders was to fall the onus of judging and sentencing the guilty. It is small wonder that I felt the blood leave my face; that my limbs trembled under me, and that I was glad to avail myself of the support of the seat near which I had come into collision with Marvel. I motioned to him to sit down also, hastily looking round, lest possible prying ears should be at hand to surprise and proclaim to the world the secret of which my companion was about to disburden himself.

"I see that you fully understand my meaning," he said, "and I don't need to beat about the bush much, for I always thought that you suspected foul play, by the way you looked at your sister and the young earl. Well, miss, it's quite true. They made away with my poor old master, for they had sworn that you shouldn't get married to him and lord it over them at the castle. Besides, they pretended to think the earl must be in his dotage, and no longer fit to be the head of the family, when he could seriously think of choosing—well, miss, not to offend you, I hope—but they said he had picked the ugliest girl he could find, and that there was no telling what crazy thing he would do next—try to cut off the entail, or something of the sort. So they laid their plans to stop the wedding, and, I swear it is true, they murdered my poor old master."

"Stop, Marvel," I said now, having at last recovered the power of speech. "The accusations you make are too terrible to be believed lightly. It is easy to say what your suspicions dictate. But you have no proofs of what you say, and I will not hear anything more. I loved the old earl for his goodness to me, a neglected, unattractive girl, whom very few people cared for. The present earl is his son and the brother of my dear stepmother. His fiancée is my sister, and thus both, though actually my enemies, have claims upon my forbearance. Marvel, I dare not believe them guilty. I will not believe them guilty! You shall tell me no more."

"You must hear all I have got to say now, Miss Dora," returned Marvel firmly. "I tell you, I must open my mind to somebody, and I reckon you are the safest. Another thing, I have to be back soon, so would like to get on with my story."

"Are you still with the present earl?"

"Yes, that's how I know so much about his black secret. And my knowing the secret is the reason why I stop on with him, for he is not very easy to put up with nowadays. But, you see, I have lived all my life in the family, and so did my father and mother before me. So I feel as if the family's trouble and disgrace were mine, too, and I would rather keep on as I am than let another man step into my shoes. For he would soon be at the bottom of the family mystery, and then what would become of us all?"

What, indeed? The result was too dreadful to contemplate, and I no longer questioned either Marvel's veracity, or the purity of his motives.

"The present earl," he went on, "was always inclined to drink a bit. But since his father's death he has really gone on awful. Every week it has got worse, and I have had to put him to bed drunk every night for this last month. This couldn't help having a serious effect on him, and last week he had a very bad attack of delirium tremens, in which his own ravings showed the whole business up as plain as daylight. I was glad he was pretty quiet when the doctor was there, as he would have been one too many in the secret. The papers said that he was laid up with an attack of pleurisy. But I knew better, and it does not pay a fashionable doctor to split about his patients. Toward the end of the week the earl got over his attack of the blues and then I had a serious talk with him.

"'My lord,' said I, 'you must drink no more.'

"'And why not?' he asked, looking at me as if he thought I had left my senses somewhere else.

"''Because,' I said, looking him straight in the face, 'dead men tell no tales, but drink makes people tell things that it's safer nobody else should know. I'll tell you what the drink has made you do and say, and then you can judge whether it's safe for you to drink anymore or not.'

"Then I described how he had gone on when unconscious of what he was doing. He had fancied every now and then that his father's ghost was standing before him with outstretched finger and threatening visage. 'For God's sake!' he would scream, 'take it away! It is drawing me down to hell! Let me go—take her! She prompted me to it! It was her crime. I would not have thought of it, but for her. I gave him the poison, but it was Belle who bought it. She swore that she would use it on her sister, if I failed with the poor old man, who deserved nothing but good at my hands. Why didn't I let her poison the girl? I shouldn't have had this to face then. Begone!'

"At this he jumped out of bed as if he meant to attack somebody. But he just fell all of a heap on the floor, and was pretty easily managed till the next paroxysm came on, which was in another hour or two.

"Now you can guess what sort of an effect my talk had upon my master. He went almost beside himself with terror, and was for offering me no end of things to bribe me to keep his secret. But I am not one of those human vultures who grow fat on the crimes and miseries of others, and I wouldn't touch a farthing from the earl except in the way of my earnings, as usual. It would burn my fingers, if I did. 'No,' I said, 'Dennis Marvel knows his duty to the family too well to betray it. Your lordship has the matter in your own hands. Keep off the drink. Keep your mouth shut, and all's safe.'

"Since then he hasn't tasted a drop of anything that could make him drunk. But he has awful nights, all the same. He wasn't really meant for a villain, and, saving your presence, Miss Dora, if that she-devil, your sister, hadn't got hold of him, things would have been all right, and we should all have been as happy as we used to be before we knew her. And now, Miss Dora, what would you advise me to do? Do you blame me for what I have done? It would kill Lady Elizabeth, and disgrace the family forever, if we didn't keep the secret. So it cannot be wicked to shield the guilty."

Thus appealed to by Marvel, I replied firmly:

"We *must* shield the guilty, Marvel, in order to protect the innocent. You wouldn't like to have Lady Elizabeth's death on your conscience, would you?"

"God forbid!"

"Then you and I, faithful friend, must breathe a word of this business to no one. And we must do all we can to prevent others from learning the terrible secret. It is a heavy burden you have put upon my shoulders, Marvel. I can only hope your burden has been eased a little in the telling, and that you will not think it necessary to share it with anyone else."

"I give you my Bible oath, Miss Dora, that not a living soul shall hear me speak of this thing but you. The weight of the secret was choking me, but, as you say, a burden shared by somebody else of like mind is half rolled away."

"And yet you have something else to tell me. What do you mean by saying that the earl has bad nights? Is he still likely to betray himself?"

"I think not; for, when awake, he knows quite well what he is saying. But his conscience is tormenting him to his doom. He cannot live long and suffer as he is doing. Sleep refuses to visit him, except when he takes an opiate, and every night the dose has to be made bigger, or it has no effect. A fine state of mind for a man to be in who is going to be married next month."

"Next month?"

"Yes, on the fifteenth."

"In London?"

"No. Lady Elizabeth is too ill to stand much fuss and excitement. So the wedding is to be as quiet as possible, and is to take place at Moorbye Church, the Rev. Mr. Garth officiating. It is just as well for everybody."

"Yes, it is just as well. And now, do you know, Marvel, I feel ill with the shock of all you have told me, and—"

Marvel at once jumped up and offered to fetch a cab for me. I gladly accepted his offer, and reached home half an hour later, while Marvel returned to his master's town house, to fulfill those duties which his long attachment to the Greatlands family, and his identification of his own honor with that of his employers, alone made it possible for him to continue.

X

"'Tis better to be born lucky than rich."

"You have been gone a long time, my dear," said madame. "I had begun to be quite anxious about you, and someone has been waiting for you who is becoming, oh! so impatient."

"Impatient to see me? Why, I shall believe myself to be quite an important individual soon," I returned, with an attempt at a smile, that was so lamentable a failure that madame's attention was aroused at once.

"What is it, my child?" she asked solicitously. "I thought, when you came in, that you were looking extra well. You had such rosy cheeks. Now I see that you are flushed with excitement. How is it? Have you had an adventure? You are trembling all over."

"Yes, I have had an adventure," I said, my pent-up emotions finding vent in tears, which soon relieved me a little, and were not checked by madame, who fully understood the value of this outlet for nature's wellsprings of feeling. She was at first somewhat alarmed as to the nature of my adventure. But I speedily reassured her on that score, telling her that I had met an old family servant, who had been giving me some news that had upset me for a time.

"Is it very bad news?" she asked.

"My stepmother is ill, and my sister is going to be married."

"But your stepmother has been ill sometime, and your sister was engaged to be married before you left home."

"Yes, but both illness and engagement have made progress, and I feel very anxious now about Lady Elizabeth."

"You must go and see her soon. That will put your mind at rest. And the dear little brother of whom you are so fond. How is he?"

How was he, indeed! Why, I had forgotten to make a single inquiry about him. Truly, my perturbation of mind must have been great to make me forget Jerry. My horror had effaced the memory of my love for the time, and I explained to my mistress that so much that was sensational had been told me that there had been no inclination to bring Jerry into the conversation.

"I shall learn all about him tomorrow," I concluded. "As you know, I have written to Mrs. Garth to send me all the news she has, and I should have her reply soon. I will also write to Lady Elizabeth at once, explaining that I am still safe and well. It is just possible that she has been anxious about me, although I wrote her a reassuring letter from the Grange before I came to you. I also gave Mrs. Garth permission to inform her that I had gone to St. Petersburg, in safe companionship."

"Not so safe as you thought, eh? But that is all over now, Heaven be thanked. And the chances are then that your stepmother and your father know already where you are, if you have imposed no special restrictions upon Mrs. Garth?"

"Yes, very likely they know already."

"I hope they will not insist upon your leaving us."

"I will not leave you. But I must see Lady Elizabeth, as she is so ill. Perhaps a visit from me might help to tranquilize her mind a little."

"Dear me! And there is someone else whose mind will want tranquilizing by this time. Sergius is waiting in the drawing-room for you all this while."

I would fain have been excused from meeting "Sergius" just then, for I knew I must be even more unpresentable than usual. But madame was inexorable, and a minute later I was *tête-à-tête* with a man in whose company I had begun of late to feel remarkably uncomfortable. It was strange that I should begin to avoid the presence of the only individual of the opposite sex whose lengthened absence was distasteful to me, and that I should become *gauché* and dull in the society of the one being whose conversation afforded me most happiness. And yet, when I come to think of it, there was nothing strange about it, after all, though I did not understand myself at the time.

I know now that I loved Sergius Volkhoffsky with a passion so great that I dreaded a betrayal of my feelings to others, with the consequent humiliation that I thought would be inevitable. He was handsome; I was ugly. He seemed to me to be one of the cleverest men under the sun, while I felt the acquirements of which I had formerly been so proud to be little more than a rudimentary education. Thanks to his prudent foresight, he had lost but a small proportion of the wealth which he had inherited from his father. And I was a penniless girl, whom disagreement with her family had compelled to go forth to earn her own livelihood.

No wonder I felt miserable when I pictured the different fate that might have been mine, had I but possessed a fair share of nature's bounties, and no wonder that I shrank, in anticipation, from the joyless existence foreshadowed in an unloved future.

ELIZABETH BURGOYNE CORBETT

I had truly loved my old earl. But my love was based entirely on gratitude and esteem. Such love is honest, honorable and pleasant to behold. It is also lasting and durable, if permitted to flow on in a gentle, uninterrupted current. But if its possessor be of an ardent nature it is as easily dispelled by a sudden passion as is froth on the surface of the breakers, and I know now how feeble is the love born of gratitude compared to the love one feels for one's ideal. There are some women so constituted that passion is powerless to assail them, and upon the whole, it is well for them that it should be so, for their lives run on in quiet, contented grooves that afford them every satisfaction.

But ask the woman of a more ardent nature if she would barter her hopes and dreams and possible disappointments for the humdrum existence associated in her mind with quiet affection, and she will answer emphatically in the negative. It was so with me now. Having once seen and known Sergius Volkhoffsky, I could but marvel how I could ever have contemplated marrying a man old enough to be my grandfather. Having arrived at this state of mind, my recollections of my past disappointments lost all their bitterness, and I could but feel thankful that my passion for Sergius, vain as it seemed, was not of an unlawful nature, since I had as yet made vows of allegiance to no other man.

But I was not thinking of all this in detail when I entered the room in which Sergius had been waiting so long for me.

"I am sorry," I said, "that I was not here to receive you when you asked for me. I am also very curious to know the nature of the business which could actually make you wait half an hour and more to see me."

He sprang up to greet me, his pleasant smile and warm hand-clasp being enough to dispel the most obstinate spirits. His glance, too, was so ardent that I felt the color rush to my cheeks, and instinctively lowered my eyelids, that he might not see what power he had over my feelings.

"I have not been dull while you were out. My friends have taken care of that. But I have that to say to you which made me very impatient for your arrival. Now that you are here, I am not in such a hurry to disburden myself, lest I be sent away in disgrace. But, first, tell me what I have been doing to offend you lately."

"Offend me! How could you offend me?" I asked, with such genuine surprise on my face that he could but see I was in earnest.

"Then why," he continued, this time taking my hands in his, as if to command my attention more effectually; "why have you been so stiff and distant with me? How do you account for that?"

How did I account for it? To this day I am unable to tell. I only know that, amazing as it may seem, Sergius loved me, and desired nothing so much as to spend the rest of his life with me. Of course I urged my own unfitness for the honor of becoming his wife. But my feeble remonstrances were so vigorously combated that at last I was able to believe myself to be as truly beloved as the most beautiful and perfect woman could wish.

There was now only one possible hindrance to my perfect happiness. Belle's secret must not be divulged in its entirety. But I could not accept an honorable man without warning him that possible disgrace—deserved disgrace—threatened my family. Disgrace, moreover, of so deadly a nature that a nation would recoil in horror from the contemplation of it.

"I have heard all your history from Madame Karniak, and can thus form some faint idea of the nature of the disgrace you hint at. It has some connection with the sudden death of the late Earl of Greatlands. You see, I know all about him, and I am not at all jealous of the affection you felt for the poor old man. But you have suffered enough in connection with that business, and anything that your sister may have been accessory to must be expiated by herself, not by you, nor by me, whose happiness depends on becoming your husband."

So said Sergius. I know of nobody so young who is half so wise and clever as Sergius. So why should I stand in the light of our mutual happiness? Truly, it would have been sheer folly. Therefore, when I went to bed that night it was as the promised bride of a man any woman would have been proud to win.

There had been much congratulation on the part of the Karniaks, who smilingly asserted that they had seen all the time "which way the wind was blowing." During the evening, we had a call from the Prince and Princess Michaelow, who warmly welcomed me as one who was speedily to become a relative.

"Not for a long time," I said, feeling just a little embarrassed because I could not prevent my face from looking ridiculously happy. "I am going to remain with madame until all the South American and Australian business is settled."

"But suppose madame no longer wants you?" observed Sergius mischievously.

"But you see she does want me."

"That remains to be proved. I believe a little bird has already

ELIZABETH BURGOYNE CORBETT

whispered something to me about alteration of plans since you came in this afternoon."

"It is quite true," supplemented madame. "What I said this afternoon to you about not leaving us was sincerely meant. But while you and Sergius were making your future arrangements, Victor and I decided that life would not be worth living so long apart. So Feo and I are going to South America with him, and may probably stay there much longer than Victor would care to stay without us."

"Meanwhile," said Nina, "you are to stay with us as our guest, until Sergius gets a house nicely furnished for you."

"And your visit is to be a very short one. A fortnight at the most. I shall make upholsterers and decorators fly around, so that when we return from our wedding-trip you will find everything to your liking."

So said Sergius, and since everybody seemed inclined to dispose of me so unceremoniously, I could but utter very feeble protests, and virtually surrender myself to their management. I only made one stipulation. My marriage must be as private as possible. My happiness seemed too great to be true, and I had a vague feeling that, if fate should dash the cup from me, I could best bear it with few onlookers. The feeling may have been morbid. But my past experience must plead my excuse.

The next morning lessons for Feo were out of the question. We elders had so much to talk about, and so many plans to discuss, that madame told Trischl to take the child for a walk, while we completed our arrangements. Trischl had been offered the option of joining her own people, who were now in Germany, but had preferred to travel with madame in the capacity of maid. So her immediate future was disposed of also. The Karniaks would have liked to stay to the wedding, but considered it advisable to secure a passage in a quick boat that was sailing in four days. There was thus little time for preparation. But I rendered all the help I could, and be sure that my dear friends and I parted from each other with tears of regret, though we expected to have the happiness of seeing each other again some day.

I had had two letters from Mrs. Garth, in which she informed me that Lady Elizabeth was very much better; that Belle was more beautiful than ever, and apparently very much delighted at the approaching consummation of her ambitious projects. Jerry was at home, and was a jolly little fellow, but said that the Grange wasn't like home without Dorrie. My father, too, I was told, had fretted somewhat about me, having evidently come to the conclusion that his treatment of me had not been the exclusive outcome of wisdom. "I am sure," continued Mrs. Garth, "that if you were to return home now, your father would welcome you as gladly as would Jerry and Lady Elizabeth. Of your sister's sentiments I know nothing, as she holds herself very much aloof from me. I have an idea that she dislikes me. By-the-by, you remember May Morris? She is going to marry Mr. Graham, the young doctor. He has bought a practice at Brightburn, and will take his bride thither next week."

I was very much amused when I remembered May's rhapsodies about the actor, but had no doubt that a healthy affection for a good man who loved her would oust all the rubbishy romance with which she had formerly been filled. It was good news to hear that my stepmother's health had improved so much. I could but hope that the improvement might continue, and that she might be spared all knowledge relating to the particulars of her father's death. I resolved that when I saw her again, I would, indirectly, try to set her mind at rest on the subject by explaining the irrational and unfounded nature of the suspicions I had, in my bitter sorrow, shared with her. Her illness had always struck me as having a mental origin, and I concluded, since she was improving, that she was already inclined to think the best of her brother and Belle.

I was just revolving all this in my mind, and thinking how glad I would be to go to the Grange again, when a servant announced a visitor for me, and my father came quickly into the room in which I sat. I was not wholly surprised by his visit, for both Sergius and I had written to him, giving him the particulars of our engagement, and asking his consent to our immediate marriage. But if I expected anything like a demonstrative greeting from him, I was disappointed, for he merely touched my hand, as though I had been a comparative stranger, and then plunged straight into the business which had brought him hither.

"I have, after an unwarrantable silence on your part," he said, "received a letter of so extraordinary a tenor that I have decided to answer it in person. You say you have promised to marry an individual who calls himself Count Volkhoffsky. What proof have you that he is a genuine count?"

"I can refer you to his cousin, Prince Alexander Michaelow, from whose house we are to be married. There are plenty of people in London who will give you proofs of the genuineness of both titles."

"A prince! You seem to have the knack of ingratiating yourself with

ELIZABETH BURGOYNE CORBETT

the aristocracy. You are not quite so ugly as you were. Your hair, curled in that fashion, looks rather pretty than otherwise. Still, I can't see what even an old and decrepit nobleman can see in you. He might get a *professional* nurse at much less expense."

My father had always trampled on my feelings without the slightest compunction, and his sneers had left many a bitter wound behind. But these were all healed now, and he had lost the power to hurt me. For the first time in my life his depreciation of me evoked nothing but a feeling of triumph. I simply rose and rang the bell, and, on its being answered, asked the servant if Count Volkhoffsky had arrived yet. On being answered in the affirmative, I sent to see if he would favor us with his company for a moment.

"And tell Mr. and Madame Karniak that I would be glad if they would permit me to introduce my father to their notice," I said, as the servant was leaving the room.

I shall never forget my father's look of indignant surprise, when I spoke of introducing *him*, to the *notice* of *my* friends. I was amply avenged for many a cut I had received, and was also convinced that, in future, he would treat me with a little more consideration. But he evidently regarded me principally as Belle's rival, and even when he, later in the day, set off to return to Courtney Grange, he was, I am sure, feeling both perplexed and sore at the idea of the apparent facility I possessed for at least equaling, if not surpassing, his beautiful darling's opportunities of happiness.

He had also taken it for granted that my fiancé was some undesirable individual, whose motive in marrying me was self-interest of some sort, and I smile yet when I remember how astonished he was when Sergius confronted him, and asked him in so courtly a fashion for his consent to his marriage with his youngest daughter. Of course that consent was given, and very glad I was, too. Although I was not anxious to see Belle again, I was thankful to be reconciled, with my family, as Jerry and Lady Elizabeth were too dear to me to be given up entirely.

The day after my father's visit to me witnessed the departure of the Karniaks to Chili and my temporary installation in the house of Prince Michaelow.

My second trousseau was already in active preparation. Madame Karniak and Princess Nina had insisted on making me handsome presents, to compensate me for the wardrobe I had lost, they said. Lady Elizabeth also sent me the most affectionate letter imaginable.

So far from resenting the fact that I was about to marry a man whom I regarded with much warmer feelings than the mild affection which I had entertained for the poor old earl, she rejoiced with me at my good fortune in having won the love of such a man as Sergius. She was also good enough to say that I fully deserved my happiness, and as an indorsement of her approval of the whole arrangement she inclosed a check for one hundred pounds as her wedding present.

Thus armed with the approbation of my friends, and all the necessary sinews of war, I entered the whirl of preparation with the lightest of hearts and the brightest of prospects. Sometimes my busy fingers would stay their work, and a cloud of dread and apprehension would settle on my brain.

Was it possible that I, utterly lacking outward beauty, and until lately the most unloved of beings, was really and truly the one and only woman with whom Sergius could be happy? Had he never loved another woman? And if he had, was she not sure to have been beautiful?

When I remembered how truly artistic was my lover's temperament, it seemed incredible to me that he could be perfectly contented with a wife whose chief function in society seemed to be to act as a foil to those women whom nature had endowed more liberally with outward charms. And if the time were to come when it would become incumbent upon me to recognize the conviction that Sergius had mistaken his sentiments for me, and that he regretted his precipitancy, how would I be able to bear my life?

Suppose, after the irrevocable knot was tied, my husband were to wake up some day to the knowledge that he loved another woman? Suppose—but by the time I had thus foolishly and fruitlessly tormented myself, it was beyond my power to endure even the thought of another self-stabbing supposition, and a reaction invariably set in. Surely Sergius, who was chivalry, gentleness and bravery personified, and who was esteemed by all his friends for his powers of observation and his clear, cool insight into human nature, would not belie his character just where I was concerned! To believe it was to doubt all his good qualities, and I rated myself an ingrate for entertaining such heretical sentiments for one moment.

If the reader is inclined to subscribe to this last opinion, perhaps he or she will kindly credit fate with at least a portion of the mental perversity which at times tormented me almost beyond endurance. It had been so often impressed upon me all my life long that I could never hope to win the true and lasting regard of any man, that it was surely natural for me to doubt the endurance of the happiness which seemed to be within my grasp.

But these freaks of fancy could not withstand the sunny presence of my worshiped Sergius himself, who was apt to flatter me almost as much as the Earl of Greatlands had done, and who seemed never tired of praising the now luxuriant silken rings of my hair, my long-lashed, expressive eyes, and my graceful figure, not to speak of my rich olive complexion. On most of these counts I let him talk without protest on my part. Although I knew that his opinion of me was ridiculously disproportionate to my deserts, my anxiously observant eyes could not blind themselves to the fact that my outward presentment was a vast improvement upon its old self.

But when Sergius actually ventured to praise my face, and above all, my inveterately snubby nose, I put down his flatteries with a firm hand. It was in vain for him to quote Tennyson, and speak of my unfortunate organ as "tiptilted." There are degrees and proportions of tiptiltedness, and I had measured the depths of unhappiness too often through "that hideous nose" to allow my vanity to persuade me into believing its disabilities removed.

Still, I was no longer miserable about it; indeed, I grew rather proud of it than otherwise. For if that nose had not had the power to repel Sergius, it was henceforth to be regarded as the most prominent existing proof of the genuineness of his affection.

And, after all, what mattered it, since, when the glamour of self-torment was off me, I knew myself to be my lover's idol and the hope of his existence, miraculous though such a state of things seemed?

My friends, too, were of the kindest and most considerate ones of the earth. Thus there seemed nothing to hinder me from being perfectly happy, and as my wedding-day approached nearer and nearer I grew more and more confident of the future, for neither envy nor hatred conspired to wreck my prospects, as had been the case before the dawning of that other wedding-day.

I was writing to Lady Elizabeth, to express my regret at her inability to come to the wedding, and to thank her for her generosity and good wishes, when Sergius was announced, and I hastily finished and sealed my missive. For was not this the last day of my spinsterhood? And did I not owe my beloved every moment I could spare?

"I hope you have finished all your preparations, sweetheart, and that no one else expects any attention from you today," said Sergius. "For I mean to monopolize you altogether."

"Indeed you won't, for Nina won't see me for sometime after tomorrow, and has exacted a promise from me that I would go with her to choose her very latest wedding-present to me. So you will have to spare me for an hour or two."

"And indeed I won't! Just picture your being selfish enough to want to go off without me! You shall do your shopping. But you must do it in my company, for, oddly enough, I also have a fancy that you should choose your most prized wedding-present from me yourself, and we can make one expedition of it. Oh, here is our gracious princess herself! She will agree to all I propose, I know."

"I must first know what it is that you propose," smiled the Princess Nina, who had just entered the room, Prince Michaelow following closely in her wake. "I don't like to make promises in the dark."

"Sergius wants to go shopping with us," I explained.

"Oh, as for that, I mean to go, too," said the prince. "If Sergius will look just a shade less bridegroomy he may also make one of the party."

The prince's sally at Sergius's ecstatically happy look was received with a laugh by us all, and half an hour later we were all four being driven toward Piccadilly behind a pair of splendid bays. Then ensued a series of excursions into various West End establishments that was even more odd than it was delightful, which is saying much. For it was strange to me to feel myself the courted and petted object of attention on the part of three such splendid specimens of humanity as my betrothed and the Prince and Princess Michaelow. Probably others also noted the disparity in our appearance and commented on it after their own fashion.

But my companions were too agreeably employed to pay attention to much beyond the business at hand, and so many presents were lavished upon me that I found it necessary to enter a protest. We were all just leaving a Regent Street jeweler's shop, preparatory to re-entering the carriage for our homeward drive, when Princess Nina suddenly said to me in a low voice: "What a beautiful woman! And she seems to know you. Who is she?"

I looked up hastily, and was confronted by my sister and her intended husband. For an instant I hesitated whether to return Belle's stare of haughty recognition by a conciliatory movement or not. My hesitation proved my salvation from what would have been an intolerable humiliation. The Earl of Greatlands and Miss Courtney passed on without vouchsafing me anything but the disapproving look due to an obnoxious stranger rather than to a sister, and we had entered our carriage before I had had time to answer Nina's question.

I felt the blood leave my face at thus meeting my mother's child as a stranger, and Nina was quick to see that I was strangely moved by the encounter. She looked the question she did not care to trouble me by repeating, and I tried to answer her in as unmoved a voice as possible.

"That was my sister who passed us. And the gentleman who is with her is the Earl of Greatlands."

"H'm! I thought as much," put in Sergius. "I was just thinking that the woman approaching us would have been quite handsome, if her face had been less soulless, when I saw her flash such a malignant look at my Dora as is never seen on the face of the good, and which a stranger certainly could not evoke. I don't envy my Lord Greatlands."

"And I would not like to be in Miss Courtney's shoes," said Nina. "For her affianced looks just like one of my father's parishioners used to look. He had been both wicked and dissipated, and finished his career in a madhouse. We will, however, hope that your sister, when married, will find her husband more desirable than he looks."

Alas! I knew too well how little happiness the future could really have in store for my misguided sister and the unhappy man who had succumbed to her evil influence. The latter looked even more ill than I had expected to see him, and I doubted whether the haunting remorse from which he suffered would not soon drive his reason from its throne.

And Belle! How could she comport herself with such queenly pride, and with such an air of self-satisfaction as she was wearing just now? It was inexplicable to me. But though the puzzle was beyond my comprehension, it had the power to damp my joy for the rest of the day.

I would much rather have been spared the sight of my enemy on my wedding-eve, and, for the life of me, I could not help wondering whether her presence in London would not prove an ill omen for me. Of course the fancy was silly. But there it was, and I could not banish it. Still, though I was less happy than before, I did not wish to spoil the pleasure of my companions, and, for their sakes, I feigned a gayety I no longer felt.

As we were being driven slowly past Hyde Park Corner, on our way back to Kensington, something else occurred to cause me an accession of surprise not unmixed with dread. A woman was waiting to cross the road as soon as it should be safe to do so.

She was carelessly glancing at the occupants of the carriages which passed her, and I was just thinking how handsome she was, and with what perfect taste she was dressed, when I felt a convulsive pressure of the hand which was clasping mine. I looked up, to see that Sergius had turned deadly pale, and that he hastily leaned back and turned his head away from the stranger.

But he was too late. She had seen him. Moreover, he was no stranger to her, as I could tell by the swift recognition which flashed across her features, and by a hasty forward movement that she made, as if to intercept our progress. The princess was not noticing the by-play. But that Prince Michaelow had seen and recognized the stranger I knew by the glances of dismayed intelligence which he exchanged with my fiancé.

Soon after this we were back at the house of my generous friends, and three of us at least were less light-hearted than when we set out early in the afternoon.

That evening I could not dismiss the stranger from my mind. Who was she? And what acquaintance could she have with Count Volkhoffsky, who had been in London so short a time? But the prince knew her too, and both men had been distinctly dismayed when they saw her. Sergius had been so little away from me since we came to London that he could not have made many acquaintances of whom I did not know.

Was it possible that he had known her in Russia? Nay, was it possible that this was the unknown rival in my lover's affections which my jealous fancy had painted? And if so, how could he have transferred his regard from so handsome a woman to my insignificant self? And in this question I found consolation and hope for my own future. For Sergius must love me, or he would not have been anxious to marry one so utterly devoid of physical and pecuniary attractions as I was. Not that I ever dreamed that he could be mercenary. But I had of late taken positive pleasure in the reflection that I owed my happiness to no external advantage which time or ill fortune could destroy.

And yet, how could I marry the man I loved, if thereby I condemned another woman, who perhaps loved him equally well, to the misery of desertion? I could not reconcile it to my conscience to do this cruel thing. So I took an opportunity of satisfying myself on that point before Sergius went back to his hotel for the night.

ELIZABETH BURGOYNE CORBETT

"Do you know," I said to him, "I do not want you to think me intrusive. But I saw the young lady at Hyde Park Corner who seems to be an old friend of yours, and whom you seemed to wish to avoid. Tell me, for God's sake, what is she to you?"

"You saw her?" he said, looking more startled than I liked to see.

"Yes. What is she to you?"

"I think, for the sake of your own peace of mind, that you had better not ask me."

"But I must know! Have you ever been her lover? If so, I must give you up to her, for I cannot purchase my paradise at the expense of another woman's salvation."

"My darling! There spoke the noble woman whom I love, and whom, God helping me, I mean to cherish through life. Thank Heaven! my past holds no dark secrets of that sort. It has been turbulent and full of danger, but, I swear before God, my love was given to no woman until I met you. Now, are you satisfied?"

"Yes, I am satisfied," I said, and I sank into his arms with a sob of relief which showed how terrible a phase of dread I had just passed through.

"You naughty child," said Sergius fondly. "How could you speak deliberately of giving me up to another woman? I am not like you. I would fight for my rights to the last breath. You have promised to marry me, and I will give you up to no one living. You are mine, mine alone!"

After this, my doubts being all dispelled, I was happy once more, and bade Sergius goodnight with the exulting conviction that henceforth the whole of my life would be spent in his beloved society.

My wedding-morn dawned bright and cloudless, and nothing intervened to prevent my marriage this time. My father came as the sole representative of my family, and explained that Lady Elizabeth had a severe cold which detained her at home. Otherwise she would have come up to town for the wedding. Belle was in London, he said, in answer to my inquiry, doing some shopping, but there was no reference made by either of us as to her absence on the occasion of her sister's marriage. Jerry had sent me a letter, full of regrets at his own enforced absence, all couched in his own boyish style, and he supplemented these regrets by the promise of a long visit to me at Christmas.

Dear boy! it did me good to read his affectionate chatter.

My father made himself uncommonly agreeable to my friends, and I think that he must have begun to doubt the correctness of his own opinions concerning me, when he saw the esteem in which others held his hitherto despised daughter. He pressed Sergius and myself so cordially to come on a visit to the Grange that I thought it would perhaps be better to bury the hatchet, even though I was inwardly convinced that if my friends had been of low rank, and that if we had been a struggling clerk and his wife, instead of the Count and Countess Volkhoffsky, he would still have preferred our absence to our company.

We were going to Torquay for a short honeymoon, after which we were to settle down in the luxurious home already prepared for our reception. As I changed my bridal gown for the dress in which I was to travel, I contrasted my present bliss with the unhappy time which already seemed to belong to the limbo of a better-to-be-forgotten past, and thanked God that I had won the love of so good and true a man as Sergius.

Sergius had laughingly bidden me to make haste with my toilet, as he was in a fever of impatience to have me to himself, and to feel that he really had secured the object he loved.

I had just as laughingly responded, little thinking of the awful blow that was even then hovering over my head. On going to the drawing-room again I expected to encounter only Sergius and the Prince and Princess Michaelow, for my father had already taken his leave.

But how shall I describe the sudden shock I experienced when I saw that Sergius was absent, and that both my friends wore such a look of commiseration and distress as convinced me that something terrible had again happened to me.

"Where is Sergius? What has happened?" I exclaimed, in sudden panic.

For a moment neither of those whom I questioned spoke. Then the prince came forward, and, clasping both my hands in his, said gently:

"You must take heart, my child. Nothing dreadful has happened to your husband."

"Then why is he not here? And why do your looks belie your words?"

"Sergius has had an unexpected summons."

"Away from me?"

"Yes, he has been compelled to go to Russia."

To Russia! To Russia, whither he had only just escaped, of all places! And without a word of farewell to me, his bride of an hour!

Surely Fate was sporting with me, when, for the second time, she robbed me of a husband on my bridal day!

But this stroke was harder than the other. The poor old earl had been claimed by Death. Sergius had left me, apparently of his own free will, and in the fullness of health and strength.

Who or what was it that had a stronger claim upon him than I had?

XI

"The grip of death."

I verily believe that for the space of half an hour I was beside myself. But so far from being violent under my emotions, I was stunned by them, and rendered temporarily incapable of connected thought. Prince Michaelow was, I think, unable to endure the look of anguish which my face must have borne; for, after whispering a few words to his wife, he quitted the room, wearing an expression which even my dulled senses were able to construe into a conviction of the hopelessness of expecting to see Sergius again.

The Princess Nina sat down beside me, clasped my hands in hers, and comforted me more by her sympathetic attitude than words could have done. Presently my thoughts were able to collect themselves again, and I began to question Nina eagerly.

"How long has Sergius known that he would have to go back to Russia?"

"Only a few minutes before he left."

"Why did he not bid me good-by first?"

"He had not time. The summons was urgent. Besides, he loves you so dearly that he could not have borne to witness your distress at his departure."

"If he loved me half so dearly as you say, he would not have forsaken me at anybody's call."

"But he was compelled to go! It was his sacred duty to do so."

"Then he ought to have taken me with him. If he is in danger, who so fit to bear him company as his wife? And to whom can he owe a more sacred duty than to me? Have I not been told more than once that all his near relatives are dead? Then who is there left to call him from me? Ah! now I have it! It is the woman whom I saw recognize him at Hyde Park Corner, and whom he tried to avoid! Who is she?"

"My dear child, now you ask of me more than I know. But you may rest assured upon this point. If any woman exerts influence over him, and has used that influence to bring about your husband's return to Russia, her motive and power are purely political. You know that Sergius has been very much involved with secret societies, and your knowledge of his character ought to assure you that nothing but the most irresistible claims upon him could have induced him to leave you at this juncture, to return to a country of which every inch is fraught with danger to him."

"Then I ought to be with him! Is it right that I should remain in a land of peace and safety, while he rushes into the jaws of death?"

"My dear child, his chances of security are much better while he is alone. If you were with him, he would perhaps have to neglect the duty to which he is called, in order to watch over your safety."

"And suppose he did?"

"Then he would meet certain and speedy death which you would no doubt share."

"I don't understand you."

"Perhaps not. I had better be more explicit. Years ago, your husband joined a society which had for its object the removal of the Emperor Alexander. It is one of the rules of this society that its members shall unhesitatingly perform any duty which the Executive Council may deem necessary for the welfare of the country. A ballot decides which of the members shall undertake any given task. Sergius has hitherto escaped the ballot. But, even as he almost ran from the house, he said that his turn had come; that he could not bid you farewell himself, and that if we never saw him again, we would know that he had done his duty. You think me cruel to tell you all this, dear; but I know your strong sense of what is right, and am sure that you would rather think of Sergius as dead than as one who could betray either his country or his wife."

Think of him as dead!

Sometimes, when I remember that scene, I wonder how it is that I did not go mad. Or that the phantom mockery of joy which had again eluded me did not leave brain and heart alike seared with hatred of all mankind.

But, after all, both hearts and brains can bear an enormous strain ere they fail their owners, and mine proved themselves to be at least of average strength. They both survived this new ordeal, and soon after this I was back in my dressing-room, anxiously trying to reduce into less chaotic sequence the thoughts which chased each other through my mind.

Was Sergius really lost to me forever? And was the errand he was bent upon as terrible as Nina's words suggested?

Alas! what room for doubt was left me? He belonged to a secret society, which had for its object the *removal* of the Emperor Alexander.

There was only one way in which an obscure society could compass that removal.

Its members would no doubt term it justice. The world would call it assassination. But to me the contemplated deed had only one name by which it could be fitly designated—murder! That was what was meant. And look where I would, that self-same word stared me in the face with demoniac persistence.

Murder! Good Heaven! was my whole life to be darkened by its foul environment? Did not my poor old earl become its victim? And was not my own sister an object of secret horror to me because I knew her to have worshiped at its shrine?

And now my newly-wedded husband, who was dearer to me than aught else on the face of the earth, was being drawn into its fearsome toils! What was it to me that he believed the czar to be a tyrant and oppressor, and that he was but doing the bidding of his superiors in office? Whatever the motive, or whatever the provocation, the deed would be the same. I have, I think, a strong sense of the duty owing to one's country. But, if a Charlotte Corday had been my ancestress, I should have made a very degenerate descendant; for I prefer moral suasion to physical force, and the assassination of the most objectionable tyrant would weigh on my conscience like lead.

And, since Sergius was now part and parcel of my being, everything that touched him touched me. Could I bear the thought that the guilt of murder lay on his conscience—on *our* conscience? I knew that I could not, and I prayed God to forbid that this evil thing should come to pass. Prayer alone would not avail me, I knew, since God helps those who help themselves. I must act, if I would compass my desire.

Yet what, after all, could I do? After an hour's almost maddened thought I succeeded in forming something like a definite plan of action. I would follow Sergius as quickly as a fast through service could take me. As to whither I was to follow him must be speedily discovered, else I might arrive on the spot too late to effect my purpose.

Said purpose was to frustrate the errand upon which my husband had been summoned. If I succeeded in doing so, what would be the consequences to him? Would the secret society to which he belonged, on finding its mandates outraged, avenge itself upon him? And would the salvation of his soul from bloodguiltiness prove his own death knell?

Truly, it was hard for me to know my own duty. But in one respect I did not hesitate. I was determined to follow my husband to Russia as soon as possible, in order that, if an opportunity offered, I might at least be on the spot to do what seemed right.

But, first, I must discover exactly where Sergius had gone to. And I must so comport myself as to hide my real intentions from Prince Michaelow and his wife. Otherwise they might decline to give me the information I sought, since I could not expect them to enter into all my thoughts and feelings respecting my husband's expedition.

Thus it happened that my outward bearing was that of one who is already resigned to her fate, when I begged them to give me some information that would enable me to picture the whereabout of my husband until he returned to me. I knew that my friends had very faint hopes that he would ever return. But they were also acting a part. They wished to blind me concerning the real gravity of the situation, in order to preserve me from the shock of sudden and hopeless bereavement. The interview was, in fact, a little comedy which had for its *motif* the enshroudment of a terrible tragedy.

But it sufficed my purpose. I learned all that my friends could tell me, and when I begged to be excused from dining with my hosts, on the plea of being too ill and sick at heart for any society but my own, I was not wasting my time in self-indulgent grief, as was imagined, but was hastily gathering together everything that I could conveniently take which would be necessary for a long journey.

I had even room to feel thankful that I had received so many valuable presents of jewelry, which might, on occasion, be turned into cash, and that the generosity of my friends had prevented me from spending much of the money which Lady Elizabeth had sent to me. Neither money nor jewelry took up much room, and it was an object with me to be as unencumbered as possible. I already knew something of the exigencies of sudden departures, and had no mind to take anything that would hinder my progress.

Luckily for my present purpose, Sergius and I, in view of a possible Continental trip, had studied Bradshaw to some purpose lately, and I now had little difficulty in extracting some information that would guide me to Moscow, whither I was told that Sergius had gone.

My newly-engaged maid was not a little bewildered by the turn of events. But she proved amenable to reason and did as she was bid without questioning. I told her to fetch me a hansom, and to tell the driver to stop at the tradesmen's entrance, where my portmanteau was put into the vehicle. Then, accompanied by my maid, I also went out by the tradesmen's entrance, my object in doing so being to escape the observation of the Prince and Princess Michaelow, who might have noticed my departure from the front door, and who would then assuredly have tried to dissuade me from following Sergius.

On arriving at Victoria Station I found that I had thirty-five minutes to spare. This I occupied in visiting a hairdresser's shop in the vicinity. Here I was enabled to purchase a gray wig and sundry etceteras which would effectually transform my outward semblance into that of a staid, elderly lady who would not be thought unfit to travel unescorted. I had already purchased a quiet black bonnet and a long black cloak from my maid, and felt sure that my ultimate transformation would be complete enough to deceive even Sergius, if he saw me.

At half-past eight I left Victoria, after giving the maid some messages for the Michaelows. She was to tell them that I thanked them for all their kindness to me, and that I felt it to be my duty to join my husband at once, without risking the delay which even my best wishers might possibly consider advisable.

I was not without hope that I might see Sergius even before I left the boat, or, at all events, before I had been long *en route*. But he had probably not taken the same direction that I was taking, and I felt bitterly disappointed when I failed to overtake him. I was at Brussels by five o'clock in the morning, and twelve hours later was in Cologne. The next morning saw me on the way to Berlin, and I pushed on thence to Alexandrovo with as little delay as possible.

I represented myself as an English lady on her way to Moscow to visit her sister's family, and had not much difficulty in obtaining a passport. In two hours from leaving Alexandrovo I was in Warsaw. Now that I had crossed the frontier I was in momentary dread of betraying myself by overanxiety, and did my best to appear as careless and joy-expecting as if I verily expected nothing more exciting than a reunion with my sister.

But in Warsaw I felt so ill with suspense, disappointment, and travel-fatigue, that I was compelled to rest at a hotel for a day, in order to recruit my strength sufficiently to complete my long journey without a breakdown. Two days later I reached Moscow, via Smolensk, and then the fever of unrest and anxiety allowed me no ease for a time.

Suppose Sergius were not here, after all! Suppose some accident had befallen him, and I had actually passed him on the way! In fact, no end of suppositions suggested themselves to me, as I drove to a hotel in which Sergius had, I knew, found a safe resting-place on more than one occasion.

Now I did not expect to encounter my husband at the public *table-d'hote*, nor, indeed, in any of the public rooms. He had come upon a secret errand, and he was not likely to ruin his chances of executing that errand by leading too open a life. I felt the burning blush of double-distilled shame on my cheeks even as I thought this. Shame at the idea of anyone whom I loved lending himself to crime even at his country's bidding, and shame that I, so much the inferior of Count Sergius Volkhoffsky, should dare to judge him by my own inexperienced standard of right and morality.

Perhaps, when I knew all his reasons for coming hither, I might even sanction the fulfillment of his task. Perhaps—but here I suddenly pulled myself up in horror, for was I not approaching perilously near to a line of argument which might ruin my peace of mind forever? Sanction murder? How could I for one single moment imagine myself capable of such an iniquity!

Rest and comfortable refreshment did wonders for me, and, on the day after my arrival in Moscow, I sat in the salon, eagerly scanning a German paper which the hotel management had provided for the use of visitors. From it I gathered that the czar was expected in Moscow, but that some rearrangement of plans at St. Petersburg had caused a postponement of the Imperial visit.

How utterly unlikely it would have seemed to those around me that the emperor's visit to Moscow could possibly concern me! And yet what a pæan of thankfulness rose from my heart as I realized that this postponement of which I had just read meant the deferring of what might prove the greatest tragedy of my life. I knew that Sergius could not hope to enter St. Petersburg without detection, and that it was hardly likely that those who at the present time had the power to direct his movements would order him thither, since he was so well known there, and had already been denounced to the government. This delay gave me a chance of meeting him soon, and of at least trying to weigh my influence against that of the terrible secret society of which he was a member.

On the second day of my stay in Moscow my wish was gratified. I saw my beloved in the flesh, safe and well, and yet, incredible as it seems to me now, I gave no outward sign of the rapture which filled my breast. He was very well disguised, but my love was so keen that it could have penetrated even more elaborate disguises than the one he had adopted, while it was so cautious that not even to himself would I betray my knowledge of him until I could feel sure that no mortal eye but ours beheld our meeting.

As I had expected, he was an inmate of the same hotel in which I had pitched my temporary habitation, and when I first saw him there he was emerging from the room next to mine, just as I approached my room door, after partaking of breakfast in the coffee-room. There were other people in the corridor at the time, so I quietly entered my own apartment and closed the door behind me, for my joy would have been too visible if I had done otherwise.

But I knew that I should see Sergius again, for I knew also that he was certain to remain in Moscow until the expected visit of the czar took place. Now that I had discovered the very location of his room, it would be easy for me to watch his movements, or at least so I thought. It was, however, nearly nightfall ere I, peeping through the chink of my partially opened door, saw him return to his own room. And even then it was impossible for me to make myself known to him, for he was accompanied by a stranger who might be either friend or foe, for anything I knew.

So I waited perforce with augmented impatience until my longed-for opportunity should come. It was very hard to know that he was within a few feet of me, yet separated from me by the barriers of caution and expediency for an indefinite period. How astonished he would be when he learned how very near I was to him! And what hopes I pitched upon my persuasive powers! No wonder that my impatience rose to an almost agonizing pitch as the hours wore on, and the stranger still lingered in my husband's room.

I would have tried to listen to the conversation of the two men, had I conceived it to be of the slightest use. But there was no conveniently placed connecting-door between the two rooms through which scraps of conversation, if not carried on in a low key, might have been heard, and the constantly frequented corridor was not an ideal resort for an eavesdropper. So I was obliged to bide my time, ere I could make any sign of my presence to Sergius.

At last the low, unintelligible murmur of voices ceased and there were indications that a move was being made in the next room. "At last!" I thought, "my weary probation is nearly over. Sergius will soon be alone, and I can then slip a note under his door that will warn him of my presence."

But picture my disappointment when the two men passed my room-door together! Sergius was going out again with the stranger, and I might not have another chance of seeing him again tonight. For a moment I hesitated as to what course to follow. Then I resolved to keep my husband in sight, and to ascertain, if possible, whither he was going.

I was convinced that, be he never so cautious, he was in danger from all sides, and, though not probable, it was certainly possible that I might be of service to him. Nina had told me that my presence near my husband would only be another source of worry and danger to him. But I could not bring myself to believe this, for I was resolved to be cautiousness itself.

Indeed, I was so cautious that Sergius and his companion were almost out of sight when I emerged from the hotel portico, and I had to accelerate my speed considerably before I succeeded in bringing myself within measurable distance of them. Sergius wore a gray wig and a flowing beard of the same venerable hue. This in itself would not have been disguise sufficient to blind anyone inclined to be suspicious of his identity. But that he never lost sight of the extreme perilousness of his position was borne into my mind by his adoption of a somewhat feeble gait and carriage, more in unison with his assumption of the character of an old man than his own light, swinging walk would have been.

The stranger seemed young, being of a lithe, supple figure, and destitute of hirsute adornment. He wore smoked glasses, and his face was disfigured by a singular contortion, which seemed to draw his features all to one side. Now and again, as they passed under a gas-lamp, I was able to scrutinize them closely, and it did not take me long to decide their errand was a secret one, for they glanced back from time to time, as if apprehensive of being followed, and doubled up one street and down another, with such a reckless disregard of distance and probable fatigue that I was convinced they were trying to elude pursuit.

By the time this sort of thing had gone on for over an hour, I began to feel desperately tired, and was seriously contemplating the necessity of returning to the hotel, when I saw something that convinced me that Sergius needed someone to give him a friendly warning, and banished all sense of fatigue.

The two men were being followed. A man stepped from a doorway after they had passed it, and, slouching into first one corner, then another, contrived to keep near them, although he did his best to avoid being seen in his turn.

In an instant I thought of Count Karenieff. Was it possible that he or his myrmidons were already on the trail? That the fiends had almost got my husband in their power, and that his denunciation was already a thing accomplished!

At thought of this awful possibility I turned sick with dread. But I no longer hesitated about revealing my own presence. At all hazards, Sergius must be warned. He must be made aware that an enemy dogged his footsteps. And he must be cautioned against betraying the secret resort of the Society to those interested in, and intent upon, its destruction.

With this object in view, I sprang forward, and would soon have reached my husband's side, but for an occurrence which was as unexpected as it was horrifying to me. The man who was acting the spy upon Sergius and his companion had also come to some sudden resolution; for he also sprang forward, but was intercepted by two individuals who appeared to have come upon the spot by magic.

I saw the glitter of gleaming steel, as a dagger flashed in the moonlight. I heard a stifled, gurgling cry, and before I could echo it, I felt myself gripped by the throat and rendered for the moment incapable of uttering a sound. It seemed to me that my last moment had come. My tongue clove to the roof of my mouth; my breath seemed to be forsaking me; my eyes felt as if they were starting from their sockets, and the horrible dread of immediate violent death possessed me.

Presently—the time may have been a few seconds; to me it seemed an age—the pressure was taken from my throat, and even as my senses were leaving me I felt a gag put in my mouth; some heavy garment was thrown over me; I was lifted from the ground, and was borne away, possibly to endure a fate which I was no longer even capable of imagining.

XII

"In mortal peril."

W hen I once more became conscious of my surroundings, I was
seated in a chair, in the center of a large, low-ceiled apartment,
of which the atmosphere was chill and damp and the light feeble. I
was supported on either side by a figure clad in a long gray cloak and
wearing a gray hood and scarlet domino. As my scared senses reasserted
themselves more fully, I could see that the room was peopled by many
other figures similarly attired, and that my presence among them was
the central subject of interest.

Nay, there was one other object that must have been of even more
horrible interest than I was! In front of the chair upon which I was
seated there lay a recumbent figure, covered by a large square of black
cloth. It was outlined with horrible distinctness, and a shudder ran
through me as I realized that this was the dead body of the man I
had seen struck down while in the act of shadowing my husband for
some purpose unknown to me, though I could not have imagined that
purpose anything but inimical to his safety.

And where was he, the beloved object for whose sake I had braved
the dangers which now encompassed me? I looked around me, hoping
to recognize his figure among the many with which I was surrounded.
But alas! the enshrouding cloaks and obscuring dominos would not
permit recognition, and my heart sank within me as I thought that even
were he here he might find it impossible to be of service to me without
endangering his own life.

At the end of the chamber in which I now found myself was a
slightly raised platform upon which were seated seven or eight of the
cloaked figures. But I noticed that in their case the cloak was black and
the domino yellow, and I conjectured rightly that they were the rulers
of the assembly. I was feeling acute bodily suffering, yet that was for the
time lost sight of in the horror of possible speedy annihilation.

Have any of my readers ever been in a situation of mortal terror? If
so, they will be able to realize the acuteness of perception with which
I regarded everything around me, and the miraculous swiftness with
which the most irrelevant ideas chased each other through my brain.
Even while trying to pierce the disguise of my possible judges, I found

myself wondering how dear little Jerry was getting on, and whether Belle's wedding would be postponed again or not.

But, after what seemed an interminable time, the silence was at last broken by a voice which ordered, in deep, impressive tones, "Remove that covering."

Instantly four figures approached the object lying in front of me, two from either side of the room, and each one silently lifted a corner of the cloth, and doubled it back, so as to expose the corpse of a man whose countenance wore such an expression of terror and agony as made me use desperate efforts to cover my face with my hands. But they were held tight by the two persons who supported me on my seat, and the same sonorous voice which I had already heard commanded me to look upon the face that lay in front of me, and ponder upon the fate mapped out for all traitors to their country.

Such a command was not reassuring, and I relapsed into trembling passivity, while black cloaks and gray cloaks proceeded to try the murdered man after he was dead.

"What is the name of that traitor?" was the question I heard, from the lips of the man who seemed to be the president of the assembly.

"Karol Gratowitzki."

"What was his crime?"

"He was a government spy."

"And his special mission?"

"To dog the footsteps of Number Finis."

"Then he deserves his fate. Who was the avenger?"

"Number Sixteen."

"Then his exemption from future death-service has been earned."

At these words the man who had replied to the above questions stepped forward, bowed to those who were seated on the platform, uttered a formula, of which I did not catch the import, and then ranged himself upon the opposite side of the room to the one he had previously been standing at.

"Remove the body," was the next command. In another moment the board upon which the dead man had been laid was re-covered, and was lifted up by four figures, who marched down the room with it, and disappeared through a low door, which was bolted after their exit, amid a dead silence on the part of those left behind.

"Now my turn is at hand," I thought, feeling sick with dread, and looking in vain for a friendly sparkle in the eyes of the silent figures

ELIZABETH BURGOYNE CORBETT

around me. My premonition was correct, for the next words I heard referred to myself.

"Who is the prisoner?"

"We do not know," was the reply.

"How came she here?"

"She was spying upon one of our chosen."

"Did she betray antagonistic intentions?"

"Yes; she sprang forward, as if to strike, simultaneously with the man who has already been removed."

"What weapons has she in her possession?"

"None that we have seen. She has not yet been searched."

"Remove her, and search her."

Up to this point I had remained silent, for my tongue refused to utter a sound. But the prospect of suffering the indignity of having my clothing removed for the purpose of examination made me utter a startled protest. There was, indeed, a tiny English revolver hidden in my dress for defensive purposes. But how was I to convince these stern martinets that I would never have dreamed of hurting anyone, unless it was absolutely necessary, in order to save either my own life or my husband's.

"Indeed!" I cried, forgetting that I was not speaking to a meeting of English people, "I assure you that I am innocent of the remotest intention of injuring anyone belonging to you. And surely I have already suffered indignity enough!"

There was a slight movement of surprise, as if my nationality had been unsuspected, and then one of the black-cloaked figures who had hitherto not spoken stepped forward, and addressed the president in a low tone. Receiving an affirmative reply to some suggestion which he offered, he proceeded to cross-question me in very good English.

I am sure that I created an unfavorable impression where I was most anxious to be conciliatory, for, after partially unfolding my story, I was seized with sudden alarm on behalf of Sergius, and forthwith became as reticent as I had a few moments before been voluble. For was it not possible that undue candor on my part might betray some secret hitherto carefully preserved by my husband? Suppose his marriage, while still a member of this dread society, was against the rules? And suppose I were betraying a secret that might prove fatal to him, if I spoke of his recent absence from the country for which he had sworn to give up his life? Of all that concerned his connection with the people who now had me in their power he had told me nothing, and in all likelihood his reticence on this subject was entirely due to considerations of personal safety. Perhaps he was under oath to reveal nothing. How, then, was I to account not merely for my knowledge of the fact that he was a member of this society, but of the still more perilous secret of his motive for returning to Russia? Or of my own object in following him?

Would not my admission that my presence in Moscow was the result of my private determination to frustrate an event which they regarded as necessary for the salvation of their country be sufficient to procure my own death-warrant as well as my husband's? Mine because they must necessarily regard me as an enemy, his because he was, even if unwillingly, the cause of my knowledge of their deadly secret. Alas! where was he? Surely, if he were present, he would at once have tried to save me from the summary fate which hung over me. And yet, to do so might be to risk his own safety.

Truly, vanity was never reproved more cruelly than mine was then! When the Princess Nina had told me that, so far from my presence near him being advantageous to Sergius, it might prove an additional source of peril, I did not believe her, since I meant to be too cautious to run into danger. And here I was, in dire extremity, and likely to involve my dear husband in my own ruin, all because I had had too much faith in the superiority of my own judgment.

The position, too, was one that was very difficult to understand. How did I come to be classed with the man who had already succumbed to the swift vengeance of this terrible society? The solution of this question was beyond my powers, but I was at least able to grasp one fact. Sergius must be the Number Finis whom the stranger was said to have been shadowing. And his safety was of such importance to the society that protectors, two and three deep, followed in his wake.

Some of these must have watched my pursuit of him, and must have imagined me to be his enemy. As this thought thrust itself forward, I began to feel less despairing, but could still not quite determine whether his speedy arrival on the scene would be conducive to my salvation, or to his undoing, and my brain became so bewildered that I hardly knew whether to pray for his prompt arrival or for his continued absence. There had been a break in the stern mode of conducting the inquiry. The door was silently opened by the janitor, in response to a signal from without, and three persons entered, who evidently brought news of stirring import, though its nature was not permitted to reach my ears. There was a buzz of excited voices, and the prevailing feeling seemed to be one of consternation. Several people who had hitherto kept silent joined in the conversation, and some hurriedly left the apartment. Although I had made wonderful progress with the Russian language, it was still beyond my power to comprehend very rapidly spoken utterances, and even if the discussion had been carried on in a louder tone I might still have been unable to grasp its full import. But I could at least tell that the news received was provocative of grief in the breasts of some of this mysterious assemblage of people, while others were stirred to menacing anger.

How this anger might affect my own fate was impossible for me to tell. But at all events I had received a momentary respite, and the dread of instant death was removed from me. Even my hands were now released, and had I been able to do so I might have stood up unhindered. But I was sick and giddy, from the combined effects of the violence to which I had been subjected, and of the mental distress under which I was laboring, and could now do no more than gaze helplessly around me, and wonder why Sergius did not come to my rescue.

Presently the excitement abated again, and the cloaked figures resumed their places, the three latest comers approaching close to where I was sitting.

"Now, Brother Finis," said the president, "look closely at this woman, who was caught dogging your footsteps, in company with a man whom we know to have been a government spy, and tell us if you have seen her before."

My heart leaped to my mouth at these words. This must be Sergius, although the ample folds of his cloak, and his hood and domino, had prevented me from recognizing him.

Hastily stepping forward, he now obtained a full view of me for the first time. He did not recognize me for a moment, owing to my disfiguring wig. But when I looked appealingly at him, clasped my hands in an attitude of distress, and sobbed just the one word. "Sergius!" he started as if struck by lightning.

The next instant he had pushed both my bonnet and my wig from my forehead, disclosing my own dark curls, and as at last I succumbed again to the faintness which had oppressed me for so long, I heard, my husband's voice exclaim:

"My God! This is my wife!"

XIII

"Paying the Penalty."

L ook up, my darling, you are safe now," were the next words of which my returning consciousness was cognizant. Opening my eyes, I saw those of Sergius bent anxiously upon me, and thankfully realized that I was embraced by his strong arms and pillowed upon his warm breast. Surely it was as he said. I was no longer in danger, and might give all necessary explanations without the paralyzing presence of an assembly which put patriotism before every other duty to humanity.

"Thank God, I have found you!" I murmured, while the tears of relief flowed down my cheeks. "Oh, Sergius! how could you leave me without one word of farewell?"

"I was compelled in honor to come here without an instant's delay. And it was hard enough to tear myself away on my wedding-day, without undergoing the agony of parting. Besides, I knew that you would refuse to let me come without you, and I dreaded to involve you in danger."

"Yet you did not dread danger for my husband, who is dearer to me than life."

"Indeed I did! But I dreaded dishonor still more. And there was another danger of which you are doubtless still ignorant. Had I not answered in person the telegram which summoned me hither, sudden death, at the hands of outraged patriotism, would have overtaken me in England. For our Society, which may strike you as a small one, has its ramifications all over Europe, and it never spares those who break their oath of obedience."

"But you barely escaped from St. Petersburg without falling into the hands of enemies, and even the strictest Society could hardly accuse you of leaving the country to evade your oath."

By this time all haziness had left my mind, and I felt altogether stronger. I raised myself into a sitting posture, and prepared for my first attempt to wean my husband from his determination to do all which his associates wished him to do. I looked around me to see that we were quite alone, in a small room, and that the door, which no doubt communicated with the larger apartment, was firmly closed. Then, with momentarily augmenting excitement, I began to tell Sergius all about my own journey hither.

ELIZABETH BURGOYNE CORBETT

"And do you know my principal object in following you?" I continued. "Nina told me that the special duty which demanded your presence here was the *removal* of the czar. For God's sake, don't lend yourself to so dreadful a deed! I could not bear to think of you as a murderer."

Even as I made this appeal I saw that it was utterly useless. Sergius had pushed his domino away from his face, and there was nothing to hinder me from noting that he had blanched considerably and that his eyes gathered an expression of mingled anger and anxiety.

"Dora," he said firmly, "you are treading on ground that is more dangerous than you dream of. Nina was a very foolish woman to make such a wild assertion, and you are still more foolish to act upon her information. Had I deemed it advisable, I would gladly have brought you with me. As I did not think such a course wise, I overconfidently imagined that my friends would have used some measure of discreetness. I certainly did not give Nina the particulars of my mission to Moscow, and even if I had done so, I should never have dreamed that she would betray my confidence."

"Indeed, Sergius," I protested, "Nina is the last woman in the world to betray her friends, and it was because she saw me tortured with all sorts of conflicting fears that she showed me the purely political nature of your sudden departure, which she no doubt knew without fresh information from you. And she certainly never dreamed that I would follow you, for I did not give her the slightest hint of my intention to do so. It was surely better for her to enlighten me than to leave me a prey to the misery of unexplained desertion."

"Perhaps you are right, Dora. All the same, your arrival here will certainly complicate matters for me. Still, I can understand your desire to learn as much as possible—and, why, I do believe you must have been suffering from jealousy! Tell me, is that so?"

"Well, I knew that you had seen a woman at Hyde Park Corner, whom you would have liked to avoid while with me. She knew you, I could tell. And she is so much handsomer than I am that you must own it was natural for me to imagine her power to be of a different nature to what it has proved."

"How do you know yet that she had anything to do with my sudden departure?"

"I don't know. I can only conjecture."

"Well, I will tell you. You have gone through such a bitter trial, and have suffered so much, that I cannot be angry with you, even for doubting my love. Vera Vassoffskoy is a member of our Fraternity. So also is her husband. Both have sad reason to hate an oppressive government, for it has robbed them both of kindred and fortune. But Madame Vassoffskoy, though at one with us in all our general plans, hates individual bloodshed. She was on a secret mission to London when she saw me. Before she left Moscow, she knew that the ballot had fallen upon me, with reversion to her husband in the event of my failure to appear on the scene in time. I shrank back when I saw her, for I regarded it as an evil omen to be confronted with my secret obligations on my wedding-day. But she was determined not to lose sight of me, and tracked us home by means of a cab which she called to her assistance. Having found my address, her next proceeding was to have an official message conveyed to me, commanding my instant return to Russia, to fulfill the great plan for relieving the sufferings of our oppressed country. Death is the reward of disobedience to the mandates of the Executive Council, and my grief at leaving you at such a time showed me that I could not have done my duty to my country if I had witnessed your distress. Hark! there is the signal! Our time is up, and we seem to have explained so little. And you still look so ill!"

"Indeed, I am quite recovered now, and will give you no trouble. To be with you is all I want to make me happy and well."

It was even so. I felt that, by his side, I could bid defiance to the threatenings of fate. Sergius tightened his arms round me and kissed me with all a young husband's devotion. But his caresses were rather those of one who is bidding a painful farewell than of one just reunited to the idol of his heart, after a trying separation.

"You must trust me, darling, whatever befalls," he whispered; and, could it be true? were those tears of grief which trickled down his cheeks? I stood up in suddenly returned alarm, but before I could question him at all there was a much louder knock at the door than the first one had been. Another second, and it was thrown open. Sergius hastily replaced his domino, and, kissing me once more, said: "I am ready."

The next moment I was standing alone in the little room. Sergius had gone. The door was closed and bolted, and I was a prisoner once more.

Still I did not, for sometime, realize that my isolation and detention were to be of a prolonged nature. But when more than an hour passed away, and I had listened to the gradual dying out of all sounds in the

ELIZABETH BURGOYNE CORBETT

outer room, I was seized by a species of panic. Was it possible that I had really brought danger upon the head of Sergius, and that he had already paid the penalty for my rashness?

I had seen with what little compunction the presumed spy had been dispatched, and my despairing fancy pictured my dear one already weltering in his blood, while I would perhaps be left to die in this cell of cold and starvation. There was a little light available for me, though not within my reach. It shone through an elevated grating which communicated with the larger apartment, and after a time this circumstance afforded me a little hope.

I concluded that, though the meeting was probably over, the place could not be entirely deserted. Otherwise the lights, feeble as they were, would most likely be extinguished. Then a new horror seized me. How many murders might have been committed on these premises! And how many corpses might be buried within a few yards of me!

I am not superstitious, in the general acceptation of the term. But I always had a horror of the near presence of death, and even the most strong-minded among those who may become acquainted with my history will admit that my circumstances and surroundings were uncanny enough to raise the hair of a much less nervous individual than myself.

My watch told me that I had been immured in this underground room for two hours, and I was feeling faint and sick with hunger; for it was now verging on dawn, and I had had very little food all the previous day, being too much engrossed in watching for Sergius to attend properly to my own bodily needs. Sleep refused me its refreshing aid, though I would gladly have welcomed the temporary oblivion of my surroundings which it might have given me.

After a time I fell into a species of semi-stupor, from which I was roused by the entrance of Sergius into my prison.

I am not sure that coherency of thought was not banished from me even after my husband had pressed wine and food upon my acceptance. I know now that I mechanically availed myself of the refreshment brought to me, but I cannot recall what transpired for a while, until a flood of tears relieved my brain from the pressure which the strength of my emotions exercised upon it.

Then I was able to comprehend all that Sergius had to tell me, and to realize how very nearly I had compassed his ruin, though I did not know until afterward what a battle he had had with the sterner members of the Society, whose motto was "Death to everything through which our plans may risk betrayal."

Briefly, the position was this.

Sergius had been strictly cross-examined concerning me, and had been able to convince his interrogators that I was really his wife. They were also satisfied as to my fidelity and attachment to him. But they declined to trust my discretion at a time when a word might betray their plans, and ruin their hopes of revolutionizing the country. It was therefore decreed that I was to be kept a close prisoner until such time as Sergius should have fulfilled the obligations that the Society demanded of him.

"In other words," I said, with a shudder, "I am never to recover my freedom until you have committed a hideous crime that would haunt us all our lives. I would rather die at once."

"My poor child! you speak out of the ignorance born of residence in a free and happy country," said Sergius sadly. "Could you but faintly realize the horror and misery that oppress the subjects of the czar, you would pray with us for the abolition of such a monstrous anomaly as a fabulously wealthy ruler at the head of a nation that is ground down to the lowest depths of poverty and degradation. While incredible sums are exacted for the support of a prodigal court, each year sees a huge holocaust of the victims of starvation and oppression! Our rulers revel in costly frivolities, while famine depopulates our country by tens of thousands! No other European state can show such a perfect system of barbaric misgovernment and corrupt officialism as Russia. If any of the czar's subjects show symptoms of originality or strivings after a better state of things, they are promptly consigned either to the state prison or to banishment, and all national reform has to be made the subject of secret plottings by a handful of men and women into whom patriotism or special provocation have instilled a greater amount of bravery than is possessed by their downtrodden and broken-spirited compatriots. The scoundrels whom despotism has put in office abuse their privileges to a brutal extent that would be tolerated nowhere else in Europe, and must come to an end even here some day. Our newspaper press is a dead letter, for it is so supervised and gagged that nothing even approaching a hint of discontent at the existing state of things is allowed to appear. A strict supervision is also exercised upon all our literature, and even that which is imported from other countries is examined so jealously that any article or paragraph which can be construed into disapproval of Russian politics is promptly detected and blocked out. Police spies intrude in our innermost sanctums, and true domestic privacy is practically unknown among us. Nor is this all. Physical oppression has been the heritage of us Russians for ages, and the slightest excuse is good enough to justify the confiscation of our property and the deprivation of our liberty. Liberty! why, even liberty of conscience is not allowed us, and we are asked to believe that God has gifted our cursed tyrants with the knowledge of the only true way in which to worship him. Whether it be Stundist or Jew, it is all the same. The Orthodox priests, who insult Christ by calling themselves Christians, are ever ready to instigate an ignorant mob into deeds of violence which are a disgrace to humanity. Dare to differ from them in creed, and you find yourself singled out for additional outrage. Your house will be wrecked, your home destroyed; your work taken from you, and all manner of vile insult heaped upon you. If you have wives and daughters, God might help them, but you can't, and the priest won't raise voice or finger to save them from the atrocities of the mob, which must be allowed to reward itself somehow for its readiness to support the Orthodox Church."

"But surely the government would not refuse to punish those guilty of such shameful deeds?"

"My dear child, the government and the Church will never fight each other, and the only reward which a complaint against the latter would bring forth would be the ruin of the man who ventured to make the complaint."

"But the czar. He is so powerful that a word from him would put an end to many of these evils. Surely if he knew—"

"The czar! He must know. He has been appealed to too often to be able to plead ignorance. But if he, who is nominally at the head of so huge a nation as ours, and who receives imperial emoluments for doing his duty to that nation, will not take the trouble to make himself acquainted with the needs of the subjects whom he is paid to govern and protect, then it is high time that he be made to give place to someone who will be honest enough to do the work for which he is paid. We want peace and prosperity at home, while our rulers neglect us in order to annex other provinces and enlarge an empire that is already too unwieldy."

"Yet if this emperor is removed by violence, he will be succeeded by his son, who will probably govern just as he is doing, so that his murder would only prove a fruitless crime."

"Not so. If his violent death does not frighten his successor into more humane methods of government, he will be removed in his turn. And so it will go on, until the rights of an oppressed people win the recognition that is demanded. You feel horrified at the idea of one man being turned over to avenging justice. How can you put his life in the scale against the lives and souls of the thousands who are the daily victims of governmental oppression and official cruelty? 'Vox Populi, vox Dei' is our watchword, and God and the People shall not always lift up their voice in vain!"

Oh, how noble my husband looked as he thus eloquently vindicated the right of the people to insist upon justice! And how strange it was that I, who had come to Russia fully resolved upon converting my husband to my own peaceable ways of thinking, should end by sharing his enthusiasm and by believing as he did. Yet so it was, and in defiance of possible subsequent conscience pricks, I began to look upon my husband's contemplated act as that of a brave, self-sacrificing hero, rather than as the assassination against which my soul had revolted. Since that eventful night a reaction has set in, and I often thank God that, after all, no bloodshed stains my husband's hands.

"You will feel your isolation very much, I am afraid," said Sergius, after we had, by tacit consent, tabooed further conversation anent the czar.

"If I can see you often, I will try to be as patient as possible. But I cannot help being anxious for your safety while you are away from me."

"My dear girl you need not worry at all on my account. You have seen for yourself how carefully I am guarded."

"Yes, that is true. But I also know that your position must be a precarious one, or you would not be under the necessity of maintaining the disguise in which I saw you. You are, too, quite aware that you may be discovered and arrested at any moment."

"How do you come to that conclusion?"

"Without much difficulty. Your manner, after leaving the hotel where I first saw you, showed that you feared to be tracked. Even the fact that your associates had mounted guard over you, and saved you from the government spy who was following you, is proof of the great danger you are in. How thankful I shall be when we are safe in England again!"

"So shall I, my darling. Meanwhile, we must make the best of the situation, which will perhaps not be quite so dreary for you as you imagine. You are to exchange this comfortless place for a room

ELIZABETH BURGOYNE CORBETT

in another part of the building, where you will have every indulgence but that of perfect freedom until it is deemed safe to permit you to go abroad again. Ah! there is the signal. Your fresh quarters are ready. Come, Dora, but remember that you must not speak by the way."

A few seconds later the door opened, and Sergius led me past two figures holding lighted candles, and in the wake of another, who pushed aside a heavy curtain, beyond which was a narrow, tortuous staircase, up which we climbed until my weary limbs found it almost impossible to go further. Fortunately, we had nearly reached the top, and Sergius half carried me into a room which was the picture of warmth and comfort.

A bright fire burned in the stove, and its enlivening rays made me suddenly conscious of the fact that I was shivering with cold. I sank quite exhausted upon a comfortable lounge, and it was like a transition to Paradise to find myself housed again in a haven of warmth and comfort, with the grateful odors of daintily prepared food assailing me. Yet I could neither eat nor drink of that which was set before me, and, so fatigued was I by my experiences, that I yielded to the languor which overpowered me, and was just conscious of being kissed affectionately by my husband, and covered over with multitudinous wraps, when I sank into a sound and refreshing slumber, from which I did not awake for several hours.

XIV

I was rested and refreshed by my long sleep, and was glad to find that the events of the night had had no ill effect upon my health. The room in which I found myself opened into a smaller one, fitted up as a bedroom, and in this place, greatly to my astonishment, I saw all the luggage I had taken with me to the hotel, which, for many reasons, had better be nameless. How Sergius had managed things so cleverly I could not tell. But I was delighted to be able to remove my disfiguring disguise, and make the most of my natural appearance.

Now that I was no longer a solitary damsel, whose movements might attract undesirable notice, I ceased to feel the need of appearing of such mature age, and I actually felt glad at the sight of my own homely presentment, after I had attired myself in a frock which I knew Sergius would like. While I was still busy touching up my toilet, an elderly woman, of serious but pleasing appearance, entered the room, and asked if I would take my breakfast, or rather lunch.

On first seeing me, she looked rather surprised, as if she had still expected to be confronted by a becurled and bespectacled old lady. I was able to understand her, and to reply to her, but was relieved to find that she relapsed into German. As I knew that language much better than Russian, it was possible to get on very well with my visitor, who told me that her name was Marie Ivanovitch, that she was the nominal lessee of this house, and that she had seen me on the previous evening.

"Then there were women, as well as men, in the assembly?" I exclaimed.

"Certainly," was the reply. "We women are as much alive to the griefs of our country as the men are, and the sexes are nearly equally balanced in our Society. Our usefulness is sometimes of a different nature to theirs, but, upon the whole, we have as much work to our hands as the men have."

"And your work just now is to prevent me from leaving this house?"

"Even so. But I trust that you will not find your detention very irksome, since it is only the consequence of necessary precautions for the safety of your husband and others. And I cannot impress upon you sufficiently the danger of attempting to elude the vigilance of those whose judgment ordered your stay here."

"I am not likely to do anything that will run counter to the wishes of the Society, provided Count Volkhoffsky approves of them."

"What! Taking my name in vain?" cried another voice at this juncture, and Sergius put in an appearance.

"I was just telling Madame Ivanovitch that I would obey any orders of the Society that are indorsed by yourself," I explained, while I smiled a glad welcome upon the face I loved.

"And the particular command in question?"

"That I do not attempt to leave these quarters."

"I hope you will not. You are safer here than elsewhere. And this is the only place in which we could see much of each other."

"Say no more, my dearest. Wild horses shall not drag me away without your approval."

"There, what do you say to that, Sister Ivanovitch?" asked Sergius. "You see, my wife has pledged her word to me to be obedient. In fact, you need be under no apprehension of indiscretion on her part. We both give you our word of honor."

"And yours is too well known to be doubted, Brother Volkhoffsky."

"Sergius," I said, as the worthy woman went to see after our lunch, "I feel thoroughly ashamed of myself for causing you so much trouble and anxiety. I shall—"

"Not another word, my darling. It does me good to see you looking something like your own bright self again. I ought never to have left you behind, for I might have known that you would have preferred to share danger with me, rather than live a life of suspense and inactivity at home."

"My life promises to be inactive enough even here now."

"But at least you know where I am and what I am doing, and that is something."

"To me it is everything. Life away from you would be such a blank that I do not care to picture anything so dreary."

Does the reader wonder at our ability to take things so quietly, even with an awful tragedy ever looming before us? I sometimes feel surprise thereat myself, until I remember that, in spite of our experiences, we were both still gifted with the elastic spirits of youth, and that the mere joy of being reunited was enough to make us temporarily forgetful of painful subjects.

Of course we had many confidences to exchange, and Sergius removed my mystification concerning several things. It seems that the man with whom I had seen him walking on the previous evening was Ivan Vassoffskoy, the husband of the handsome young woman I had seen at Hyde Park Corner, and the individual who would have had to officiate as my husband's substitute in the event of his failure to respond to the injunction to repair to Moscow at once. Ivan Vassoffskoy had even more reason to dread recognition by government spies than had Sergius, for it was in Moscow itself that he had been denounced, and, but for the injunction of the Society, would ere now have sought safety in flight. His wife was already in England, having been deputed to carry out some plans for the Fraternity, of which she also was a member.

"Ivan has wonderful powers of contortion, which have saved him from discovery more than once," said Sergius, when speaking of his colleague. "It would take his dearest friend all his time to recognize his naturally handsome face in the twisted and distorted visage which he presents to the public gaze. I have only heard of three people who could equal him in this direction. These were an English actor, a Japanese contortionist, and an English murderer. All three used their peculiar talent to good purpose, and were able to mystify whom they liked. The murderer even went so far as to masquerade in your Scotland Yard, although he knew that detectives were on the lookout for him. If Ivan's powers of contortion serve him as well as they served the English malefactor he will have cause to be thankful for them."

"I thought he looked very singular," I said. "But I would never have dreamed that he could by any possibility be regarded as a handsome man. But tell me, where were you going when I saw you together?"

"We were going to visit and take pecuniary help to the wife of a man who has fallen a victim to official rancor. He had the misfortune to have a pretty daughter, who was beloved by a youth in every way worthy of her. Now, although both Olga and her father and mother favored this young suitor, he had several rivals for her hand. Olga is a very nice girl, but I fancy that the good pecuniary position of the family had something to do with the love of at least one of those who proposed for her hand. Be this as it may, on finding himself rejected, he swore to be revenged both upon his rival and upon the girl who had had the temerity to award a man of his standing the insult of a refusal."

"His threats were heard with dread, for he was in a position of some importance, in which he had facilities for dealing underhand

ELIZABETH BURGOYNE CORBETT

blows at those who were unfortunate enough to offend him. A large proportion of the denunciations, which result in death, imprisonment or banishment, are the outcome of personal malice; and when once a man or woman is in the position of an accused prisoner, there is small hope of delivery, especially if there is property to confiscate."

"And did this bad man fulfill his threats?"

"Indeed he did. You shall judge what difference this enmity made to Olga and her parents when I tell you that her father and brother have been sent to Siberia as political exiles. The mother and daughter are reduced to poverty, and have found it impossible to support the younger children without help from friendly sympathizers, who have to exercise the greatest precautions in visiting them, lest they, too, fall into the power of iniquitous officialism."

"And Olga's lover—what of him? Can he not help them in their emergency?"

"Poor Paul! I fear there is little doubt that he languishes in that living grave—the fortress on the Neva."

"How horrible! It makes me shudder to think of it. Oh, Sergius, for Heaven's sake take care of yourself! What shall I do if evil befalls you, and how can you escape it in this dreadful country? I hardly dare hope that you will reach England alive. How thankful I would be if we could leave at once."

"My dear girl, there are many things worse than death. *That* I must risk. But I could not retain your respect for a man whose oath has been broken, and whose word of honor is worthless. I will be as careful as is consistent with my duty. More I cannot promise, even to you."

Was it true that I would rather welcome the death of my hero than that which he conceived to be dishonor? I think not. But I had not the temerity to argue the question with him, and, rather than distress him again, I tried to put the ghastly picture of his so-called duty from my mind.

"Tell me, if you may," I said, "what special information it was that produced such a sensation at the meeting last night?"

"There is no reason why I should not tell you. Some members of our St. Petersburg branch have been denounced and tracked by informers in the pay of Count Karenieff and his myrmidons. Six of them have been arrested, and it is not likely that they will ever recover their liberty again. One lady, who was arrested some weeks ago, and who was really innocent of conspiracy, has been so monstrously treated that she has died in prison. The circumstance of her death would be regarded as an opportune release from a life that could never again become tolerable to her, were not the predisposing details so horrible. She was grossly insulted by the governor of the jail in which she was immured, but refused to forget that she was an honorable wife and mother. Nothing daunted by her indignant rebuff, the scoundrel again insulted her. This time the unhappy lady slapped her tormentor's face, and aroused in him the demon of revenge. She was accused of attempting to take the governor's life, and was ordered to be subjected to the frightful indignity of the knout. In spite of her alternate prayers for mercy and screams of resistance, she was dragged to the place of punishment, forcibly stripped, and mercilessly beaten.

"The physical pain was something terrible to endure, but one survives even worse things than that. It was the moral degradation that ate into her soul, and induced her to end her unhappy life. How she obtained it no one knows. But it is certain that she had poison in her possession, and that she used it to good purpose."

"How can such iniquities be permitted! You make even me feel a longing to take part in the downfall of a government that can sanction such atrocities! To think that a noble woman's end should be so sad!"

"Her end? That has not come. She lives in our souls, and cries aloud from the grave for vengeance! Her death has revived the ardor of both the enthusiasts and the lukewarm adherents of the cause of the people, and will do freedom more service than her life has done."

We had much more conversation in the same strain, for I fully sympathized with my husband's accounts of the cruelties inflicted upon his compatriots. But all subjects come to an end sometime, and our talk varied itself by excursions to Greenby and to Courtney Grange, not to speak of all we hoped to do when we were once more at liberty to return to England and take possession of the handsome house intended for our reception.

"And I have already written to the Michaelows," said Sergius. "Of course, neither their name nor ours appeared in the letter. But they will receive it indirectly, and they will understand that we are together. This will allay their anxiety about you, and all the particulars of our adventures can be related when we see them."

"I wonder if such an event will really come to pass?"

"To be sure it will. I can't have you always imagining the worst. You must look at the bright side of things."

"Do you know what I would do if I had the power?"

"Something wonderful, no doubt."

"I would give you a drug, if such were obtainable, that would make you oblivious of everything but my presence and my wishes. Then I would take you far away from Russia, and would keep you there until there was no longer any danger of your being recalled."

"Ah! Dora, I'm afraid I shall never make a patriot of you.—But, whatever can be the matter! Do you hear the commotion?"

"Sergius! for Heaven's sake, fly! Someone has betrayed you! Those are government men who are rushing upstairs! Oh, what shall we do? How can you escape?"

But my husband appeared much more astonished than frightened, and hardly seemed to notice what I was saying, for all his attention was apparently concentrated upon the hurrying footsteps without.

In another moment our room door was flung open without ceremony, and half a dozen people entered, among them being Madame Ivanovitch.

"The country is saved! Hurrah! Death to the tyrant!"

These and other exclamations became mixed in an inextricable jumble, so excited were all the speakers. Sergius saw that some great news had arrived, and became as excited as the rest.

"Silence, some of you," he cried, "until I know what has happened! You, Vassoffskoy, what is it?"

"We have been anticipated. The czar will never come to Moscow now! Our St. Petersburg contingent has achieved the great deed. The tyrant has been assassinated! Long live the people!

XV

It was all quite true. The czar had been assassinated. Though he was not killed outright by the bomb which was thrown under his carriage, it was known that he was mortally injured, and could not live long. The messenger who brought the news to Sergius had started from St. Petersburg to Moscow as soon as the deed was done, being previously armed with a railway ticket and a passport, and was already on his way to the frontier, whither it was advisable for all other suspects to proceed at once, if they would escape the tremendous hue and cry which would doubtless be raised without delay.

In spite of the fact that I was the associate of conspirators, the news which elated them horrified me, and I was more than ever convinced that my rightful avocation lay among scenes of peace and domesticity. It was, therefore, all the more strange that the whole of my grown-up life so far should have been one of danger, turmoil and excitement.

Yet, as all things have their limit of prominence in the ever-shifting kaleidoscope of life, even so would that fever of existence, which is variously termed "patriotism" and "treason," cease to influence my daily being ere long. Such, at all events, was my hope, and I no longer doubted that Sergius would at once use his utmost endeavors to escape to England.

But, for a time, it was difficult to obtrude individual interests into the jumble of excited comment in which the ever-increasing number of fresh arrivals discussed the tragedy which had taken place at St. Petersburg, and its probable effects upon the members of the Society.

"I suppose it will be no longer safe to meet here after today," said a man, whom I heard addressed as Ivan Vassoffskoy, but whom I would not have recognized as the man whom I had seen with Sergius on that never-to-be-forgotten night of adventure.

"I do not think it was safe to meet here today," said another, who had just arrived. "Just as I entered the passage leading round to our secret entrance I fancied that a man brushed past me, and I feel rather alarmed."

"One of ours," remarked Sergius.

"I think not," was the reply, which seemed to imbue all the company with a sense of insecurity. "I challenged him in our usual way, but received no answer, as must have been the case if he had been one of us."

ELIZABETH BURGOYNE CORBETT

"Then why did you come in if you fancied yourself followed?"

"Because I concluded that the 'house' was already suspected. I did retrace my steps for a few yards, but did not succeed in drawing the man away from the vicinity of the passage. This being the case, I thought it better to come in, after all, in order to warn you. It is quite possible that the passage is guarded already, and that everybody emerging from it will be arrested."

"You did well, brother," was the verdict of a tall, imposing man who had hitherto said little. "I had already begun to doubt the wisdom of meeting here much oftener, but was anxious to await the great event before altering our plans. As you all know, that event has taken place, and, by the terms of our oath, we are no longer a Society, although the consummation aimed at has been not our work, but the work of our brave St. Petersburg contingent. I proclaim us morally and patriotically disbanded, and absolved from all further duty or allegiance to the rules of our Brotherhood. If, in the future, it becomes necessary to give the government another severe lesson, you all know how to communicate with me, if I am still alive and in freedom, and you all know that my sole aim in life is to avenge the wrongs of the people. Before the setting of another sun some of us will be on our way to other lands, to seek that safety and freedom of speech which is denied us here. Some of us may have fallen into the hands of the tyrants, and have no longer a hope left. Others, confident that nobody suspects their connection with us, will continue to live in and about Moscow in comparative security, pursuing a life of honest toil, and always ready to afford an asylum to a patriot. But, whatever be the fate in store for us, we have nothing to reproach ourselves with, unless it be that our fight for God and our right has not been drastic enough."

All the details of this conversation were fully explained to me by Sergius some days later, when it was no longer dangerous to speak even in whispers, as was the case while we were flying toward the frontier. But although I had not understood all that was said, I had gathered enough to know that our situation was already one of extreme peril, and I own that I felt terribly alarmed. I was also angry with myself for my husband's sake, for I was sure that my presence could not fail to hamper his escape from Moscow. But I was not a little surprised to see how stoically all these dangerous conspirators received the news that their arrival had been watched, and that their exit was probably cut off by an outraged government at whose hands they would find little mercy.

This seeming mystery was, however, soon explained. There were, on the upper landing, and partly within the four rooms whose doors opened on to this landing, over twenty people present, none of whom appeared in the cloaks and dominos which had imparted such an awful solemnity to their meeting when I was taken captive by them. This, Sergius told me afterward, was because they knew that the catastrophe at St. Petersburg had virtually disbanded them.

"Take off your shoes, Dora," whispered Sergius. "And don't be alarmed, darling. Our danger is not nearly so imminent as you seem to fear. We have long expected this crisis, and have not allowed ourselves to be trapped like rats in a hole."

While Sergius was speaking, he rapidly unlaced his boots and took them off. Greatly to my amazement I saw that all the other people present were engaged upon the same task, and I followed the general example, feeling sure that it would eventually prove to be justified, by reason.

As soon as their noise-producing foot covering was removed, all present began to throng into the bedroom I had occupied for so short a time. Someone touched a secret spring in the wainscoting, which noiselessly yielded to a slight pull given to it by Sergius, and revealed a cavernous opening into which, with whispered injunctions against making much noise, first one and then another of the conspirators disappeared with either boots or shoes in hand. One man fetched a short ladder into the room, besides a boot and a shoe, which had evidently been previously in readiness for some special purpose.

Sergius held back until all the others had passed through the secret door. Then he raised the bedroom window, which was one that opened on to the roof. His next proceeding was to throw the two shoes some distance along the flat roofs of the adjoining buildings. Then, leaving the window open, and the ladder by which he had reached it still standing, he took my hand and drew me into the space in which our companions were making cautious and laborious progress. Carefully closing the door behind us, he stooped for a moment, and I heard a sharp click, as of breaking metal.

"There," he said, in a low tone. "It would take pursuers sometime to follow us, for I have broken the spring, and that door will never yield again to gentle persuasion. Are your shoes all right?"

"Yes, I have them in my hand."

"And your money and jewelry is already stowed in our pockets.

Everything else you must sacrifice. You are unfortunate with your clothes."

"Never mind, so long as I have you left. But why did you throw those shoes out of the window? And why did you leave the window open?"

"To lead probable pursuers off the scent, and induce them to believe that we have escaped through the window, dropping our shoes in our hurry. A couple of houses along the flat roof there is an easy means of descent to the ground, by way of out-house tops, and thence into an unfrequented back street. It will seem the most natural way in the world to escape, and while the enemy is following up the false scent we shall all be making good progress in another direction."

"But suppose it is a false alarm, after all?"

"Listen!"

I did listen, and no longer hesitated about groping my way into the darkness beyond. For noises, loud and threatening, penetrated to my shrinking ears, and told me that the house had already been forcibly entered. Of course the doors had been locked behind us, and I could hear that these were being beaten down with heavy weapons.

"Now, silence, for your life!" whispered Sergius. "Trust me to lead you to safety."

Not another word was exchanged between us for several minutes, during which, having crawled on to a sort of shelf, and covered the opening by means of a spring sliding panel, we found it necessary to crawl for some distance on all fours, in a stifling atmosphere which threatened to choke us. But at last this ordeal was also over, and we emerged into another chamber, similarly arranged to the one by which we had entered the species of tunnel which we had just traversed.

I was by this time almost exhausted with terror and haste, and was thankful indeed to be told that the worst danger was now over. But I exerted myself womanfully to hide the full extent of my distress from Sergius, and have since felt rather ashamed at times when he has insisted upon praising my courage and fortitude.

"You may put your shoes on again now," he said, "and we shall no doubt find someone in the next room ready to give us a good brushing."

It was as he said. But it took a good wash, as well as a good brush, to make us at all presentable, and every requisite facility for furbishing up one's toilet was to be found here.

"How strange it seems," I said, "to have come into such handy quarters. I understand the comforts of the other end. But these two little rooms seem to be only used for dressing, and don't communicate with a bedroom at all."

"That is easily explained. We are now actually in a theater, and these are the manager's dressing-rooms. He is one of us, and the whole plan of escape is of his devising. That passage along which we crawled is space taken from the front upper rooms of three houses that we have crossed. It was necessary to take off our shoes, in order not to make too much noise over other people's heads; but even the chance of betrayal on this score is practically guarded against, since all these front rooms have been taken by various members of our Fraternity. They would know what a scrambling noise overhead meant, but there is a possibility of antagonistic strangers being sometimes present in some of the rooms, so we are always as careful as possible. There, now, if you have quite recovered your breath, we will follow the rest of our friends downstairs."

In a few minutes we found our way down staircases along corridors into what proved to be the manager's private room, and here the manager himself was conversing with several of those who had so recently escaped a mortal danger.

"Ah! here you are, Brother Volkhoffsky," he said. "Do you think the alarm has been a false one, or that the flight was unnecessary?"

"If my wife and I had been one minute later," was the reply, "all would have been lost. I had only just broken the secret spring, when I heard loud commands to surrender, while the door was being violently assailed."

"Ugh!" shuddered one or two. "It's as well we're out of it. But what had we better do next?"

"I do not think that it would be advisable for anymore of you to leave the theater now," said the manager. "The police will be watching the whole neighborhood very carefully just now. You very likely all need refreshment badly, or will before you have a chance of obtaining any elsewhere. Four of you shall have some wine and such substantial fare as I have already provided, while the rest walk boldly on to the stage. You must refresh yourselves in relays of four. I don't want too many people in this room at once, as we are likely to be interrupted at any moment, and my advice is that you spend as short a time here as is consistent with a substantial meal, which I again warn you will be needed. I will give you all part of some play to masquerade on the stage with, and if any prying spies intrude, you will be supposed to be rehearsing for tonight's performance. As evening approaches, the theater will be lighted up, and before the real artists arrive you must so dispose yourselves as to be able to join the audience unobtrusively. You will then be comparatively safe, as no one will imagine that people who know the police to be on their track would spend the evening listening to a comic opera, thus apparently wasting valuable time. After the play is over, you can emerge with the crowd, and go your several directions in comparative safety. After that it will be each one for himself, and the God of nations for us all. And now, my friends, I have my daily duties to perform, and must attend to them at once, if I would avoid the curse of suspicion. So good-by, and may our unhappy country be no more under the necessity of fighting against those whose duty it is to help instead of to oppress!"

This wish was fervently echoed by the rest of those present. There was a solemn ceremony of handshaking, and then the Society which had exacted such a horrible duty from my husband was disbanded forever, although many of its members found it advisable to follow the manager's advice and abide in the theater until after the evening performance. Sergius and I were of the number; and, greatly to our relief, the tickets and passports with which Sergius was already provided were accepted at the railway stations without suspicion.

Our journey to the frontier, although desperately fatiguing, proved uneventful, and when, having traveled by the Brest-Litovsk route, we found ourselves in Berlin, we felt able to express to each other without fear our thankfulness at our escape. In Berlin we stayed for a couple of days, to take much needed rest, and to replenish our shabby and scanty wardrobe, since we did not care to return to England with nothing but the clothes we stood up in.

There was no need for Sergius to sell any of our jewelry to provide ready money. He was well supplied with cash, and had this not been so he could have drawn upon a Berlin banker whom he knew.

A couple of days later we presented ourselves, somewhat travel-worn, but otherwise in good health, at the house of Prince Michaelow, in Kensington, and I shall never forget the delighted astonishment with which he and Nina welcomed us "home" again.

"Thank God!" said the former. "We never expected to see either of you alive again."

"You see, I fetched him home," I said to Nina, and I hardly know whether smiles or tears most prevailed as I received my friend's enraptured caresses.

"I can't think how you have managed so beautifully," said Nina; "unless, indeed, you only went part of the way."

"We went all the way, and Dora has gone through all sorts of terrible adventures with no end of pluck," asserted Sergius.

"It's just wonderful! After the news of that horrible assassination reached England, I felt sure you were both doomed," said Nina, with a shudder, accompanied by another hug. "But how did you escape so easily?"

"Perhaps we had better defer explicit particulars for a little while," interposed Prince Michaelow. "I am thinking that one never knows what may happen, and that it will be as well not to betray the fact of your having been in Russia again to anyone. I suppose you were in St. Petersburg?"

This was said so significantly that I knew what awful thing he was hinting at, and at once exclaimed: "No, thank Heaven! Sergius has been no further than Moscow. *That* was done without him."

"I am so thankful!" chimed in Nina. "Of course, I feel for the people. But it is an immense relief to me to know that none of my friends have killed the poor, misguided man."

"You see," said the prince, "we shall never be able to make true patriots of our wives. They are too English for that. But how will this affect your future?"

"I am just as much absolved from further duty as if mine had been the hand which threw the bomb. Our Society is disbanded, and will never be reorganized on the same lines. While still a member of it, I was resolved to fulfill the terms of my oath to the letter. But that sort of work does not suit me, and though I long for the regeneration of my country, I am now convinced that violence on the part of secret societies can never cure the evils we deplore."

"Then you are not likely to join another secret society?"

"Never! My political career is over. I cannot sympathize with the government. I may not work openly in the interests of the people. And I will not lend myself again to secret plotting. This much I have already told Dora. But she does not know yet that I have resolved never to return to Russia. Henceforth my life is devoted to her happiness and comfort."

This was indeed glorious news, which helped me to throw off the last talon of the incubus of dread, and speedily recover the happiest spirits imaginable. We decided to adopt the prince's advice, and to say

ELIZABETH BURGOYNE CORBETT

nothing to anyone about having been elsewhere than on our originally projected wedding-tour. We had returned within the time expected, and I for one would not have put it in Belle's power to betray the fact that Sergius was in Russia when the czar was assassinated.

So we duly took possession of our own beautiful house; and then, as I really longed to see Lady Elizabeth and Jerry, we went down to the Grange, to pay a visit which my father had strongly urged us to pay.

And how different this journey to Moorbye was to the last one! Then I was lonely, unloved, miserable and homeless. Now I was the possessor of everything that goes to make life happy. And yet only a few months had elapsed between the two visits. Early summer had but given way to late autumn. Certainly, many events had been crowded into a short space of time. Nevertheless, it was nothing short of wonderful that such results should have sprung so rapidly from the ashes of what I had deemed an almost incurable grief.

I could not complain of my reception, for all but Belle greeted me with warmth, and I was positively thankful that she held aloof from me. I was also glad that no one witnessed our meeting. She had kept her room, when we first arrived, on the plea of a headache, to which I inwardly gave the name of envy. For, knowing the superiority of Sergius to the Earl of Greatlands, and thoroughly understanding Belle's envious nature, I knew that my good fortune could but be a very bitter pill for her to swallow. We encountered each other in the corridor, when I was on my way to the dressing-room assigned me, and it was characteristic of the nature of us both that we merely bowed when we saw each other. There was no sisterly kiss. Not even a handshake. Apparently there was to be an armed truce between us, and Belle's first words prepared me to understand that she hated me as much as ever.

"So," she said, drawing her superb figure up to its full height, and looking scornfully at me, "you have managed to secure a title, after all! Had you lived in the middle ages you would have been burned as a witch, for nobody would have believed that you used aught but magic arts to ensnare your victims. And you have not shown much decency, either, or you would not have married so soon after—"

Here Belle, callous and hardened as she was, paused for a moment, and I finished the sentence for her in a manner she little expected.

"Since the death of *your* victim," I said, now feeling as relentless as she was herself. "Take care how you goad me, or I may be tempted to betray your secrets. For I know everything, and one word from me could shatter your castle of cards. While I am at it I will tell you something else. Not long ago you deliberately meditated my removal by the same means which made your fiancé an earl. Take care how you attempt to repeat such experiments. I am not the only one in the secret. But it will be safely kept, if you behave yourself, for the sake of others, who would suffer by your downfall. I hardly need hint that you would precipitate that downfall by any attack upon my life, since I am less likely to die unavenged than the poor old earl. And now I have only one stipulation to enforce. You must henceforth be civil and polite to me and mine. In return I will refrain from ever alluding to this wicked business again. The possessors of your secret are as anxious to guard it as if they were alike guilty with you."

Had Belle been struck into stone she could not have been more rigid than she was. Her face petrified with horror, and her eyes betrayed the consciousness of guilt. She made no attempt to interrupt me. But the look of relief which overspread her face when I reassured her that her secret was safe showed me that she thoroughly understood the meaning of every word I said, and convinced me that I need fear no further insults from her in future. I had not meant thus openly to confront her with her own wickedness. But her insults stung me to it, and my words certainly had the effect I desired.

When, shortly afterward, I joined the others in the dining-room, there was ample balm for my wounded feelings. My father, having got over the pique which he had first felt on discovering that I was capable of carving my own fortunes, and that I was not inclined to eat humble pie, was becoming quite cordial with me, and had evidently come to the conclusion that there must be something in me, after all, since others seemed to appreciate me so highly. As for Sergius, it was impossible to resist him, and there was every evidence that Mr. Courtney was already feeling very proud of his new son-in-law.

Lady Elizabeth was looking much better, and plied me with a great many questions relative to my early Russian adventures. "I have missed you very much," she said. "But I have not felt so anxious about you as might have been the case had you been less energetic and self-reliant. Besides, you knew that I loved you, and I expected you would apply to me at once, if you were in need of money. I also thought that, as the friction was connected with Belle, you would return to us as soon as she was married. But I never dreamed that you would be the possessor of a wealthy husband and a title. Certainly, in your case, it has been proved that it is better to be born lucky than rich. I wonder what Belle thinks of it. She has never said anything to me. She knows I would not listen to a word against you. But I hope she does not mean to be rude, or that her headache is not a mere pretext to avoid you."

"You need have no fear," I replied confidently. "I met Belle in the corridor, and received her congratulations. I think she means to let bygones be bygones as much as possible now. I daresay she felt that she had sufficient cause to be ill-natured before. And, you know, she must have been awfully disappointed when she found she was not to live at the castle."

"You said some strange words that morning," said Lady Elizabeth, sinking her voice to a whisper. "The thought of what they implied has almost killed me. The whole affair was so dreadful that I did not know what to think. Do you still—"

"Mother," I interrupted hastily, "for Heaven's sake, pay no more heed to the ravings of a grief stricken girl. It was unfortunate for us all that your brother should have gained his title under such tragic circumstances. But pray do not think that anything but nature interfered with my wedding. It served me right. I was selfish and headstrong, and ought to have remembered how cruelly Belle was disappointed. It was a shame to say wicked things of her besides."

"Oh, Dorrie! how thankful you make me. I have of late begun to think it impossible that either Cyril or Belle would stoop to criminality. It was too awful to believe. Now that you are also convinced, I feel thoroughly happy. And how nice you are looking, too! You have such pretty hair, and such a fine complexion. Your figure, too, since you have become less thin, is as good as Belle's own. Your father remarked a little while ago that it was wonderful what an amount of good looks you were developing."

"I believe I am too happy and well-cared forever to recover my former perfection of ugliness."

"Now, Dorrie," chimed in another voice, "it's really too bad of you. You don't seem to be able to spare me a minute. I don't believe you are half so jolly as you used to be."

"Why, Jerry!" I said, kissing him affectionately. "Didn't I talk with you nearly all the way from the station? And didn't I discover what a little fraud you are, for you couldn't answer my most simple French questions? And haven't you taken possession of Sergius ever since?"

"Yes, to be sure. I forgot that. But, oh my! isn't he a brick? He's given me a sovereign, and he's going to buy me the jolliest pony he can get, so that I can have plenty of riding in the holidays."

Just at this juncture Mr. and Mrs. Garth, who, it seems, had been invited to dine with us, arrived on the scene, and there was a considerable amount of congratulating and handshaking. Then Belle came down, looking as quietly elegant and beautiful as ever, though perhaps a shade paler. She was very gracious when introduced to Sergius, and impressed everyone very favorably by her brilliant conversation and ready wit.

Both my father and Lady Elizabeth looked very happy and contented, and the evening was spent sociably and harmoniously. There was only one cankerous secret hidden beneath the smiling surface of family unity. But that was to be buried forever, I devoutly hoped.

"What a pity Greatlands isn't here," said my father, sometime after we had all adjourned to the drawing-room. "I'm sorry business kept him in town this week. You see, Volkhoffsky, he is doing the thing in style, and is very busy making all necessary preparations for next week's grand event. Yes, one week more, and then Belle, too, will have passed the portals of matrimony."

Yes, one week more, and the final scene in this life-drama will have been played. One turn more of Fortune's wheel, and we will ring the curtain down upon these reminiscences of an ugly girl's life.

XVI

"Life and thought have gone away."

Never had such a brilliant company been assembled within the walls of Moorbye Church. It was Belle's wedding-day, and the sun shone kindly upon the face of nature. Only a few family friends had been invited down, but the little church was filled to overflowing by the gentlefolks of the neighborhood, who did not think it *infra dig.* to undergo a lot of crowding and elbowing for the privilege of witnessing an earl's wedding.

Belle looked superb in her pearl-embroidered satin gown as she walked up the aisle with my father, and her bearing must have struck the onlookers as unusually calm and dignified. I fancied that I could detect a sign of anxiety in the hurried glance she cast around in search of Cyril, and that her face paled on discovering that he had not yet arrived. Possibly she thought of that other bridal morning, when the bridegroom did not put in an appearance. As yet, however, there was no need for uneasiness. The train by which the Earl of Greatlands was to come from town was only just due, and it might possibly be a little late.

"I feel very anxious," said Lady Elizabeth to me, in a voice low enough only to be heard by myself. "Cyril ought to have contrived to be here first. He has behaved very strangely altogether of late, and I cannot help thinking that something must be wrong with him. I hope he is not ill."

Alas! I knew what was wrong with him, and by this time my fears exceeded Lady Elizabeth's own. When I say that I feared, I speak advisedly. For it had seemed to me that an interruption to this marriage was a thing to be dreaded, for everybody's sake. True, real happiness was not to be expected for either Belle or her husband. But it was more fitting that these two, who had sinned together, should spend the rest of their conscience-haunted days together, than that either of them should be left at liberty to cast a shadow upon the life of anyone else. Perhaps it was very presumptuous of me to constitute myself judge in such a case as this; for to encourage criminals in the achievement of that for which they have schemed and planned hardly seems a justifiable way of making the punishment fit the crime. Certainly the demands of justice would appear to point to a very different ending to our family troubles.

But what woman in my place would not have tried to pit silence and oblivion against naked justice?

It was a relief to us all when the Earl of Greatlands, accompanied by Mr. Alwyn Gardener, his best man, hurriedly entered the church and walked toward the altar. But Mr. Gardener appeared flushed and troubled, and the bridegroom seemed to me to be looking like one demented. For at one moment he bit his lip and clinched his hand with all the air of one who is doing a thing that is distasteful to him. The next he was smiling at Belle, and gazing at her with the exultant admiration of a proud and happy bridegroom.

Presently Mr. Garth and his two chosen assistants began the marriage service, and the interest of the onlookers was quickened in an endeavor to hear the responses. Even yet I felt apprehensive of interruption. But, so far, my fears were unfounded, for the ceremony was concluded, and soon all was smiles and congratulation. The bride was kissed by relatives and bridemaids, and I hoped that, among all the fuss and excitement, the fact that I neither kissed my sister nor shook hands with my brother-in-law would pass unnoticed.

There was to be a reception after the wedding, and then the newly-married pair were to go to Scotland for their honeymoon. We were quite a merry party at the Grange, and even I, who was so much behind the scenes, felt as if I almost dared hope that the family troubles were now over.

Jerry was in high glee, for everybody liked him, and the tips he got were enough to have turned any ordinarily lucky schoolboy green with envy. His holidays were almost over, and no doubt some of the school-chums of whom he spoke to me would soon show him how to get rid of his pocket-money.

The Earl of Greatlands excused himself somewhat earlier than had been expected, on the plea of feeling the need of half an hour's quiet, as he was considerably out of sorts. "It will be time enough for you to get into your traveling dress in three-quarters of an hour, dear," he said to Belle, whom he kissed again with all the ardor of a lover. Then he went up to his room, while Belle supported her honors a while longer in a manner that won admiring encomiums from certain individuals of the toadying order, who never lose an opportunity of flattering their superiors in station. When at last the bride went upstairs, she had little time to spare for dressing, but declined to take her two bridemaids with her to facilitate the process.

ELIZABETH BURGOYNE CORBETT

A minute later Marvel, who had accompanied his master to Moorbye, rushed into the room in which the rest of us were toying with time, and, throwing his hands up with a despairing gesture, screamed rather than shouted his dreadful tidings—

"My master is dead!"

That was what he had to tell us, and a moment later all was confusion and excitement, which was augmented by the sound of despairing shrieks from above.

In common with others, my first impulse was to rush upstairs to Belle's room. I arrived first, and found her standing in the middle of the floor, alternately screaming and laughing, both screams and laughter being such as can but proceed from the tortured bosom of insanity. Beside her, on the floor, lay an open letter. I instinctively picked it up and hid it in my pocket before anyone else saw it. I knew, without being told, that whatever awful tragedy had taken place in the next room was explained in that letter, and that it was the reading of it which had driven my sister mad.

There were plenty of affectionate hands ready to help the stricken bride, and plenty of loving hearts that would fain have lightened her woe. But the blow had been too awful in its suddenness, and had struck when she was least prepared for it, just when she was at the zenith of her triumph and satisfaction. It had extinguished forever the light of reason from that beautiful face, and had transformed the erstwhile smiling bride into a hopeless maniac.

Strangely enough, she seems to have forgotten the present, and all memory of aught connected with the family of Greatlands has been wiped off her darkened mind. She will never betray the part she bore in that other tragedy, and the world speaks very pityingly of the beautiful girl whose mental and social life ended on the very day which had witnessed the climax of her ambition.

The new Earl of Greatlands, being tender and pitiful, would have established his father's bride of an hour in the dower-house, surrounded by such comforts as she is capable of enjoying. But to this plan neither my father nor Lady Elizabeth were willing to consent, and she still lives at Courtney Grange, one of the saddest wrecks of humanity it is possible to meet with. Interest in her surroundings she takes none, but will sit and babble by the hour of the time when she was a little one, and had no greater trouble than to please an indulgent governess.

My father has aged very much of late, and always bears about him the impress of one who has been cruelly stricken by fate. He had almost worshiped his eldest daughter, in whom he saw nothing but physical, mental and moral perfection. To gaze upon her as she is, and to contrast her present condition with what might have been, is a daily torture to him, which robs his life of much of its former animation and spirit. Seeing how he takes the changed order of things to heart, I often feel thankful that he is quite unsuspicious of the fact that, but for herself, Belle might now have been happy in the love of husband and children, even as I am.

Lady Elizabeth, too, was greatly grieved for a time. But as her sympathies are widely scattered, and her interest in human nature is keen, she finds sufficient employment for mind and body to keep both in a healthy state of activity. If there is one thing that she is more sorry about than another, it is the fact that she could ever have harbored unworthy suspicions against two people whom she now firmly believes to be entitled to be numbered among the innocents. Thank God that she is spared the knowledge which I possess! It would kill her.

Jerry is now at Cambridge, and bids fair to reward all the hopes centered upon him.

As for myself, there is a perpetual problem facing me, and that is—What have I done to deserve all the love and happiness which are showered upon me? Yes, there is one other—How shall I repay Sergius for the transformation he has wrought in my life? I am constantly trying to do it, but never manage it quite to my own satisfaction, though I believe my Russian friends, all of whom now live within a short distance of our house, entertain very exaggerated views concerning my capabilities of making a good wife.

There is one other subject upon which the future reader of these memoirs may possibly desire a little enlightenment. He shall have it.

Cyril, earl of Greatlands, who is said to have accidentally poisoned himself by swallowing a large dose of chloral in mistake for a milder drug, sleeps by the side of his ancestors in the Greatlands mausoleum, and only Dennis Marvel, who is now the young earl's valet, and myself ever dream that despair and remorse drove an apparently happy man to sever the life-chords which had become a torture to him.

So soon as I had an opportunity to do so unobserved, I read the letter which had been the last thing upon which Belle had gazed with the light of reason.

"My darling wife," it ran, "I thought to have overcome the horror which has been resting upon me ever since I became an accursed parricide. My God! how could I do it! And how could you urge me to it! You, whom it would not have been difficult to worship as the outward embodiment of all that is pure and holy! I have often asked myself if I were mad. For I could not otherwise understand how it was possible for me to continue loving the temptress whose ambition has wrought my father's doom and mine. For I am doomed and accursed! My days are filled with loathing of myself, and my nights are one long dream of horror. For me there is no salvation. I see my father's frowning face, and hear his curses even amid the gay talk of the happy folk around us, and it is more than I can bear. Therefore I have put an end to it. When you pick this up from your dressing-table, the man who murdered his own father to gratify your ambition and his own greed will be numbered among the dead. But for you, who could coolly plan a murder, and yet not be haunted by remorse, life still holds many possibilities. You are now the Countess of Greatlands. I have enabled you to gratify your ambition. In return, you can make expiation for your own guilt by devoting your gifts to the interests and benefit of others. This I pray you to do, repentant sinner that I am! This I implore you to do, madly-loving husband that I am! This I command you to do, wretched—but but my strength fails me. I must bid you an eternal farewell. God bless you, my darling, and may His mercy be given to us both.

CYRIL

I read this letter through, but though it moved me terribly, it told me nothing I did not know already. How would it be with others, though? Would it not enlighten them more than was desirable about secrets that were better kept? I thought so, and I carefully burned the letter, anxiously watching it shrivel beneath the action of the flames, and guarding against the possibility of the smallest fragment escaping to betray the dark mysteries of the past.

Does the reader blame me?

THE END

A Note About the Author

Elizabeth Burgoyne Corbett (1846–1930) was an English novelist, journalist, and feminist. In addition to her work for the *Newcastle Daily Chronicle*, Corbett was a popular adventure and detective writer whose work appeared in some of the Victorian era's leading magazines and periodicals. In response to Mrs. Humphrey Ward's "An Appeal Against Female Suffrage," published in *The Nineteenth Century* in 1889, Corbett wrote *New Amazonia: A Foretaste of the Future* (1889), a feminist utopian novel set in a futuristic Ireland. Despite publishing a dozen novels and two collections of short fiction, Corbett—who was once described by *Hearth and Home* as a master of the detective novel alongside Arthur Conan Doyle—remains largely unheard of by scholars and readers today.

A Note from the Publisher

Spanning many genres, from non-fiction essays to literature classics to children's books and lyric poetry, Mint Edition books showcase the master works of our time in a modern new package. The text is freshly typeset, is clean and easy to read, and features a new note about the author in each volume. Many books also include exclusive new introductory material. Every book boasts a striking new cover, which makes it as appropriate for collecting as it is for gift giving. Mint Edition books are only printed when a reader orders them, so natural resources are not wasted. We're proud that our books are never manufactured in excess and exist only in the exact quantity they need to be read and enjoyed.

Discover more of your favorite classics with Bookfinity™.

- Track your reading with custom book lists.
- Get great book recommendations for your personalized Reader Type.
- Add reviews for your favorite books.
- AND MUCH MORE!

Visit **bookfinity.com** and take the fun Reader Type quiz to get started.

Enjoy our classic and modern companion pairings!